Frank Merriwell's Triumph

Or; The Disappearance of Felicia

BURT L. STANDISH

Author of the celebrated "Merriwell"
stories, which are the favorite reading of
over half a million up-to-date (1904)
American boys.

BOOKS FOR ATHLETICS

LONDON
IBOO PRESS HOUSE
86-90 PAUL STREET

FRANK MERRIWELL'S TRIUMPH

OR

THE DISAPPEARANCE OF FELICIA

BURT L. STANDISH

Author of the famous Merriwell Stories.

BOOKS FOR ATHLETICS

Layout & Cover © Copyright 2020 iBooPress, London

Published by
iBoo Press House

3rd Floor
86-90 Paul Street
London, EC2A4NE UK

t: +44 20 3695 0809
info@iboo.com II iBoo.com

ISBNs
978-1-64226-290-2 (h)
978-1-64226-291-9 (p)

Printed in the United States

Frank Merriwell's Triumph

Or; The Disappearance of Felicia

BURT L. STANDISH

Author of the celebrated "Merriwell" stories, which are the favorite reading of over half a million up-to-date (1904) American boys.

BOOKS FOR ATHLETICS

MERRIWELL SERIES
Stories of Frank and Dick Merriwell
Fascinating Stories of Athletics

A half million enthusiastic followers of the Merriwell brothers will attest the unfailing interest and wholesomeness of these adventures of two lads of high ideals, who play fair with themselves, as well as with the rest of the world.

These stories are rich in fun and thrills in all branches of sports and athletics. They are extremely high in moral tone, and cannot fail to be of immense benefit to every boy who reads them.

They have the splendid quality of firing a boy's ambition to become a good athlete, in order that he may develop into a strong, vigorous, right-thinking man.

Contents

CHAPTER I.

A COMPACT OF RASCALS.

They were dangerous-looking men, thirty of them in all, armed to the teeth. They looked like unscrupulous fellows who would hesitate at no desperate deed. Some of them had bad records, and yet they had served Frank Merriwell faithfully in guarding his mine, the Queen Mystery, against those who tried to wrest it from him by force and fraud.

Frank had called these men together, and he now stood on his doorstep in Mystery Valley, Arizona, looking them over. Bart Hodge, Frank's college chum and companion in many adventures, was behind him in the doorway. Little Abe, a hunchback boy whom Merriwell had rescued from ruffians at a mining camp and befriended for some time, peered from the cabin. Merry smiled pleasantly as he surveyed the men.

"Well, boys," he said, "the time has come when I shall need your services no longer."

Some of them stirred restlessly and looked regretful.

"To tell you the truth," Frank went on, "I am genuinely sorry to part with you. You have served me well. But I need you no more. My enemies have been defeated, and the courts have recognized my rightful claim to this property. You fought for me when it was necessary. You risked your lives for me."

"That's what we is paid for, Mr. Merriwell," said Tombstone Phil, the leader. "We tries to earn our money."

"You have earned it, every one of you. I remember the day we stood off a hundred painted ruffians in the desert; I remember the hunting of Jim Rednight; and I don't forget that when Hodge and I stood beneath a tree near Phœnix, with ropes about our necks, that you charged to the rescue and saved us. Have I paid you in a satisfactory manner?"

"Sure thing!"

"You bet!"

"That's whatever!"

"You don't hear us kick any!"

"We're satisfied!"

These exclamations were uttered by various men in the gathering.

"I am glad to know, boys," declared Frank, "that you are all satisfied. If you must leave me, I like to have you leave feeling that you have been treated on the square."

"Mr. Merriwell," said Mexican Bob, a wizened little man, "I ken chew up the galoot what says you ain't plumb on the level. Thar's nary a critter in the bunch whatever makes a murmur about you."

"You can see, boys," Frank went on, "that I have no further use for you as a guard to my property. If any of you wish to remain, however, I shall try to find employment for you. There's work enough to be done here, although it may not be the sort of work you care to touch. I need more men in the mine. You know the wages paid. It's hard work and may not be satisfactory to any of you."

The men were silent.

"As we are parting," Merry added, "I wish to show my appreciation of you in a manner that will be satisfactory to you all. For that purpose I have something to distribute among you. Hand them out, Hodge."

Bart stepped back and reappeared some moments later loaded down with a lot of small canvas pouches.

"Come up one at a time, boys," invited Merry, as he began taking these from Bart. "Here you are, Phil."

He dropped the first pouch into Tombstone Phil's hand, and it gave forth a musical, clinking sound that made the eyes of the men sparkle.

One by one they filed past the doorstep, and into each outstretched hand was dropped a clinking canvas pouch, each one of which was heavy enough to make its recipient smile.

When the last man had received his present, they gathered again in front of the door, and suddenly Tombstone Phil roared:

"Give up a youp, boys, for the whitest man on two legs, Frank Merriwell!"

They swung their hats in the air and uttered a yell that awoke the echoes of the valley.

"Thanks, men," said Merry quietly. "I appreciate that. As long as you desire to remain in Mystery Valley you are at liberty to do so; when you wish to depart you can do so, also. So-long, boys.

Good luck to you."

He waved his hand, and they answered with another sharp
yell. Then they turned and moved away, declaring over and over
among themselves that he was the "whitest man." One of those
who repeated this assertion a number of times was a leathery,
bowlegged, bewhiskered individual in greasy garments known
as Hull Shawmut. If anything, Shawmut seemed more pleased
and satisfied than his companions.

The only one who said nothing at all was Kip Henry, known as
"the Roper," on account of his skill in throwing the lariat. Henry
was thin, supple, with a small black mustache, and in his appearance was somewhat dandified, taking great satisfaction in bright
colors and in fanciful Mexican garments. He wore a peaked Mexican hat, and his trousers were slit at the bottom, Mexican style.
Several times Shawmut glanced at Henry, noting his lack of en-
thusiasm. When the Thirty retired to their camp down the valley
and lingered there, Henry sat apart by himself, rolling and smoking a cigarette and frowning at the ground.

"What's the matter, pard?" asked Shawmut, clapping him on
the shoulder. "Didn't yer git yer little present?"

"Yes, I got it," nodded the Roper.

"Then what's eating of yer?"

"Well, Shawmut, I am a whole lot sorry this yere job is ended.
That's what's the matter. It certain was a snap."

"That's right," agreed Kip, sitting down near the other. "We gits
good pay for our time, and we works none to speak of. It certain
was a snap. Howsomever, such snaps can't last always, partner.
Do you opine we've got any kick coming?"

"The only thing I was a-thinking of," answered Kip, "is that
here we fights to keep this yere mine for him, we takes chances o' being called outlaws, and—now the job is done—we gits
dropped. You knows and I knows that this yere mine is a mighty
rich one. Why don't we have the luck to locate a mine like that?
Why should luck always come to other galoots?"

"I ain't explaining that none," confessed Shawmut, as he filled
his pipe. "Luck is a heap singular. One night I bucks Jimmy
Clerg's bank down in Tucson. I never has much luck hitting the
tiger, nohow. This night things run just the same. I peddles and
peddles till I gits down to my last yeller boy. If I loses that I am
broke. I has a good hoss and outfit, and so I says, 'Here goes.'
Well, she does go. Jim's dealer he rakes her in. I sets thar busted wide. When I goes into that place I has eight hundred in my
clothes. In less than an hour I has nothing.

"Clerg he comes ambling along a-looking the tables over. I sees him, and I says: 'Jim, how much you let me have on my hoss and outfit?' 'What's it wurth?' says he. 'Three hundred, cold,' says I. 'That goes,' says he. And he lets me have the coin. Then I tackles the bank again, and I keeps right on peddling. Yes, sir, I gits down once more to my last coin. This is where I walks out of the saloon on my uppers. All the same, I bets the last red. I wins. Right there, Kip, my luck turns. Arter that it didn't seem I could lose nohow. Pretty soon I has all the chips stacked up in front of me. I cashes in once or twice and keeps right on pushing her. I knows luck is with me, and I takes all kinds o' long chances. Well, pard, when I ambles out of the place at daylight the bank is busted and I has all the ready coin of the joint. That's the way luck works. You gits it in the neck a long time; but bimeby, when she turns, she just pours in on yer."

"But it don't seem any to me that my luck is going to turn," muttered the Roper.

"Mebbe you takes a little walk with me," said Shawmut significantly. "Mebbe I tells you something some interesting."

They arose and walked away from the others, so that their talk might not be heard.

"Did you ever hear of Benson Clark?" asked Shawmut.

"Clark? Clark? Why, I dunno. Seems ter me I hears o' him."

"I knows him well once. He was a grubstaker. But his is hard luck and a-plenty of it. All the same, he keeps right on thinking sure that luck changes for him. Something like two years ago I loses track of him. I never sees him any since. But old Bense he hits it rich at last. Somewhere in the Mazatzals he located a claim what opens rich as mud. Some Indians off their reservation finds him there, and he has to run for it. He gits out of the mountains, but they cuts him off and shoots him up. His luck don't do him no good, for he croaks. But right here is where another lucky gent comes in. This other gent he happens along and finds old Bense, and Bense he tells him about the mine and gives him a map. Now, this other lucky gent he proposes to go and locate that mine. He proposes to do this, though right now he owns two of the best mines in the whole country. Mebbe you guesses who I'm talking about."

"Why," exclaimed Henry, "you don't mean Mr. Merriwell, do yer?"

"Mebbe I does," answered Shawmut, glancing at his companion slantwise. "Now, what do yer think of that?"

"What do I think of it?" muttered the Roper. "Well, I will tell yer.

I think it's rotten that all the luck is to come to one gent. I think Mr. Merriwell has a-plenty and he can do without another mine."

"Just what I thinks," agreed Shawmut. "I figgers it out that way myself. But he has a map, and that shows him where to find old Bense's claim."

"See here," said Kip, stopping short, "how do you happen to know so much about this?"

"Well, mebbe I listens around some; mebbe I harks a little; mebbe I finds it out that way."

"I see," said Henry, in surprise; "but I never thinks it o' you. You seem so satisfied-like I reckons you don't bother any."

"Mebbe I plays my cards slick and proper," chuckled Shawmut. "You sees I don't care to be suspected now."

"What do you propose to do?"

"Well, partner, if I tells you, does you opine you're ready to stick by me?"

"Share even and I am ready for anything," was the assurance.

"Mr. Merriwell he proposes hiking out soon to locate that thar claim o' Benson Clark's. I am none in a hurry about getting away from here, so I lingers. When he hikes I follers. When he locates the claim mebbe he has to leave it; mebbe I jump it; mebbe I gits it recorded first. If he don't suspect me any, if he don't know I'm arter it, he don't hurry any about having it recorded. That gives me time to get ahead of him. If you're with me in this, we goes even on the claim. It's a heap resky, for this yere Merriwell is dangerous to deal with. Is it settled?"

"Yere's my hand," said Kip Henry.

Shawmut clasped the proffered hand, and the compact was made.

CHAPTER II.

DAYS OF RETRIBUTION.

When Merry had dismissed the men, he turned back into the cabin and sat down near the table.

"Well, that's the end of that business, Bart," he said.

"Yes," nodded Hodge, sitting opposite. "I congratulate you on the way you handled those men, Merry. No one else could have done it as well. If ever I saw a collection of land pirates, it was that bunch."

Frank smiled.

"They were a pretty tough set," he confessed; "but they were just the men I needed to match the ruffians Sukes set against me."

Milton Sukes was the chief conspirator against Frank in the schemes to deprive him of the Queen Mystery Mine.

"Sukes will hire no more ruffians," said Hodge.

"I should say not. He has perpetrated his last piece of villainy. He has gone before the judgment bar on high."

"And the last poor wretch he deluded is an imbecile."

"Poor Worthington!" said Merry. "I fear he will never be right again. It was his bullet that destroyed Sukes, yet no man can prove it. What he suffered after that during his flight into the desert, where he nearly perished for water, completely turned his brain."

"You want to look out for him, Frank. I think he is dangerous."

Merry laughed.

"Ridiculous, Hodge! He is as harmless as a child. When I let him, he follows me about like a dog."

Even as Frank said this, a crouching figure came creeping to the door and peered in. It was a man with unshaven, haggard face and eyes from which the light of reason had fled.

"There he is!" exclaimed this man. "There is my ghost! Do you want me, ghost?"

"Come in, Worthington!" called Frank.

The man entered hesitatingly and stood near the table, never taking his eyes from Merry's face for a moment.

"What you command, ghost, I must obey," he said. "You own me, body and soul. Ha! ha! body and soul! But I have no soul! I bartered it with a wretch who deceived me! I was an honest man before that! Perhaps you don't believe me, but I swear I was. You must believe me! It's a terrible thing to be owned by a ghost who has no confidence in you. But why should my ghost have confidence! Didn't I deceive him? Didn't I kill him? I see it now. I see the fire! It is burning—it is burning there! He has found me as I am setting it. He springs upon me! He is strong—so strong! Ha! his feet slip! Down he goes! His head strikes! He is unconscious!"

The wretch seemed living over the terrible experiences through which he had passed on a certain night in Denver, when he set fire to Merriwell's office and tried to burn Frank to death. He thought he had accomplished his purpose, and the appearance of his intended victim alive had turned his brain.

As he listened Hodge shivered a little.

"Never mind, Worthington," said Frank. "He is all right. He will escape from the fire."

"No, no, no!" gasped the man, wringing his hands. "See him lying there! See the fire flashing on his face! See the smoke! It is coming thick. I must go! I must leave him. It is a fearful thing to do! But if he escapes he will destroy me. He will send me to prison, and I must leave him to die!"

He covered his eyes with his hands, as if to shut out a terrible spectacle.

"No one sees me!" he whispered. "Here are the stairs! It is all dark—all dark! I must get out quick, before the fire is discovered. I have done it! I am on the street! I mustn't run! If I run they will suspect me. I will walk fast—walk fast!"

Merry glanced at Hodge and sadly shook his head.

"Now the engines are coming!" exclaimed the deranged man. "Hear them as they clang and roar along the streets! See the people run! See the horses galloping! They are coming to try to put out the fire. What if they do it in time to save him! Then he will tell them of my treachery! Then he will send me to prison! I must see—I must know! I must go back there!"

"He shall not send you to prison, Worthington," asserted Merry soothingly. "He shall be merciful to you."

"Why should he? Here is the burning building. Here are the engines, panting and throbbing. See! they pour streams of water on

13

the building. No use! It is too late; you cannot save him. He is dead long before this. Who shall say I was to blame? What if they do find his charred body? No man can prove I had a hand in it. I defy you to prove it!"

Shaking his trembling hands in the air, the wretch almost shrieked these words.

"This," muttered Bart Hodge, "is retribution."

"I must go away," whispered Worthington. "I must hide where they can't see me. Look how every one stares at me! They seem to know I have done it! These infernal lights betray me! I must hide in the darkness. Some one is following me everywhere. I am afraid of the darkness! I will always be afraid of the darkness! In the darkness or in the light, there is no rest for me—no rest! Did you hear that voice? Do you hear? It accuses me of murder! I am haunted! My God! Haunted, haunted!"

With this heartbroken cry he sank on his knees and crept toward Frank.

"You're the ghost that haunts me!" he exclaimed. "It is my punishment! I must always be near you, and you must haunt me forever!"

Merry touched him gently.

"Get up, Worthington," he said regretfully. "Your punishment has been too much. Look at me. Look me straight in the eyes, Worthington. I am not dead. You didn't kill me."

"No use to tell me that; I know better."

"It is hopeless now, Hodge," said Merry, in a low tone. "The only chance for him is that time will restore his reason. You may go, Worthington."

"I must stay near by, mustn't I?"

"You may stay outside."

With bowed head and unsteady steps the man left the cabin and disappeared.

Little Abe had remained speechless and frightened in a corner. Now he picked up his fiddle, and suddenly from it came a weird melody. It was a crazy tune, filled with wild fancies and ghostly phantoms.

"He is playing the music of that deranged soul," murmured Frank.

The sound of the fiddle died in a wail, and the boy sat shivering and silent in the corner.

"This is a little too much of a ghostly thing!" exclaimed Merry as he arose and shook himself. "Let's talk of something else, Hodge. To-morrow we start for the Mazatzals, and I have everything ready. If we can locate that mine, one-half of it is yours."

He took from his pocket a leather case and removed from it a torn and soiled map, which he spread on the table. Together he and Bart examined the map once more, as they had done many times before.

"There," said Frank, "is Clear Creek, running down into the Rio Verde. Somewhere to the northwest of Hawley Peak, as this fellow indicated here on the map, in the valley shown by this cross, is Benson Clark's claim."

"The location is vaguely marked," said Bart. "We may search for it a year without discovering it."

"That's true; but we know approximately somewhere near where it is."

"Well," said Hodge, "we will do our best. That's all any one can do. It is your fortune, Frank, to be lucky; and for that reason we may be successful."

"Something tells me we shall be," nodded Merriwell.

The start was made next day, and the journey continued until one afternoon Merry and Bart Hodge stood looking down into a deep, oblong valley in the heart of the Northern Mazatzals. With them was Cap'n Walter Wiley, a former seafaring man, who had been Frank's friend in many thrilling adventures in the West. Little Abe had come with them from Mystery Valley, as had Worthington, but they were at the camp Merry had established some distance behind.

"I believe this valley is the one," Merry declared; "but how are we going to get into it? That's the question that bothers me."

"There must be an inlet or outlet or something to the old valley," said Hodge. "It cannot be just a sink hole dropped down here like a huge oval basin in the mountains. There is a stream running through it, too. It is wooded and watered, and there is plenty of grass for grazing."

"I am almost positive this valley is the one Benson Clark told me of. I am almost positive it is the one marked on my map. Clark was shot and dying when I found him. He didn't have time to tell me how to get into the valley."

"We seem to have struck something that impedes navigation and investigation and causes agitation," put in Cap'n Wiley. "I would truly love to have the wings of a dove that I could fly from these heights above. Poetry just bubbles from me occasionally. I must set my colossal intellect at work on this perplexing problem and demonstrate my astounding ability to solve entangling enigmas. (Webster's Dictionary does contain the loveliest words!) Let me think a thought. Let all nature stand hushed and silent while I thunk a think."

His companions paid little heed to him; but he continued to discuss the problem of descending into the valley.

"I have visited the northern end and the southern end," said Frank, "and I have explored this side and surveyed the other side through my field glasses. There seems no break in these perpendicular walls. This valley seems like one of those Southwestern mesas inverted. They rise sheer from the plains, and it is impossible to reach the top of many of them. This drops straight down here, and it seems impossible to reach its bottom."

"The more difficult it is," said Bart, "the greater becomes my desire to get down there."

"Same here," smiled Frank. "The difficulty makes it something of a mystery. Scientific expeditions have spent thousands of dollars in reaching the top of the Mesa Encantada, in New Mexico. By Americans it is called the Enchanted Mesa. Now, the mere fact that we can't seem to get down into this valley throws an atmosphere of mystery over it, and to me it is an enchanted valley."

"Hush!" whispered Wiley, with one finger pressed against his forehead. "A mighty thought is throbbing and seething in my cohesive brain. If I only had my gravity destroyer here! Ha! Then I could simply jump down into the valley and look around, and, when I got ready, jump back up here. By the way, mates, did you ever know why it was that Santos-Dumont retired from this country in confusion and dismay? You know he came over here with his old flying machine, and was going to do stunts to amaze the gaping multitudes. You know he suddenly packed his Kenebecca and took passage to foreign shores. The secret of his sudden departure has never been told. If you will promise to whisper no word of it to the world, I will reveal the truth to you.

"Just before Santy arrived in the United States I succeeded in perfecting my great gravity destroyer. As I have on other occasions explained to you, it was about the size of an ordinary watch, and I carried it about in my pocket. By pressing a certain spring I immediately destroyed the force of gravity so that, by giving an easy, gentle sort of a jump into the air, I could sail right up to the top of a church steeple. When I got ready to come down, I just let go and sailed down lightly as a feather. When I heard that Santy was going to amaze this country with his dinky old flying machine, I resolved to have a little harmless amusement with him.

"With this object in view, I had a flying machine of my own invented. It was made of canvas stretched over a light wooden frame, and along the bottom, to keep it upright, I had a keel of lead. My means of expulsion was a huge paddle wheel that I could work with my feet. That was the only thing about the machine that I didn't like. There was some work connected with it. To the rear end of the arrangement I attached a huge fanlike rudder that I could operate with ropes running to the cross pieces, like on ordinary rowboats.

"Mates, there never was a truer word spoken from the chest than that the prophet is not without honor save in his own country. I had this flying machine of mine constructed in Cap'n Bean's shipyard, down in Camden, Maine, my home. The villagers turned out in swarms, and stood around, and nudged each other in the ribs, and stared at my contrivance, and tried to josh me. Even Billy Murphy gave me a loud and gleeful ha-ha! They seemed to think I had gone daffy, but I kept right on about my business, and one day the Snowbird, as I called her, was finished. She was a beauty, mates, as she lay there, looking so light and airy and fragile.

"By that time I had become decidedly hot under the collar on account of so much chaffing from the rustic populace. Says I to myself, says I: 'Cap'n, these Rubes don't deserve to see you fly. If you let them see you fly you will be giving every mother's son of them two dollars' worth of entertainment free of charge.' Now, it isn't my custom to give anything free of charge. Therefore I advertised in the Herald that on a certain day I would sail the aërial atmosphere. I stated that before doing so I would pass around the hat, and I expected every person present to drop two dollars into it. I thought this was a clever idea of mine.

"On the day and date the people came from near and far. They journeyed even from Hogansville, South Hope, and Stickney's Corner. When I saw them massed in one great multitude in and around that shipyard and on the steamboat wharf, I made merry cachinnation.

"But alas! when I passed through that crowd with my hat and counted up the collection, I found I had a lead nickel, a trousers button, and a peppermint lozenger. That was all those measly, close-fisted people donated for the pleasure of seeing me navigate the ambient air. Although I am not inclined to be over-sensitive, I felt hurt, and pained, and disappointed. I then made a little speech to them, and informed them that over in Searsmont there was a man so mean that he used a wart on the back of his neck for a collar button to save the expense of buying one, but I considered him the soul of generosity beside them. I further in-

17

formed them that I had postponed sailing. I minded it not that they guffawed and heaped derision upon me. I was resolute and unbending, and they were forced to leave without seeing me hoist anchor that day.

"In the soft and stilly hours of the night which followed I seated myself in the Snowbird, applied my feet to the mechanism, pressed the spring of the gravity destroyer, and away I scooted over Penobscot Bay. When the sun rose the following morning it found Cap'n Bean's shipyard empty and little Walter and his flying machine gone.

"I was on hand when Santos-Dumont arrived in New York. I sought an interview with him, and I told him I proposed making him look like a plugged quarter when he gave his exhibition. I challenged him to sail against me and told him I would show him up. Santy didn't seem to like this, and he made remarks which would not look well in the Sabbath School Herald. Indeed, he became violent, and, though I tried to soothe him, I discovered myself, when the interview ended, sitting on the sidewalk outside of the building and feeling of my person for bumps and sore spots.

"You can imagine with what dignity I arose to my feet and strode haughtily away. More than ever was I determined to make old Santy look like an amateur in the flying business. However, he took particular pains while in New York to scoot around in his machine when he knew I was not informed that such was his intention. With a great deal of craft and skill he avoided coming in competition with me. One day some part of his jigger got out of gear and he had it removed into the country to fix it. I located him and followed him up. I have forgotten the name of the village where I found him; but the people were getting much excited, for he had stated that at a certain time he would show them what he could do.

"He had gathered scientific men from Oshkosh, Skowhegan, Chicago, and other centres of culture and refinement. Among them was Professor Deusenberry, of the Squedunk Elementary College of Fine Fatheads. I succeeded in getting at Professor Deusenberry's ear. He had a generous ear, and there was not much trouble in getting at it. I told him all about my Snowbird, and informed him that I had her concealed near at hand and proposed to show up Santos when he broke loose and sailed. I took him around to see my craft; but when he looked her over he shook his head and announced that she'd never rise clear of the skids on which I had her elevated above the ground.

"Well, mates, the great day came around, and promptly at the hour set Santos rose like a bird in the air. I was watching for him, and when I saw him gliding about over the village I promptly started the Snowbird going. The moment I shut off the power of gravitation I scooted upward like a wild swan. I made straight for Dumont's old machine, and there before the wildly cheering people, whose shouts rose faint and sweet to my ear, I proceeded to do a few stunts. I circled around Santos when he was at his best speed. I sailed over him and under him, and I certain gave him an attack of nervous prostration. In his excitement he did something wrong and knocked his machine out of kilter, so that he suddenly took a collapse and fell into the top of a tree, where his old craft was badly damaged. I gently lowered myself to the ground, and as I stepped out of the Snowbird Professor Deusenberry clasped me to his throbbing bosom and wept on my breast.

"'Professor Wiley!' he cried, 'beyond question you have solved the problem of aërial navigation. Professor Wiley——' 'Excuse me, Professor Deusenberry' said I, 'but I am simply plain Cap'n Wiley, a salty old tar of modesty and few pretensions. I have no rightful claim to the title of professor.'

"'But you shall have—you shall have!' he earnestly declared. 'I will see that you're made professor of atmospheric nullity at the Squedunk Elementary College of Fine Fatheads. Your name shall go ringing down through the corridor of the ages. Your name shall stand side by side in history with those of Columbus, Pizarro, and Richard Croker.'

"That night I was wined, and dined, and toasted in that town, while Santos-Dumont stood outside and shivered in the cold. The scientific men and professors and men of boodle gazed on me in awe and wonderment and bowed down before me. Professor Deusenberry was seized with a determination to own the Snowbird. He was fearful lest some one else should obtain her, and so he hastened to get me to set a price upon her. I was modest. I told him that I was modest. I told him that in the cause of science I was ready to part with her for the paltry sum of five thousand dollars. In less than ten minutes he had gathered some of the moneyed fatheads of his college and bought my flying machine.

"I suggested to them that the proper way to start her was to get her onto some eminence and have some one push her off. The following morning they raised her to the flat roof of a building, and, with no small amount of agitation, I saw that Professor Deusenberry himself contemplated making a trip in her. When they pushed her off he started the paddle wheels going, but without the effect of my little gravity destroyer to keep her from falling.

She dropped straight down to the ground. When they picked the professor up, several of his lateral ribs, together with his dispendarium, were fractured. I thought his confidence in me was also broken. At any rate, I hastened to shake the dust of that town from my feet and make for the tall timber.

"Nevertheless, mates, my little experience with Santos-Dumont so disgusted and discouraged him that he immediately left this country, which explains something that has been puzzling the people for a long time. They wondered why he didn't remain and do the stunts he had promised to do. Even now I fancy that Santy often dreams in terror of Cap'n Wiley and his Snowbird."

CHAPTER III.

THE MAP VANISHES.

hile Cap'n Wiley had been relating this yarn Merriwell seemed utterly unconscious of his presence. Having produced his field glasses from the case at his side, he was surveying the impregnable valley. Suddenly he started slightly and touched Bart's arm.

"Look yonder, Hodge," he said, in a low tone. "Away up at the far end of the valley where the timber is, I can see smoke rising there."

"So can I!" exclaimed Hodge. "What does it mean?"

"There is but one thing it can mean, and that is——"

"There's some one in the valley."

"Sure, sure," agreed Cap'n Wiley. "Somebody has found a passage into that harbor."

"Do you suppose," asked Hodge, in consternation, "that there are other parties searching for that mine?"

"It's not unlikely."

"But you were the only one told of its existence by Benson Clark."

"Still, it's likely others knew he was prospecting in this vicinity."

"It will be hard luck, Merry, if we find that some one has relocated that claim ahead of us."

"That's right," nodded Frank. "The fact that there is smoke rising from that part of the valley proves it is not impossible to get down there. It's too late to-day to make any further effort in that direction. We will return to the camp and wait for morning."

"And if you find other men on the claim, what will you do?"

"I haven't decided."

"But it belongs to you!" exclaimed Hodge earnestly. "Clark located it, and when he died he gave you the right to it."

"Nevertheless, if some one else has found it and has registered his claim, he can hold it."

"Not if you can prove Clark staked it off and posted notices. Not if you can prove he gave it to you."

"But I can't prove that. Clark is dead. He left no will. All he left was quartz in his saddlebags and some dust he had washed from the placer, together with this map I have in my pocket. You see, I would find it impossible to prove my right to the mine if I discovered other parties in possession of it."

Bart's look of disappointment increased.

"I suppose that's right, Merry," he confessed; "but it doesn't seem right to me. The Consolidated Mining Association of America tried to take your Queen Mystery Mine from you on a shabbier claim than you have on this mine here."

"But I defeated them, Bart. You must not forget that."

"I haven't forgotten it," Hodge declared, nodding his head. "All the same, you had hard work to defeat them, and, later, Milton Sukes made it still harder for you."

"But I triumphed in both cases. Right is right, Bart; it makes no difference whether it is on my side or the other fellow's."

"That's so," Hodge confessed. "But it would be an almighty shame to find some one else squatting on that claim. I'd like to get down into that valley now!"

"It can't be done before nightfall, so we will go back to camp."

They set out, and an hour later they reached their camp in a small valley. There they had pitched a tent near a spring, and close at hand their horses grazed. As they approached the tent, little Abe came hobbling up to them.

"I am glad you're back," he declared. "That man has been going on just awful."

"Who? Worthington?" questioned Merry.

"Yes; he said over and over that he knew his ghost would be lost. He declared his ghost was in danger. He said he could feel the danger near."

"More of his wild fancies," said Hodge.

"Mates," observed Cap'n Wiley, "if there's anything that upsets my zebro spinal column it is a crazy gentleman like that. I am prone to confess that he worries me. I don't trust him. I am afraid that some morning I will wake up and find a hatchet sticking in my head. I should hate to do that."

"I am positive he is harmless," declared Merry. "Where is he, Abe?"

"I don't know now. A while ago he just rushed off, calling and calling, and he's not come back."

Frank looked alarmed. "He promised me he would stay near the camp. He gave me his word, and this is the first time he has failed to obey me implicitly in everything."

"He said he'd have to go to save you."

"It was a mistake bringing him here, Frank," asserted Hodge.

"But what could I do with him? He wouldn't remain behind, and I knew the danger of leaving him there. Any day he might escape from the valley and lose himself in the desert to perish there."

"Perhaps that is what will happen to him now."

Merry was sorely troubled. He made preparations to go in search of Worthington without delay. But even as he was doing so the deranged man came running back into the camp and fell panting at his feet.

"I have found you again, my ghost!" he cried. "They are after you! You must beware! You must guard yourself constantly!"

"Get up, Worthington!" said Merry. "I am in no danger. No one can hurt a ghost, you know."

"Ah! you don't know them—you don't know them!" excitedly shouted the lunatic. "They are wicked and dangerous. I saw them peering over those rocks. I saw their evil eyes. Abe was asleep. I had been walking up and down, waiting for you to return. When I saw them I stood still as a stone and made them believe I was dead. They watched and watched and whispered. They had weapons in their hands! You must be on your guard every minute!"

"I have heard about crazy bedbugs," muttered Wiley; "but I never saw one quite as bad as this. Every time I hear him go on that way I feel the need of a drink. I could even partake of a portion of Easy Street firewater with relish."

Worthington seized Frank's arm.

"You must come and see where they were—you must come and see," he urged.

"Never mind that now," said Merry. "I will look later."

"No! no! Come, now!"

"Be still!" commanded Merry sharply. "I can't waste the time."

But the maniac continued to plead and beg until, in order to appease him, Merry gave in.

Worthington led him to a mass of bowlders at a distance, and, pointing at them, he declared in a whisper:

"There's where they were hiding. Look and see. There is where they were, I tell you!"

More to pacify the poor fellow than anything else, Frank looked around amid the rocks. Suddenly he made a discovery that caused him to change countenance and kneel upon the ground. Bart, who had sauntered down, found him thus.

"What is it, Frank?" he asked.

"See here, Hodge," said Merry. "There has been some one here amid these rocks. Here's a track. Here's a mark where the nails of a man's boot heel scratched on the rocks."

Hodge stood looking down, but shook his head.

"You have sharper eyes than I, Frank," he confessed. "Perhaps Worthington has been here himself."

"No! no!" denied the deranged man. "I was afraid to come! I tell you I saw them! I tell you I saw their wicked eyes. This is the first time I have been here!"

"If he tells the truth," said Frank, "then it is certain some one else has been here."

Behind Worthington's back Bart shook his head and made signals expressive of his belief that whatever signs Frank had discovered there had been made by Worthington.

"Now, you see," persisted the madman; "now you know they were here! Now you know you must be on your guard!"

"Yes, yes," nodded Merry impatiently. "Don't worry about that, Worthington. I will be on my guard. They will not take me by surprise."

This seemed to satisfy the poor fellow for the time being, and they returned to the tent. There a fire was again started and supper was prepared. Shadows gathered in the valley and night came on. Overhead the bright stars were shining with a clear light peculiar to that Southwestern land.

After supper they lay about on the ground, talking of the Enchanted Valley, as Merry had named it, and of the mysterious smoke seen rising from it. Later, when little Abe and Cap'n Wiley were sleeping and Worthington had sunk into troubled slumber, through which he muttered and moaned, Frank and Bart sat in the tent and examined the map by the light of a small lantern.

"Beyond question, Merry, the mine is near here. There is not a doubt of it. Here to the east is Hawley Peak, to the south lies Clear Creek. Here you see marked the stream which must flow through that valley, and here is the cross made by Clark, which indicates the location of his claim."

They bent over the map with their heads together, sitting near the end of the tent. Suddenly a hand and arm was thrust in through the perpendicular slit in the tent flap. That arm reached over Frank's shoulder, and that hand seized the map from his fingers. It was done in a twinkling, and in a twinkling it was gone.

With shouts of astonishment and dismay, both Frank and Bart sprang up and plunged from the tent. They heard the sounds of feet running swiftly down the valley.

"Halt!" cried Merry, producing a pistol and starting in pursuit.

In the darkness he caught a glimpse of the fleeing figure.

"Stop, or I fire!" he cried again.

There was no answer. Flinging up his hand, he began shooting into the gloom. He did not stop until he had emptied the weapon. Having run on some distance, he paused and listened, stopping Bart with an outstretched hand.

Silence lay over the valley.

"Did you hit him?" asked Bart.

"I don't know," confessed Frank.

"I can hear nothing of him."

"Nor I."

"You may have dropped him here."

"If not——"

"If not, my map is gone."

As he was talking, Frank threw open his pistol and the empty shells were ejected. He deftly refilled the cylinder.

"By George, Merry!" whispered Bart, "Worthington may have been right when he told you he saw some one beyond those bowlders."

"He was."

"Then we have been followed! We have been spied upon!"

"No question about it."

"Who did it?"

"That's for us to find out."

Together they searched for the man at whom Frank had fired in the darkness. They found nothing of him. From the tent little Abe began calling to them. Then Worthington came hurrying and panting through the darkness seeking them.

"They have gone!" declared the man wildly. "They were here! In my sleep I felt them! In my sleep I saw them!"

"We must have a light, Hodge," said Frank. "Bring the lantern."

Bart rushed back to the tent and brought the lantern. With it Frank began examining the ground.

"Poor show of discovering any sign here," he muttered.

After a time, however, he uttered an exclamation and bent over.

"What have you found?" questioned Hodge excitedly.

"See here," said Frank, pointing on the ground before him.

On a rock at their feet they saw fresh drops of blood.

"By Jove, you did hit him!" burst from Bart's lips. "If we can follow that trail——"

"We will find the man who has that map," said Merry grimly. "I wonder how badly he is wounded."

"Blood!" moaned Worthington. "There is blood on the ground! There is blood in the air! There is death here! Wherever I go there is death!"

"Keep still!" said Frank sharply. "Look out for Abe, Bart."

Then he began seeking to follow the sanguine trail with the aid of the lighted lantern. It was slow work, but still he made some progress.

"We're taking big chances, Merry," said Bart, who had a pistol in his hand.

"It's the only way we can follow him."

"Beware!" warned Worthington, in a hollow whisper. "I tell you there is death in the air!"

They had not proceeded far when suddenly a shot rang out and the bullet smashed the lantern globe, extinguishing the light. Hodge had been expecting something of the sort, and he fired almost instantly in return, aiming at the flash he had vaguely seen.

"Are you hurt, Merry?" he asked.

"No; the lantern was the only thing struck. Did you see where the shot came from?"

"I caught a glimpse of the flash."

Then a hoarse voice hailed them from the darkness farther down the valley.

"You gents, there!" it called.

They did not answer.

"Oh, Frank Merriwell!" again came the call.

"It's somebody who knows you," whispered Hodge.

"What is it?" called Merry, in response.

"You holds up where you are!" returned the voice, "or you eats lead a-plenty."

"Who are you?"

"That's what you finds out if you come. If you wants to know so bad, mebbe you ambles nearer and takes your chances o' getting shot up."

"It's sure death to try it," warned Hodge, in a whisper.

"Death and destruction!" Worthington screamed. "It is here! Come away! Come away!"

He seized Merry and attempted to drag him back. Frank was forced to break the man's hold upon him.

"I must save you!" the deranged man panted. "I knew it would come! Once I left you to perish in the flames; now I must save you!"

He again flung himself on Frank, and during the struggle that followed both Hodge and Wiley were compelled to render assistance. Not until the madman had been tripped and was held helpless on the ground did he become quiet.

"It's no use!" he groaned; "I can't do it! It is not my fault!"

Merry bent close and stared through the gloom at the eyes of the unfortunate man.

"You must obey me," he said, in that singular, commanding tone of his. "You have to obey me! Go back to the tent!"

Then he motioned for Hodge to let Worthington up, and Bart did so. Without further resistance or struggling, the man turned and walked slowly back to the tent.

"Go with him, Wiley, and take Abe with you."

Although Wiley protested against this, Frank was firm, and the sailor yielded. Then, seeking such shelter as they could find amid the rocks and the darkness, Bart and Frank crept slowly toward the point from which that warning voice had seemed to come. A long time was spent in this manner, and when they reached the spot they sought they were rewarded by finding nothing.

"He has gone, Frank," muttered Hodge. "While we were struggling with Worthington, he improved the opportunity to escape."

"I fear you are right," said Merriwell.

Further investigation proved this was true. In vain they searched the valley. The mysterious unknown who had snatched the map and who had been wounded in his flight by Frank had made good his escape.

CHAPTER IV.

THE NIGHT WATCH.

hey were finally compelled to give up the search, although they did so with the greatest reluctance.

"Unless it aids the other fellow to locate the claim
first," said Bart, "the loss of the map cannot be much of a disadvantage to you, Merry. It could give us no further assistance in
finding the claim."

"That's true," muttered Frank. "But the fact that mysterious men
have been prowling around here and one of them has secured the
map seems to indicate there are others who are searching for Benson Clark's lost claim. If they locate it first——"

"It's rightfully yours!" growled Hodge. "No one else has a real
claim to it. Clark gave it to you."

"But he made no will."

"All the same, you know he gave it to you."

"We have discussed all that, Hodge," said Merry as they returned to the tent. "If other parties find the claim first and begin
work on it, they can hold it."

Wiley was teetering up and down in front of the tent, apparently
in an uneasy state of mind.

"I have faced perils by sea and land!" he exclaimed, as they approached. "It doesn't behoove any one to shunt me off onto a
lunatic and a cripple when there is danger in the air. My fighting
blood is stirred, and I long to look death in the mouth and examine his teeth."

Neither Merry nor Bart paid much attention to the spluttering
sailor. They consulted about the wisdom of changing their camping place for the night.

"I don't think it is necessary," said Frank. "Whoever it was, the
prowler secured the map, and I fancy it will satisfy him for the
present. Something assures me that was what he was after, and
we have nothing more of interest to him now."

After a time they decided to remain where they were and to take turns in guarding the camp. The first watch fell on Bart, while Frank was to take the middle hours of the night, and Wiley's turn came toward morning. It was found somewhat difficult to quiet Worthington, who remained intensely wrought up over what had happened; but in time Merry induced him to lie down in the tent.

Little Abe crept close to Frank and lay there, shivering somewhat.

"You have so many enemies, Frank," he whispered. "Who are these new enemies you have found here?"

"I don't know at present, Abe; but I will find out in time."

"Why must you always have enemies?"

"I think it is the fortune of every man who succeeds to make enemies. Other men become jealous. Only idiots and spineless, nerve-lacking individuals make no enemies at all."

"But sometime your enemies will hurt you," muttered the boy fearfully. "You can't always escape when they are prowling about and striking at your back."

"Of course, there is a chance that some of them may get me," confessed Frank; "but I am not worrying over that now."

"Worthington frightens me, too," confessed the boy. "He is so strange! But, really and truly, he seems to know when danger is near. He seems to discover it, somehow."

"Which is a faculty possessed by some people with disordered brains. I fancied the fellow was dreaming when he declared he saw some one hiding behind those rocks to-day; but now I know he actually saw what he claimed to see."

"Oh, I hope they don't get that mine away from you! You have taken so much trouble to find it!"

"Don't worry," half laughed Merry. "If they should locate the mine ahead of me, I can stand it. I have two mines now, which are owned jointly by myself and my brother."

"Your brother!" exclaimed Abe, in surprise. "Why, have you a brother?"

"Yes; a half-brother."

"Where is he?"

"He is attending school far, far away in the East. I received some letters from him while you were in Denver."

"Is he like you?"

"Well, I don't know. In some things he seems to be like me; in others he is different."

"He is younger?"

"Yes, several years younger."

"Oh, I'd like to see him!" breathed Abe. "I know I'd like him. What's his name?"

"Dick."

"Perhaps I'll see him some day."

"Yes, Abe, I think you will. By and by we will go East, and I will take you to see him at Fardale. That's where he is attending school."

"It must be just the finest thing to go to school. I never went to school any. What do they do there, Frank?"

"Oh, they do many things, Abe. They study books which prepare them for successful careers, and they play baseball and football and take part in other sports. They have a fine gymnasium, where they exercise to develop their bodies, which need developing, as well as their brains. In some schools, Abe, the development of the body is neglected. Scholars are compelled to study in close rooms, regardless of their health and of their individual weaknesses. And many times their constitutions are wrecked so that they are unfitted to become successful men and women through the fact that they have not the energy and stamina in the battle of life, at which successes must be won.

"I don't know that you understand all this, Abe, but many parents make sad mistakes in seeking to force too much education into the heads of their children in a brief space of time. It is not always the boy or girl who is the smartest as a boy or girl who makes the smartest and most successful man or woman. Some of the brightest and most brilliant scholars fail after leaving school. Although at school they were wonders in their classes, in after life others who were not so brilliant and promising often rise far above them."

"I don't know nothing about those things, Frank," said the boy. "You seem to know all about everything. But I want you to tell me more about the school and the games they play and the things they do there."

"Not to-night, Abe," said Merry. "Go to sleep now. Sometime I will tell you all about it."

Long after Merry's regular breathing indicated that he was slumbering, little Abe lay trying to picture to himself that wonderful school, where so many boys studied, and lived, and prepared themselves for careers. It was a strange school his fancy pictured. At last he slept also, and he dreamed that he was in the school with other boys, that he was straight, and strong, and handsome, and that Dick Merriwell was his friend and companion. He dreamed that he took part in the sports and games, and was successful and admired like other lads. It was a joyful dream, and in his sleep he smiled and laughed a little. But for the poor little cripple it was a dream that could never come true.

In the night Frank was aroused by Bart, who lay down, while Merry took his place on guard outside the tent. The night was far spent when Frank awakened Wiley to take a turn at watching over the camp.

"Port your helm!" muttered the sailor thickly, as Merry shook him. "Breakers ahead! She's going on the rocks!"

"Turn out here," said Frank. "It's your watch on deck!"

"What's that?" mumbled the sailor. "Who says so? I am cap'n of this ship. I give off orders here."

Merry seized him by the shoulders and sat him upright.

"In this instance," declared Frank, "you're simply the man before the mast. I am captain this voyage."

"I deny the allegation and defy the alligator," spluttered Wiley, waving his arms in the dark. "I never sailed before the mast."

Frank was finally compelled to drag him bodily out of the tent, where at length Wiley became aware of his surroundings and stood yawning and rubbing his eyes.

"This is a new turn for me, mate," he said. "It has been my custom in the past to lay in my royal bunk and listen to the slosh of bilge water and the plunging of my good ship through the billows, while others did the real work. I always put in my hardest work at resting. I can work harder at resting than any man I know of. I have a natural-born talent for it. Nevertheless, Cap'n Merriwell, I now assume my new duties. You may go below and turn in with the perfect assurance that little Walter will guard you faithfully from all harm. Though a thousand foes should menace you, I will be on hand to repel them."

"That's right, Wiley; keep your eyes open. There may be no danger, but you know what happened early this night."

"Say no more," assured Wiley. "I am the embodied spirit of active alertness. Permit rosy slumber to softly close your dewy eyes and dream sweet dreams of bliss. Talk about real poetry; there's a sample of it for you."

Smiling a little at the eccentricities of the sailor, Frank slipped into the tent and again rolled himself in his blanket.

Rosy dawn was smiling over the eastern peaks when Frank opened his eyes. The others were still fast asleep, and Merry wondered if Wiley had already started a fire preparatory for breakfast. It seemed singular that the sailor had not aroused them before this. Stealing softly from the tent, Merry looked around for the captain. At first he saw nothing of him, but after some minutes he discovered Wiley seated on the ground, with his back against a bowlder and with his head bowed. Approaching nearer, Frank saw the sailor was fast asleep, with a revolver clutched in his hand.

"Sleeping at your post, are you?" muttered Frank, annoyed. "Had there been enemies near, they might have crept on us while you were sleeping and murdered the whole party. You deserve to be taught a lesson."

Making no noise, he drew nearer, keeping somewhat to one side and behind the sailor, then bent over and uttered a piercing yell in Wiley's ear. The result was astonishing. With an answering yell, the sailor bounded into the air like a jack-in-the-box popping up. As he made that first wild, electrifying leap he began shooting. When his feet struck the ground he started to run, but continued shooting in all directions.

"Repel boarders!" he yelled. "Give it to them!"

Frank dropped down behind the bowlder to make sure that he was protected from the bullets so recklessly discharged from the cap'n's revolver. Peering over it, he saw Wiley bound frantically down the slope toward the spring, catch his toe, spin over in the air, and plunge headlong. By a singular chance, he had tripped just before reaching the spring, and he dived into it, splashing the water in all directions. This termination of the affair was so surprising and ludicrous that Merry was convulsed with laughter. He ran quickly out, seized the sailor by the heels, and dragged him out. Wiley sat up, spluttering and gurgling and spouting water, very stupefied and very much bewildered.

This sudden commotion had brought Hodge leaping from the tent, a weapon in hand, while Abe and Worthington crawled forth in alarm.

Merry's hearty laughter awoke the echoes of the valley.

"Why do you disturb the placid peacefulness of this pellucid morning with the ponderous pyrotechnics of your palpitating pleasure?" inquired Wiley. "Did it amuse you so much to see me take my regular morning plunge? Why, I always do that. I believe in a cold bath in the morning. It's a great thing. It's a regular thing for me. I do it once a year whether I need it or not. This was my morning for plunging, so I plunged. But what was that elongated, ear-splitting vibration that pierced the tympanum of my tingling ear? Somehow I fancy I heard a slight disturbance. I was dreaming just at that moment of my fearful encounter with Chinese pirates in the Indian Ocean some several years agone. Being thus suddenly awakened, I did my best to repel boarders, and I fancy I shot a number of holes in the ambient atmosphere around here."

"You did all of that," smiled Merry. "I found it necessary to get under cover in order to be safe. Cap'n, you certainly cut a queer caper. It was better than a circus to see you jump and go scooting down the slope; and when you plunged into the spring I surely thought you were going right through to China."

"Well," said the sailor, wiping his face and hands on the tail of his coat, "that saves me the trouble of washing this morning. But I still fail to understand just how it happened."

"You were sleeping at your post."

"What? Me?"

"Yes, you."

"Impossible; I never sleep. I may occasionally lapse a little, but I never sleep."

"You were snoring."

Wiley arose, looking sad and offended.

"If I did not love you even as a brother I should feel hurt by your cruel words," he muttered, picking up an empty pistol that had fallen near the spring. "But I know you're joking."

"You just said you were dreaming, Wiley," reminded Frank. "Is this the way you are to be trusted? What if our enemies had crept upon us while you were supposed to be guarding the camp?"

"Don't speak of it!" entreated the marine marvel. "It hurts me. In case I closed my eyes by accident for a moment, I hope you will forgive me the oversight. Be sure I shall never forgive myself. Oh, but that was a lovely dream! There were seventeen pirates coming over the rail, with cutlasses, and dirks, and muskets, and cannon in their teeth, and I was just wading into them in earnest when you disturbed the engagement.

"In that dream I was simply living over again that terrible contest with the Chinese pirates in which I engaged while commanding my good ship, the Sour Dog. That was my first cruise in Eastern waters. The Sour Dog was a merchantman of nine billion tons burthen. We were loaded with indigo, and spice, and everything nice. We had started on a return voyage, and were bound southward to round the Cape of Good Hope. I had warned my faithful followers of the dangers we might encounter in the Indian Ocean, which was just literally boiling over with pirates of various kinds.

"One thing that had troubled us greatly was the fact that our good ship was overrun with rats. I set my nimble wits to work to devise a scheme of ridding us of those rats. I manufactured a number of very crafty traps, and set them where I believed they would be the most efficacious. You should have seen the way I gathered in those rats. Every morning I had thirty or forty rats in those traps, and soon I was struck with a new scheme. Knowing the value of rats in China, I decided to gather up those on board, put about, and deliver them as a special cargo at Hongkong. With this object in view, I had a huge cage manufactured on the jigger deck. In this cage I confined all the rats captured, and soon I had several hundred of them. These rats, Mr. Merriwell, saved our lives, remarkable though it may seem to you. Bear with me just a moment and I will elucidate.

"We had put about and set our course for the Sunda Islands when an unfortunate calm befell us. Now, a calm in those waters is the real thing. When it gets calm there it is so still that you can hear a man think a mile away. The tropical sun blazed down on the blazing ocean, and our sails hung as still and silent as Willie Bryan's tongue after the last Presidential election. The heat was so intense that the tar in the caulking of the vessel bubbled and sizzled, and the deck of the Sour Dog was hot as a pancake griddle. Suddenly the watch aloft sent down a cry, 'Ship, ho!' We sighted her heaving up over the horizon and bearing straight down on us."

"But I thought you said there was no wind," interrupted Merry. "How could a ship come bearing down upon you with no wind to sail by?"

"It was not exactly a ship, Mr. Merriwell; we soon saw it was a Chinese junk. She was manned with a great crew of rowers, who were propelling her with long oars. We could see their oar blades flashing in the sun as they rose and fell with machine-like regularity. I seized my marine glasses and mounted aloft. Through them I surveyed the approaching craft. I confess to you, sir, that the appearance of that vessel agitated my equilibrium. I didn't like her looks. Something told me she was a pirate.

"Unfortunately for us, we were not prepared for such an emergency. Had there been a good breeze blowing, we could have sailed away and laughed at her. As there was no breeze, we were helpless to escape. It was an awful moment. When I told my crew that she was a pirate they fell on their knees and wept and prayed. That worried me exceedingly, for up to that time they had been the most profane, unreligious set of lubbers it was ever my fortune to command. I told them in choice language just about what I thought of them; but it didn't seem to have any effect on them. I told them that our only chance for life was to repel those pirates in some manner. I warned them to arm themselves with such weapons as they could find and to fight to the last. We didn't have a gun on board. One fellow had a good keen knife, but even with the aid of that we seemed in a precarious predicament.

"The pirate vessel came straight on. When she was near enough, I hailed her through my speaking trumpet and asked her what she wanted. She made no answer. Soon we could see those yellow-skinned, pigtailed wretches, and every man of them was armed with deadly weapons. Having heard the fearful tales of butcheries committed by those monsters, I knew the fate in store for us unless we could repulse them somehow. Again I appealed to my men, and again I saw it was useless.

"The pirate swung alongside and fastened to us. Then those yellow fiends came swarming over the rail with their weapons in their teeth, intent on carving us up. The whole crew boarded us as one man. Just as they were about to begin their horrid work a brilliant thought flashed through my brain. I opened the rat cage and let those rats loose upon the deck. As the Chinamen saw hundreds of rats running around over the deck they uttered yells of joy and started in pursuit of them.

"When they yelled they dropped their cutlasses and knives from their teeth, and the clang of steel upon the deck was almost deafening. It was a surprising sight to see the chinks diving here and there after the rats and trying to capture them. To them those rats were far more valuable than anything they had expected to find on board. For the time being they had wholly forgotten their real object in boarding us.

"Seeing the opening offered, at the precise psychological moment I seized a cutlass and fell upon them. With my first blow I severed a pirate's head from his body. At the same time I shouted to my crew to follow my example. They caught up the weapons the pirates had dropped, and in less time than it takes to tell it that deck ran knee-deep in Chinese gore. Even after we had attacked them in that manner they seemed so excited over those rats that they continued to chase the fleeing rodents and paid little attention to us.

"If was not more than ten minutes before I finished the last wretch of them and stood looking around at that horrible spectacle. With my own hand I had slain forty-one of those pirates. We had wiped out the entire crew. Of course, I felt disappointed in having to lose the rats in that manner, but I decided that it should not be a loss, and straightway I began shaving the pigtails from the Chinamen's heads. We cut them off and piled them up, after which we cast the bodies overboard and washed the deck clean.

"When I arrived in New York I made a deal with a manufacturer of hair mattresses and sold out that lot of pigtails for a handsome sum. It was one of the most successful voyages of my life. When Congress heard of the wonderful things I had done in destroying the pirates, it voted me a leather medal of honor. That's the whole story, Mr. Merriwell. I was dreaming of that frightful encounter when you aroused me. Perhaps you may doubt the veracity of my narrative; but it is as true as anything I ever told you."

"I haven't a doubt of it," laughed Frank. "It seems to me that the most of your wonderful adventures are things of dreams, cap'n. According to your tell, you should have been a rich man to-day. You have had chances enough."

"That's right," nodded the sailor. "But my bountiful generosity has kept me poor. In order to get ahead in this world a fellow has to hustle. He can't become a Rockefeller or a Morgan if he's whole-souled and generous like me. I never did have any sympathy with chaps who complain that they had no chance. I fully agree with my friend, Sam Foss, who wrote some touching little lines which it would delight me to recite to you. Sam is the real thing when it comes to turning out poetry. He can oil up his machine and grind it out by the yard. Listen, and I will recite to you the touching stanzas in question."

In his own inimitable manner Wiley began to recite, and this was the poem he delivered:

"Joe Beall 'ud set upon a keg,
Down to the groc'ry store, an' throw
One leg right over t'other leg,
An' swear he'd never had a show.
'O, no,' said Joe,
'Hain't hed no show;'
Then shift his quid to t'other jaw,
An' chaw, an' chaw, an' chaw, an' chaw.

"He said he got no start in life,
Didn't get no money from his dad
The washing took in by his wife
Earned all the funds he ever had.
'O, no,' said Joe,
'Hain't hed no show;'
An' then he'd look up at the clock,
An' talk, an' talk, an' talk, an' talk.

"'I've waited twenty year—let's see——

36

Yes, twenty-four, an' never struck,
Altho' I've sot roun' patiently,
The fust tarnation streak er luck.
'O, no,' said Joe,
'Hain't hed no show;'
Then stuck like mucilage to the spot,
An' sot, an' sot, an' sot, an' sot.

"'I've come down regeler every day
For twenty years to Piper's store;
I've sot here in a patient way,
Say, hain't I, Piper?' Piper swore.
'I tell yer, Joe,
Yer hain't no show;
Yer too dern patient'——ther hull raft
Just laffed, an' laffed, an' laffed, an' laffed."

"That will about do for this morning," laughed Frank. "We will
have breakfast now."

That day Frank set about a systematic search for some method
of getting into the Enchanted Valley, as he had called it. Having
broken camp and packed everything, with the entire party he set
about circling the valley. It was slow and difficult work, for at
points it became necessary that one or two of them should take
the horses around by a détour, while the others followed the rim
of the valley.

Midday had passed when at last Merry discovered a hidden cleft
or fissure, like a huge crack in the rocky wall, which ran downward and seemed a possible means of reaching the valley. He had
the horses brought to the head of this fissure before exploring it.

"At best, it is going to be a mighty difficult thing to get the horses down there," said Bart.

"We may not be able to do it," acknowledged Merry; "but I am
greatly in hopes that we can get into the valley ourselves at last."

When they had descended some distance, Frank found indications which convinced him that other parties had lately traversed
that fissure. These signs were not very plain to Bart, but he relied
on Merry's judgment.

They finally reached a point from where they could see the bottom and look out into the valley.

"We can get down here ourselves, all right," said Hodge. "What
do you think about the horses?"

"It will be a ticklish job to bring them down," acknowledged
Merry; "but I am in for trying it."

"If one of the beasts should lose his footing and take a tumble——"

"We'd be out a horse, that's all. We must look out that, in case such a thing happens, no one of us is carried down with the animal."

They returned to the place where Wiley, Worthington, and little Abe were waiting. When Frank announced that they could get into the valley that way, the deranged man suddenly cried:

"There's doom down there! Those who enter never return!"

"That fellow is a real cheerful chap!" said the sailor. "He has been making it pleasant for us while you were gone, with his joyful predictions of death and disaster."

They gave little heed to Worthington. Making sure the packs were secure on the backs of the animals, they fully arranged their plans of descent and entered the fissure. More than an hour later they reached the valley below, having descended without the slightest mishap.

"Well, here we are," smiled Merry. "We have found our way into the Enchanted Valley at last."

"Never to return! Never to return!" croaked Worthington.

"It's too late to do much exploring to-night, Merry," said Hodge.

"It's too late to do anything but find a good spot and pitch our tent."

"Where had we better camp?"

After looking around, Merriwell suggested that they proceed toward the northern end of the valley, where there was timber.

"It's up that way we saw smoke, Frank," said Hodge.

"I know it."

As they advanced toward the timber they came to a narrow gorge that cut for a short distance into the side of a mighty mountain. The stream which ran through the valley flowed from this gorge, and further investigation showed that it came from an opening in the mountainside itself. Beside this stream they found the dead embers of a camp fire.

"Who built it, Frank?" asked Bart, as Merry looked the ground over. "Was it Indians, do you think?"

Merriwell shook his head.

"No; it was built by white men."

Hodge frowned.

"It makes little difference," he said. "One is likely to be as dangerous as the other."

"We will camp here ourselves," decided Merry.

The animals were relieved of their packs, and they busied themselves in erecting a tent and making ready for the night. Little Abe was set to gathering wood with which to build a fire. Darkness came on ere they had completed their tasks, but they finished by the light of the fire, which crackled and gleamed beside the flowing stream.

Wiley had shown himself to be something of a cook, and on him fell the task of preparing supper. He soon had the coffeepot steaming on a bed of coals, and the aroma made them all ravenous. He made up a batter of corn meal and cooked it in a pan over the fire. This, together with the coffee and their dried beef, satisfied their hunger, and all partook heartily.

"Now," said Wiley, as he stretched himself on the ground, "if some one had a perfecto which he could lend me, I would be supinely content. As it is, I shall have to be satisfied with a soothing pipe."

He filled his pipe, lighted it, and lay puffing contentedly. Bart and Merry were talking of what the morrow might bring forth, when suddenly Worthington uttered a sharp hiss and held up his hand. Then, to the surprise of all, from some unknown point, seemingly above them, a voice burst forth in song. It was the voice of a man, and the narrow gorge echoed with the weird melody. Not one of them could tell whence the singing came.

"Where dead men roam the dark
The world is cold and chill;
You hear their voices—hark!
They cry o'er vale and hill:
'Beware!
Take care!
For death is cold and still.'"

These were the words of the song as given by that mysterious singer. They were ominous and full of warning.

"That certainly is a soulful little ditty," observed Wiley. "It is so hilariously funny and laughable, don't you know."

Frank kicked aside the blazing brands of the fire with his foot and stamped them out, plunging the place into darkness.

"That's right," muttered Hodge. "They might pick us off any time by the firelight."

A hollow, blood-chilling groan sounded near at hand, and Wiley nearly collapsed from sudden fright. The groan, however, came from the lips of Worthington, who was standing straight and silent as a tree, his arms stretched above his head in a singular manner.

"The stars are going to fall!" he declared, in a sibilant whisper that was strangely piercing. "Save yourselves! Hold them off! Hold them off! If they strike you, you will be destroyed!"

"Say, Worth, old bughouse!" exclaimed Wiley, slapping the deranged man on the shoulder; "don't ever let out another geezly groan like that! Why, my heart rose up and kicked my hair just about a foot into the air. I thought all the ghosts, and spooks, and things of the unseen world had broken loose at one break. You ought to take something for that. You need a tonic. I would recommend Lizzie Pinkham's Vegetable Compound."

"Keep still, can't you!" exclaimed Hodge, in a low tone. "If we hear that voice again, I'd like to locate the point from whence it comes."

"Oh, I will keep still if you will guarantee to muzzle Worth here," assured the sailor.

The deranged man was silent now, and they all seemed to be listening with eager intentness.

"Why doesn't he sing some more, Merry?" whispered Bart.

After some moments, the mysterious voice was heard again. It seemed to come from the air above them, and they distinctly heard it call a name:

"Frank!"

Merry stood perfectly still, but, in spite of himself, Bart Hodge gave a start of astonishment.

"Frank Merriwell!"

Again the voice called.

"Great Cæsar's ghost!" panted Hodge in Merry's ear. "Whoever it is, he knows you! He is calling your name. What do you think of that?"

"That's not so very strange, Bart."

"Why not?"

"Since we came into the valley, either you, or Wiley, or Abe have spoken my name so this unknown party overheard it."

"Frank Merriwell!" distinctly spoke the mysterious voice; "come to me! You must come! You can't escape! You buried me in the shadow of Chaves Pass! My bones lie there still; but my spirit is here calling to you!"

"Booh!" said Wiley. "I've had more or less dealings with spirits in my time, but never with just this kind. Now, ardent spirits and spritis fermenti are congenial things; but a spooky spirit is not in my line."

"I tell you to keep still," whispered Hodge once more.

"I am dumb as a clam," asserted the sailor.

"Do you hear me, Frank Merriwell?" again called the mysterious voice. "I am the ghost of Benson Clark. I have returned here to guard my mine. Human hands shall never desecrate it. If you seek farther for it, you are doomed—doomed!"

At this point Worthington broke into a shriek of maniacal laughter.

"Go back to your grave!" he yelled. "No plotting there! No violence—nothing but rest!"

"Now, I tell you what, mates," broke in Cap'n Wiley protestingly; "between spook voices and this maniac, I am on the verge of nervous prostration. If I had a bottle of Doctor Brown's nervura, I'd drink the whole thing at one gulp."

Having shouted the words quoted, Worthington crouched on the ground and covered his face with his hands.

"What do you think about it now?" whispered Bart in Frank's ear. "Whoever it is, he knows about Benson Clark and his claim. He knows you buried Clark. How do you explain that?"

"I can see only one explanation," answered Frank, in a low tone. "This man has been near enough at some time when we were speaking of Clark to overhear our words."

"This man," muttered Wiley. "Why, jigger it all! it claims to be an ethereal and vapid spook."

"Don't be a fool, Wiley!" growled Hodge. "You know as well as we do that it is not a spook."

"You relieve me greatly by your assurance," said the sailor. "I have never seen a spook, but once, after a protracted visit on Easy Street, I saw other things just as bad. I don't think my nerves have gained their equilibrium."

"What will we do about this business, Merry?" asked Hodge.

"I don't propose to be driven away from here by any such childish trick," answered Frank grimly. "We will not build another fire to-night, for I don't care to take the chances of being picked off by any one shooting at us from the dark. However, we will stay right here and show this party that he cannot frighten us in such a silly manner."

"That's the talk!" nodded Hodge. "I am with you."

"Don't forget me," interjected the sailor.

"You!" exclaimed Frank sharply. "How can we depend on a fellow who sleeps at his post when on guard?"

"It's ever thus my little failings have counted against me!" sighed Wiley. "Those things have caused me to be vastly misunderstood. Well, it can't be helped. If I am not permitted to take my turn of standing guard to-night, I must suffer and sleep in silence."

Having said this in an injured and doleful manner, he retreated

41

to the tent and flung himself on the ground.

Frank and Bart sat down near the tent, and listened and waited a long time, thinking it possible they might hear that voice once more. The silence remained undisturbed, however, save for the gurgle of the little brook which ran near at hand.

CHAPTER V.

WILEY'S DISAPPEARANCE.

ight passed without anything further to disturb or annoy them. The morning came bright and peaceful, and the sun shone pleasantly into the Enchanted Valley. Wiley turned out at an early hour, built the fire, and prepared the breakfast.

"Seems like I had an unpleasant dream last eve," he remarked. "These measly dreams are coming thick and fast. Night before last it was pirates; last night it was spooks. It seems to be getting worse and worse. If this thing keeps up, I will be in poor condition when the baseball season opens in the spring."

"Then you intend to play baseball again, do you, cap'n?" asked Merry.

"Intend to play it! Why, mate, I cannot help it! As long as my good right arm retains its cunning I shall continue to project the sphere through the atmosphere. To me it is a pleasure to behold a batter wildly swat the empty air as one of my marvelous curves serenely dodges his willow wand. I have thought many times that I would get a divorce from baseball and return to it no more. But each spring, as the little birds joyfully hie themselves northward from their winter pilgrimage in the Sunny South, the old-time feeling gets into my veins, and I amble forth upon the turf and disport myself upon the chalk-marked diamond. Yes, I expect to be in the game again, and when little Walter gets into the game he gets into it for keeps."

"What if some one should offer you a prominent position at a salary of ten thousand a year where you would be unable to play baseball?" inquired Merry, with a sly twinkle in his eye. "You'd have to give it up then."

"Not on your tintype!" was the prompt retort.

"What would you do?"

"I'd give up the position."

Frank laughed heartily.

"Cap'n, you're a confirmed baseball crank. But if you live your natural life, there'll come a time when your joints will stiffen, when rheumatism may come into your good arm, when your keen eye will lose its brightness, when your skill to hit a pitched ball will vanish—then what will you do?"

The sailor heaved a deep sigh.

"Don't," he sadly said, wiping his eye. "Talk to me of dreadful things—funerals, and deaths, and all that; but don't ever suggest to me that the day will dawn when little Walter will recognize the fact that he is a has-been. It fills my soul with such unutterable sadness that words fail me. However, ere that day appears I propose to daze and bewilder the staring world. Why, even with my wonderful record as a ball player, it was only last year that I failed to obtain a show on the measly little dried-up old New England League. I knew I was a hundred times better than the players given a show. I even confessed it to the managers of the different teams. Still, I didn't happen to have the proper pull, and they took on the cheap slobs who were chumps enough to play for nothing in order to get a chance to play at all.

"I knew my value, and I refused to play unless I could feel the coin of the realm tickling my palm. I rather think I opened the eyes of some of those dinky old managers. But even though Selee, McGraw, and others of the big leagues have been imploring me on their knees to play with them, I have haughtily declined. What I really desire is to get into the New England League, where I will be a star of the first magnitude. I had much rather be a big toad in a little puddle than a medium-sized toad in a big puddle. The manager who signs me for his team in the New England League will draw a glittering prize. If I could have my old-time chum, Peckie Prescott, with me, we'd show those New England Leaguers some stunts that would curl their hair.

"Speaking of Peckie, Mr. Merriwell, reminds me that there is a boy lost to professional baseball who would be worth millions of dollars to any manager who got hold of him and gave him a show. Play ball! Why, Peckie was born to play ball! He just can't help it. He has an arm of iron, and he can throw from the plate to second base on a dead line and as quick as a bullet from a rifle. As a backstop he is a wizard. And when it comes to hitting—oh, la! la! he can average his two base hits a game off any pitcher in the New England League. To be sure, the boy is a little new and needs some coaching; but give him a show and he will be in the National or American inside of three seasons."

"Are you serious about this fellow, cap'n?" asked Frank. "I am aware that you know a real baseball player when you see him, but you have a little way of exaggerating that sometimes leads people to doubt your statements."

"Mr. Merriwell, I was never more serious in all my life. I give you my word that everything I have said of Prescott is true; but I fear, like some sweet, fragile wild-woods flower, he was born to blush unseen. I fear he will never get the show he deserves. While these dunkhead managers are scrabbling around over the country to rake up players, he remains in the modest seclusion of his home, and they fail to stumble on him. He is a retiring sort of chap, and this has prevented him from pushing himself forward."

"You should be able to push him a little yourself, cap'n."

"What! When I am turned down by the blind and deluded managers, how am I to help another? Alas! 'tis impossible! Coffee is served, Mr. Merriwell. Let's proceed to surround our breakfast and forget our misfortunes."

After breakfast Frank and Bart discussed the programme for the day. They decided to make an immediate and vigorous search for the lost mine. It was considered necessary, however, that one of the party should remain at the camp and guard their outfit. Neither Abe nor Worthington was suitable for this, and, as both Frank and Bart wished to take part in the search, Wiley seemed the only one left for the task.

"Very well," said the sailor, "I will remain. Leave me with a Winchester in my hands, and I will guarantee to protect things here with the last drop of my heroic blood."

In this manner it was settled. The sailor remained to guard the camp and the two pack horses, while the others mounted and rode away into the valley.

Late in the afternoon they returned, bringing with them a mountain goat which Merry had shot. As they came in sight of the spot where the tent had stood they were astonished to see that it was no longer there.

"Look, Frank!" cried Bart, pointing. "The tent is gone!"

"Sure enough," nodded Merriwell grimly. "It's not where we left it."

"What do you suppose has happened?"

"We will soon find out."

Not only had the tent and camping outfit disappeared, but the two pack horses were missing. Nor was Wiley to be found.

Hodge looked at Merry in blank inquiry.

"Where is this fellow we left to guard our property?" he finally

45

exclaimed.

"You know as well as I," confessed Frank.

"As a guard over anything, he seems to be a failure."

"We can't tell what has happened to him."

"What has happened to him!" cried Bart. "Why, he has taken French leave, that's what has happened! He has stolen our horses and piked out of the valley."

Merry shook his head.

"I don't believe that, Hodge," he said. "I don't think Wiley would do such a thing."

"Then, why isn't he here?"

"He may have been attacked by enemies."

"If that had been the case, we would see some signs of the struggle. You can see for yourself that no struggle has taken place here."

"It's true," confessed Merry, "that there seem to be no indications of a struggle."

"Do you know, Frank, that I never have fully trusted that chap."

"I know, Bart, you made a serious mistake on one occasion by mistrusting him. You must remember that yourself."

"I do," confessed Hodge, reproved by Merry's words. "All the same, this disappearance is hard to explain. Our tent and outfit are gone. We're left here without provisions and without anything. In this condition it is possible we may starve."

"The condition is serious," Frank acknowledged. "At the same time, I think it possible Wiley decided this location was dangerous and transferred the camp to some other place. That's a reasonable explanation of his disappearance."

"A reasonable one perhaps; but if that had happened! he should be here on the watch for our return."

"Perhaps we have returned sooner than he expected."

"Well, what's to be done, Merry?"

"We will sit here a while and see if he doesn't turn up. At least, we can make some sort of a meal off this mountain goat."

"A mighty poor meal it will be!" muttered Hodge disgustedly.

A fire was built, however, and the mountain goat served to appease their hunger somewhat, although without salt it was far from palatable. There was plenty of feed and drink for the horses, therefore the animals did not suffer. In vain they waited for Wiley to return. Afternoon faded into nightfall and the sailor came not.

"Do you propose to remain here all night, Merry?" inquired Bart.

Frank shook his head.

"I don't think it advisable. We will find another spot."

With the gloom of night upon them, they set out, Frank in the lead. He had taken notice of a clump of thick timber in another part of the valley, and toward this he rode. In the timber they ensconced themselves and prepared to pass the night there. Worthington was strangely silent, but seemed as docile and as harmless as a child. When all preparations to spend the night in that spot were made, Frank announced to Bart that he proposed to go in search of their missing companion.

"What can you do in the night?" questioned Hodge. "You can't find him."

"Perhaps not," said Merry; "but I am going to try."

"I hate to have you do it alone."

"You must remain here to look out for Abe and Worthington."

When this was settled, Merry set out on foot. During their exploration of the valley he had observed a deep, narrow fissure near the southern extremity, into which the stream plunged before disappearing into the underground channel. To him on discovering this it had seemed a possible hiding place for any one seeking to escape observation. Something caused him to set his course toward this spot.

An hour later, from a place of concealment high up on a steep bank, Frank was peering into the fissure. What he discovered there surprised and puzzled him not a little. On a little level spot close by the stream a tent had been pitched. Before the tent a small fire was burning, and squatted around this fire were three persons who seemed to be enjoying themselves in fancied security. The moment Merry's eyes fell on two of them he recognized them as having been members of the Terrible Thirty. They were the ruffians Hank Shawmut and Kip Henry. The third person, who seemed perfectly at his ease as he reclined on the ground and puffed at a corn-cob pipe, was Cap'n Wiley!

Was Wiley a traitor? This question, which flashed through Frank's mind, seemed answered in the affirmative by the behavior of the sailor, who was chatting on intimate terms with his new associates.

Of course Frank had decided at once that Shawmut and Henry had somehow learned of his expedition in search of Benson Clark's lost mine and had followed him. Henry's left hand was swathed in a blood-stained bandage, the sight of which convinced the watching youth that it was this fellow who had snatched the map and who afterward had been winged in the pursuit. In spite of appearances, Frank did not like to believe that Cap'n Wiley had played him false. From his position he was able to hear the conversation of the trio, and so he lay still and listened.

"We sartain is all right here fer ter-night," observed Shawmut. "We will never be disturbed any afore morning."

"Perchance you are right, mate," said the sailor; "but in the morning we must seek the seclusion of some still more secure retreat. My late associate, the only and original Frank Merriwell, will be considerable aroused over what has happened. I am positive it will agitate his equipoise to a protracted extent. My vivid imagination pictures a look of supine astonishment on his intellectual countenance when he returns and finds his whole outfit and little Walter vanished into thin, pellucid air."

Shawmut laughed hoarsely.

"I certain opine he was knocked silly," he said.

"But he is a bad man," put in Henry. "To-morrow he rakes this valley with a fine-toothed comb. And he is a heap keerless with his shooting irons. Look at this yere paw of mine. He done that, and some time I'll settle with him."

The fellow snarled the final words as he held up his bandaged hand.

"Yes," nodded the sailor, "he has a way of shooting in a most obstreperous manner. The only thing that is disturbing my mental placitude is that he may take to the war path in search of my lovely scalp."

"Confound you!" thought Frank, in great anger. "So you are a traitor, after all! Hodge was right about you. You're due for a very unpleasant settlement with me, Cap'n Wiley."

"What binds me to you with links of steel, mates," said the sailor, "is the fact that you are well supplied with that necessary article of exuberancy known to the vulgar and unpoetical as tanglefoot. Seems to me it's a long time between drinks."

"You certain must have a big thirst," observed Shawmut, as he produced a cold bottle and held it toward the sailor, who immediately arose and clutched it with both hands.

"Mates, it has been so long since I have looked a drink in the face that it seems like a total stranger to me. Excuse me while I absorb a small portion of mountain dew."

His pipe was dropped, and he wiped the mouth of the bottle with his hand after drawing the cork. He then placed the bottle to his lips and turned its bottom skyward.

"So it is for that stuff you sell your friends, is it?" thought Frank.

Having remained with his eyes closed and the bottle upturned for some moments, the sailor finally lowered it and heaved a sigh of mingled satisfaction and regret.

"My only sorrow," he said, "is that I haven't a neck as long as a giraffe's. If the giraffe should take to drink, what delight he would enjoy in feeling the ardent trickle down his oozle! Have something on me, boys."

He then returned the bottle, and the ruffians drank from it.

"There," said Wiley, picking up his pipe, "my interior anatomy glows with golden rapture. I am once more myself. Oh, booze, thou art the comforter of mankind! You cause the poor man to forget his sorrows and his misfortunes. For him you build bright castles and paint glorious pictures. For him you remove far away the cares and troubles of life. You make him a king, even while you make him still more of a pauper. You give him at first all the joys of the world and at last the delirium tremens.

"Next to women, you are the best thing and the worst thing in this whole wide world. Mates, you see I am both a poet and a philosopher. It's no disparagement to me, for I was born that way, and I can't help it. Ever since my joyful boyhood days on Negro Island I have looked with a loving eye on the beauties of nature and on the extracted fluid of the corn. But what of this world's riches has my mighty intellect and my poetic soul brought me? I am still a poor man."

"But you won't be long arter we diskeevers this mine," said Shawmut. "If you sticks by us, we gives you a third share."

"Your generosity overwhelms me. But it must not be forgotten that we yet have Frank Merriwell to dispose of. It is vain for you to try to frighten him away from this valley. Last night you attempted it with your spook trick, but it didn't work."

"What's that?" exclaimed Henry. "What are you talking about?"

"Oh," said the sailor, "you can't deceive little Walter. We heard you doing that spook turn. But it was time wasted."

Henry and Shawmut exchanged puzzled looks.

"You certain will have to explain what you are driving at," growled Shawmut.

"Don't you know?"

"None whatever."

"I fear you are still seeking to deceive me."

"Not a bit of it," averred Henry. "Whatever was yer talking about, Wiley?"

"Why, last eve, after we had partaken of our repast and were disporting ourselves in comfort on the bosom of mother earth, there came through the atmosphere above us a singing voice which sang a sweet song all about dead men and such things. Afterward the voice warned us to hoist anchor, set sail, and get out of this port. It claimed to be the voice of Benson Clark, the man who first found the mine here, and who was afterward shot full of holes by some amusement-seeking redskins. I surely fancied you were concerned in that little joke, mates."

Both the ruffians shook their heads.

"We has nothing to do with it," denied Shawmut.

"Well, now it is indeed a deep, dark mystery," observed the sailor. "Do you suppose, mates, that the spook of Benson Clark is lingering in this vicinity?"

"We takes no stock in spooks," asserted Henry.

"And thus you show your deep logical sense," slowly nodded the sailor. "I congratulate you; but the mystery of that voice is unsolved, and it continues to perplex me."

The listening man high up on the embankment was also perplexed. If Shawmut and Henry knew nothing of the mysterious warning voice, the enigma was still unsolved. As he thought of this matter, Merry soon decided that these ruffians had spoken the truth in denying all knowledge of the affair. These men talked in the rough dialect of their kind. The unseen singer had not used that dialect; and, therefore, the mystery of the valley remained a mystery still.

Frank continued to watch and listen.

"It's no spook we're worried about," declared Henry. "If we dispose of this yere Merriwell, we will be all right. With you ter help us, Wiley, we oughter do the trick."

"Sure, sure," agreed the sailor.

"Thar is three of us," said Shawmut, "and that certain makes us more than a match for them. The kid and the crazy galoot don't count. We has only Merriwell and Hodge to buck against."

"They are quite enough, mates—quite enough," put in the sailor. "We will have to get up early in the morning to get ahead of them."

"This yere Merriwell certain is no tenderfoot," agreed Shawmut.

Wiley arose and slapped the speaker on the shoulder in a friendly, familiar manner.

"Now you're talking," he nodded. "He is a bad man with a record longer than your arm. I have dealt with hundreds of them, however; and I think my colossal brain will be more than a match for him. Did you ever hear how I got the best of Bat Masterson? It's a thrilling tale. Listen and I will unfold it to you. You know Bat was the real thing. Beyond question, he was the worst bad man that ever perambulated the border. Yet I humbled him to his knees and made him beg for mercy. That was some several years ago. At that time—"

Wiley was fairly launched on one of his yarns, but at that moment Frank Merriwell heard a slight movement and attempted to turn quickly, when he was given a thrust by a powerful pair of hands, which hurled him forward from the embankment and sent him whirling down toward the tent below.

Frank struck on the tent, which served to break his fall somewhat, but he was temporarily stunned. When he recovered, he found himself bound hand and foot and his three captors surveying him by the light of the fire.

"Well, wouldn't it jar you!" exclaimed the sailor. "It was almost too easy. Why, mates, he must 'a' been up there listening to our innocent conversation, and somehow he lost his hold and took a tumble."

Shawmut laughed hoarsely.

"It was a mighty bad tumble for him," he said. "He falls right into our paws, and we has him foul. Now we're all right. Talk about luck; this is it!"

Kip Henry shook his wounded and bandaged hand before Frank's eyes.

"You did that, hang you!" he snarled. "Now you gits paid fer it!"

As the ruffian uttered these words he placed a hand on his revolver and seemed on the point of shooting the helpless captive.

"Wait a minute, mate," urged Wiley. "Let's not be too hasty. There are three of us here, and I have a sagacious opinion that any one of us will take morbid pleasure in putting Mr. Merriwell out of his misery. I propose that we draw lots to see who will do the little job."

"You seem mighty anxious to take a hand at it!" growled Henry.

"I wish to prove my readiness to stand by you through thick and thin," asserted the sailor. "In this way I shall win your absolute confidence. Should it fall on me to do this unpleasant task, you will see the job most scientifically done."

As he made this assertion Wiley laughed in a manner that seemed wholly heartless and brutal.

"I didn't think it of you, cap'n!" exclaimed Frank.

"That's all right," returned the sailor brazenly. "I'm a solicitor of fortune; I am out for the dust. These gents here have assured me that I shall have a third interest in the mine when it is located. Every bird feathers its own nest. I have a chance to feather mine, and I don't propose to lose the opportunity. If the task devolves upon me to transport you to the shining shore, rest easy in the assurance that I'll do a scientific job. I will provide you in short order with a pair of wings."

"That's the talk!" chuckled Shawmut. "How does we settle who does it?"

"Have you a pack of cards?" inquired Wiley.

"Sartin," said Shawmut, fishing in his pocket and producing a greasy pack. "We has 'em."

"Then I propose that we cut. The one who gets the lowest does the trick."

That was agreed to, and a moment later the cards had been shuffled and placed on a flat stone near the fire. Henry cut first and exposed a king.

"That lets you out," said the sailor. "I can beat that. Come ahead, Mate Shawmut."

Shawmut cut and turned up a trey.

"I reckon I'm the one," he said.

Then Wiley cut the cards and held up in the firelight a deuce!

Both Henry and Shawmut uttered exclamations.

"Well, you has your wish," said the latter. "Now it's up to you to go ahead with the business."

Wiley actually smiled.

"Let me take your popgun, mate," he said, extending his hand toward Henry. "Mine is a little too small to do the trick properly."

Henry handed over his pistol.

Wiley examined it critically, finally shaking his head.

"It's a mighty poor gun for a man of your standing to carry, mate," he asserted. "Perhaps you have a better one, Shawmut? Let me see."

Shawmut also gave up his pistol.

Having a revolver in each hand, Cap'n Wiley cocked them both.

"They seem to be in good working order," he said. "I should fancy either of them would kill a man quicker than he could wink his eye."

"You bet your boots!" said Henry.

"That being the case," observed Wiley, "I will now proceed to business."

Then, to the surprise of the two ruffians, he leveled the pistols straight at them.

"Now, you double-and-twisted yeller dogs!" he cried, "if you so much as wiggle your little finger, I will perforate both of you! I have the pleasure to inform you that I am a fancy pistol shot, and I think I can soak you with about six bullets each before you can say skat."

The astounded ruffians were taken completely by surprise.

"What in blazes does you mean?" snarled Shawmut.

"I mean business," declared the sailor. "Did you low-born whelps think that Cap'n Wiley would go back on his old side pard, Frank Merriwell? If you fancied such a thing for the fraction of a momentous moment, you deceived yourselves most erroneously. Now you keep still where you are, for I give you my sworn statement that I will shoot at the first move either of you make."

As Wiley said this he stepped close to Frank, beside whom he knelt, at the same time keeping the ruffians covered. He placed one of the revolvers on the ground and drew his hunting knife. With remarkable swiftness he severed the cords which held Frank helpless.

"Pick up that shooting iron, Merry," he directed. "I rather think we have these fine chaps just where we want them."

Frank lost no time in obeying, and the tables were completely turned on Shawmut and Henry.

"Stand up, you thugs!" ordered Merry. "Stand close together, and be careful what you do."

Infuriated beyond measure, they obeyed, for they were in mortal terror of their lives.

"Take those ropes, Wiley, and tie their hands behind their backs," directed Frank.

"With the greatest pleasure," laughed the sailor. And he proceeded to do so.

When the ruffians were thus bound Merry turned to Wiley, whose hand he grasped.

"Cap'n, forgive me!" he cried. "I was mistaken in you. I couldn't believe it possible; still, everything was against you. How did it happen?"

"A few words will clear up my seeming unworthiness," said the sailor. "When you departed to-day I found everything calm, and peaceful, and serene about the camp, and, after smoking my pipe a while, I fell asleep beside the tent. When I awoke these fine gentlemen had me. They proceeded to tie me up to the queen's taste. Seeing my predicament, I made no resistance. I permitted them to do just as they liked. I depended on my tongue, which has never failed me, to get me out of the predicament, I saw them gather up the outfit, pack it on the horses and prepare to remove it. During this I craftily assured them that I would gleefully embrace the opportunity to join issues with them.

"It's needless to enter into details, but they decided that it was best to let me linger yet a while on this mundane sphere while thinking my proposition over. So I was brought thither, along with the goods and chattels, and I further succeeded in satisfying them that they could trust me. It was my object, when I found they were well supplied with corn juice, to get them both helplessly intoxicated, after which I hoped to capture them alone and unaided. Your sudden tumble into this little nest upset my plans in that direction, but everything has worked out handsomely."

CHAPTER VI.

WILEY MEETS MISS FORTUNE.

hen they returned with their captives and the stolen horses and outfit to the timber in which Frank had left Hodge and the others it was learned that Worthington had disappeared. In vain they searched for him. He had slipped away without attracting Hodge's attention, and he failed to answer their calls. In the morning the search was continued. They returned to their former camping place at the head of the valley where the mysterious voice had been heard, and there Frank finally discovered some rude steps in the face of the cliff, by which he mounted to an opening which proved to be the mouth of a cave.

There were evidences that this cave had been occupied by some person. Merry saw at once that this unknown person might have been in the mouth of the cave at the time the mysterious voice was heard, and that beyond question he was the singer and the one who had warned them.

It was midday when Worthington was found. They discovered him in a thicket, locked fast in the arms of another man, whose clothes were ragged and torn, and who looked like a hermit or a wild man. The thicket in that vicinity was smashed and broken, and betrayed evidences of a fierce struggle. Worthington's hands were fastened on the stranger's throat, and both men were stone-dead.

"I know that man!" cried Merry, in astonishment. "I met him in Holbrook last spring. I told him of Benson Clark's death. He was once Clark's partner. Since that time he must have searched for Clark's mine and made his way to this valley. This explains the mystery. This explains how he knew me and knew of Benson Clark."

"Yes, that explains it," nodded Hodge. "But now, Frank—what are we to do?"

"We will give these poor fellows decent burial, and after that——"

"After that—what?"

"Shawmut and Henry must be turned over to the law. We must dispose of them as soon as possible. Then there will be plenty of time to return here and locate Benson Clark's lost mine."

And that plan was carried out. In a few days Frank Merriwell, Bart Hodge, Cap'n Wiley and little Abe rode into Prescott, Arizona, escorting their captives, whom they turned over to the officers of the law. Merry was ready to make a serious charge against the men, but, after listening to his story, the city official said:

"Better not trouble yourself about it, Mr. Merriwell. Those chaps are old offenders! They have been wanted for some time for stage robbing, horse stealing, and for the malicious murder of a man in Crown King and another in Cherry. Did you ever hear of Spike Riley?"

"Seems to me," said Frank, "I have heard of him as a bad man who was associated with the Kid Grafton gang."

"Well, sir, this chap you call Shawmut is Spike Riley. Since then little has been heard from him. I am glad to get my hands on him."

"Then I'll leave him to your gentle care," said Frank, with a smile. "You will relieve me of further bother on his part. As for Henry——"

"Henry!" laughed the official. "Why, he's got a record pretty nearly as bad as that of Riley. He is known down in Northern Mexico as one Lobo, and he has been concerned with Juan Colorado in some few raids. I think there is a reward offered for both of these men. In that case I presume you will claim it, sir."

Cap'n Wiley, who had listened with his head cocked on one side and a peculiar look in his eyes, now coughed suggestively. Frank glanced at the sailor and smiled.

"In case there is a reward, sir," he said, "it belongs to this gentleman."

As he rested a hand on Wiley's shoulder the latter threw out his chest and swelled up like a toad taking in air.

"Thanks, mate," he said. "My modesty would have prevented me from mentioning such a trifling matter."

"Oh, I will give you all the credit that's your due, cap'n," assured Merry. "You pulled me out of a bad pickle and tricked those ruffians very handsomely."

"That will do, that will do," said the sailor. "Let it go at that, Frank, old side partner. It is as natural for me to do such things as for the sweet flowers to open in the blooming spring. I never think anything about them after I do them. I never mention them to a soul. Why, if I were to relate half of the astounding things that have happened to me some people might suspect me of telling what is not strictly true. That's what binds my tongue to silence. That's why I never speak of myself. Some day my history will be written up, and I shall get great glory even though I do not collect a royalty."

"This is a pretty good thing, Merry," said Hodge. "It relieves you of all responsibility in regard to those ruffians, and you can now go about your business."

In this manner it was settled, and Frank left the two ruffians to be locked up in the Prescott jail.

Rooms were obtained at the best hotel in the place, and both Frank and Bart proceeded without delay to "spruce up." Having bathed, and shaved, and obtained clean clothes, they felt decidedly better.

It was useless for Cap'n Wiley to indulge in such needless trouble, as he regarded it.

"This is not my month to bathe," he murmured, as he sat with his feet on the sill of Frank's window and puffed leisurely at a cigar. "Besides, I am resting now. I find myself on the verge of nervous prostration, and therefore I need rest. Later I may blossom forth and take the town by surprise."

Later he did. Although he had jocosely stated that it was not his month to bathe, he indulged in such a luxury before nightfall, was shaved at a barber's shop and purchased a complete outfit of clothes at a clothing store. He even contemplated buying a silk hat, but finally gave this up when he found that silk hats of the latest style were decidedly scarce in Prescott. When he swaggered into Frank's room, where Merry and Hodge were holding a consultation, they both surveyed him in surprise.

"I am the real thing now," he declared.

"What has brought about this sudden change on your part?" questioned Frank.

"Hush!" said the sailor. "Breathe it softly. When I sat by yonder window musing on my variegated career I beheld passing on the street a charming maiden. I had not fancied there could be such a fair creature in this town. When I beheld her my being glowed. I decided that it was up to me to shed my coat of dust and grime and adorn myself. I have resolved to make my ontray into the midst of society here."

"But aren't you going back with us to the Mazatzals?" questioned Merry.

"When do you contemplate such a thing?"

"We expect to leave to-morrow."

"Why this agitated haste?"

"You know we've not definitely located Benson Clark's lost claim, although we feel certain it must be in the Enchanted Valley or in that vicinity. We're going back to prospect for that mine. If you return with us and we discover it, of course you will have an interest in it."

"Thanks for your thoughtful consideration, mate. At the same time, it seems to me that I have had about enough prospecting to do me for a while."

"Do you mean that you're not going with us?" exclaimed Hodge, in surprise. "Why, if we discover that mine it may make you rich!"

"Well, I will think the matter over with all due seriousness," said Wiley easily. "I know you will miss my charming society if I don't go."

"It may be the chance of your lifetime," said Merry.

"I'm not worrying about that. Wherever I go, Dame Fortune is bound to smile upon me. I have a mash on that old girl. She seems to like my style."

"I think you will make a mistake, Wiley, if you don't go," asserted Frank.

"Possibly so; but I've made so many mistakes in the brief span of my legitimate life that one or two more will hardly ruffle me. If I have to confess the truth to you, that valley is to me a ghastly and turgid memory. When I think of it I seem to hear ghostly voices, and I remember Worthington raving and ranting about death and destruction, and I picture him as we discovered him in the thicket, dead in the clutch of another dead man. These things are grewsome to me, and I fain would forget them."

"All right, cap'n," said Frank; "you are at liberty to do as you like."

Then he and Bart continued arranging their plans.

That evening Wiley disappeared. Frank and Bart left little Abe at the hotel and went out to "see the sights." In the biggest gambling place of the town they found the sailor playing roulette. Wiley had a streak of luck, and he was hitting the bank hard. Around him had gathered a crowd to watch his plunging, and the coolness with which he won large sums of money commanded their admiration.

"It's nothing, mates," he declared—"merely nothing. When I

was at Monte Carlo I won eleventeen thousand pesoses, or whatever they call them, at one turn of the wheel. Such a streak of luck caused the croupier to die of apoplexy, broke the bank, and put the Prince of Monte Carlo out of business for twenty-four hours. The next day the prince came to me and besought me to leave the island. He declared that if I played again he feared he would die in the poorhouse. As it was, he found it necessary to mortgage the Casino in order to raise skads to continue in business. To-night I am merely amusing myself. Five thousand on the red."

"Well, what do you think of that?" asked Hodge in Frank's ear.

"I think," said Frank, "that it is about time for Cap'n Wiley to cash in and stop playing."

He pushed his way through the throng and reached the sailor.

"Now is the time for you to stop," said Frank in Wiley's ear, speaking in a low tone, in order not to attract attention, for he knew such advice would not be relished by the proprietor and might get him into trouble.

"Never fear about me, mate," returned the sailor serenely. "Ere morning dawns I shall own this place. Talk about your gold mines! Why, this beats them all!"

"It's a wise man who knows when to stop," said Frank.

"It's a wise man who knows how to work a streak clean through to the finish," was the retort. "I have my luck with me to-night, and the world is mine. In the morning I shall build a fence around it."

"Red wins," quietly announced the croupier.

"You observe how easy it is, I presume," said Wiley, smiling. "I can't help it. It's as natural as breathing."

Frank saw that it was useless to argue with the sailor, and so he and Hodge left him still playing, while they strolled through the place. There was a dance hall connected, which provided amusement for them a while, although neither danced. Barely half an hour passed before Frank, who was somewhat anxious about Wiley, returned to note how Wiley was getting along.

Luck had turned, and Wiley was losing steadily. Still he continued to bet with the same harebrained carelessness, apparently perfectly confident that his bad luck could not keep up.

"He will go broke within twenty minutes if he sticks to it, Frank," said Hodge.

Merry nodded.

"That's right," he agreed; "but he won't listen to advice. If we attempt to get him away, we will simply kick up a disturbance and find ourselves in a peck of trouble. Even if he should cash in now and quit ahead of the game, he'd come back to it and lose all he's won. Therefore we may as well let him alone."

They did so, and Bart's prophecy came true. The sailor's reckless betting lowered his pile so that it seemed to melt like dew before the sun. Finally he seemed to resolve on a grand stroke, and he bet everything before him on the red.

The little ball clicked and whirred in the whirling wheel. The spectators seemed breathless as they watched for the result of that plunge. Slower and slower grew the revolutions of the wheel. The ball spun around on its rim like a cork on the water. At length it dropped.

"He wins!" panted an excited man.

"No—see!" exclaimed another.

The ball had bobbed out of its pocket and spun on again.

"Lost!" was the cry, as it finally settled and rested securely in a pocket.

Wiley swallowed down a lump in his throat as the man behind the table raked in the wager.

"Excuse me," said the sailor, rising. "I hope you will pardon me while I go drown myself. Can any one direct me to a tub of tanglefoot?"

As he left the table, knowing now that it would cause no disturbance, Frank grasped his arm and again advised him to leave the place.

"I admit to you," said Wiley, "that I was mistaken when I stated that I had a mash on Dame Fortune. I have discovered that it was her daughter, Miss Fortune. Leave me—leave me to my fate! I shall now attempt to lap up all the liquids in the place, and in the morning I'll have a large aching head."

Frank insisted, however, and his command led Wiley reluctantly to permit them to escort him from the place.

"I might read you a lecture on the evils of gambling, cap'n," said Merry; "but I shall not do so to-night. It strikes me that you have learned your lesson."

"It is only one of many such lessons," sighed the sailor. "By this time I should have them by heart, but somehow I seem to forget them. I wish to tell you a secret that I have held buried in my bosom these many years. It is this:

"Somewhere about my machinery there is a screw loose. In vain I have sought to find it. I know it is there just as well as I know that I am Cap'n Wiley. Now, you are a perfect piece of machinery, with everything tight, and firm, and well oiled, and polished. As an example you are the real thing. Perhaps to-morrow I may conclude to follow in your footsteps. Just tuck me in my little bed and leave me to dreamy slumber."

After being left in his room, however, Wiley did not remain long in bed. Knowing they would not suspect such a thing of him, he arose, and dressed, and returned to the gambling house. When morning came he was not only broke, but he had pawned everything of value in his possession and was practically destitute.

"Well," said Merry, having discovered the cap'n's condition, "I presume now you will return with us to the Mazatzals?"

"No use," was the answer; "I shall stay here in Prescott. I have my eye on a good thing. Don't worry about me."

It was useless to urge him, for he persisted in his determination to stay there. And so before leaving Frank made some final arrangements with him.

"I have wired for my mail to be forwarded here, Wiley," he said. "If anything of importance comes, anything marked to be delivered in haste, I wish you would see that it reaches me. Cannot you do so?"

"Depend upon me, Frank," assured the sailor. "I will not fail you in this. But before departing it seems to me that you should make arrangements that any such message be delivered into my hands."

"I will do so," said Merry. "Now, see here, cap'n, I don't like to leave you strapped in this town. At the same time, I don't care to let you have money of mine to gamble with. If I provide you with some loose change, will you give me your word not to use it in gambling?"

"Your generosity is almost ignoble!" exclaimed Wiley. "However, I accept it in the same manner that it is tendered. I give you my word."

"Well, that goes with me," nodded Merry. "Before leaving I shall see that you are fixed with ready money."

CHAPTER VII.

A STARTLING TELEGRAM.

Sunset in the Enchanted Valley. Below the little waterfall which plunged down into the fissure at the southern end of the valley Frank and Bart had toiled hard all through the day. Their sleeves were rolled up and their clothes mud-bespattered. There they had worked in the sandy soil near the stream, and there they had found the shining stuff for which they sought. Every panful was carefully washed in the stream, showing dull yellow grains in the bottom when the last particles remained.

Not far away, on the level of the valley above them, set near the stream, was their tent. In front of it little Abe was building a fire and was seeking to prepare supper for them, knowing they would be ravenously hungry when they quit work for the night. At intervals the cripple hobbled to the brink of the fissure and looked down at them as they toiled.

No one had troubled them since their return to the valley. No longer did the place seem enchanted or mysterious. All the mysteries were solved, and it lay sleeping and silent amid that vast mountainous solitude.

"Well, Bart," said Frank, as he dropped his spade, "it seems to me that the thing is done to our satisfaction. At the northern end of the valley we have found Clark's quartz claim, and the specimens we have taken from it seem decidedly promising. Here we have located this placer, and we know from what we have washed out that it is rich and will prove extremely valuable while it lasts. Now it's up to us to register our claims and open them for operation in the proper manner. We ought to be satisfied."

"Satisfied!" exclaimed Bart. "You bet I am satisfied! What if I had remained in Boston, Merry? Why, I would be plugging away to-day on a poor paying job, with decidedly poor prospects ahead of me. It was a most fortunate thing for me when I decided to stick by you and come West."

Frank smiled.

"It was lucky, Hodge," he agreed. "But I don't forget that you came without a selfish thought on your part. You came to help me in my fight against Milton Sukes. I am far better pleased for your sake than for my own that we have had this streak of luck. Let's knock off for the night, old man. There's no reason why we should stick to it longer."

As they were climbing from the fissure by the narrow and difficult path, little Abe came rushing excitedly to the brink above and called to them.

"Come quick! Come quick!" he cried.

"What's the matter, Abe?" asked Frank, alarmed by the boy's manner.

"Somebody's coming," said the hunchback; "a man on a horse. He is coming right this way. He has seen the tent!"

"We may have some trouble after all, Merry," said Hodge.

Ere they could reach the head of the path near the waterfall they plainly heard the thudding hoofs of the horse coming rapidly in that direction. When they had reached the level ground above they beheld the horseman approaching. It seemed that he observed them at the same time, for he suddenly waved his hat in the air and gave a yell.

"By Jove!" exclaimed Merry, "I know him! It is Wiley!"

"Right you are!" agreed Hodge. "What the dickens could have brought him here at this time?"

"Perhaps he has some message for me. You know I made arrangements with him to bring any message of importance."

The sailor drew up his horse as he approached.

"Ahoy there, mates!" he cried. "At last I have struck port, although I'd begun to wonder if I'd ever find it. This confounded old valley has moved since I was here last. I thought I knew just where it was, but I have spent two whole days cruising around in search of it."

"Hello, cap'n!" said Frank. "You're just in time for supper."

"Supper!" exclaimed the sailor. "Say it again! Supper! Why, I have been living on condensed air for the last twenty-four hours. Look at me! I am so thin and emaciated that I can't cast a shadow. Hungry! Mates, a bootleg stew would be a culinary luxury to me. I will introduce ravage and devastation among your provisions. This morning I found an empty tomato can and another that once contained deviled ham, and I lunched off them. They were rather hard to digest, but they were better than nothing."

He sprang down from his horse, which betrayed evidence of hard usage.

"How did you happen to come?" asked Merry.

Wiley fumbled in his pocket and brought forth a telegram.

"I believe I made arrangements to deliver anything of importance directed to you," he said. "This dispatch arrived in Prescott, and I lost no time in starting to fulfill my compact."

Merry took the telegram and quickly tore it open. There was a look of anxiety on his face when he had read its contents.

"Anything serious the matter?" asked Hodge.

"It's a message from my brother, Dick," answered Frank. "You know I wired him to address his letters to Prescott. He didn't stop to send a letter. Instead he sent this telegram. You know Felicia Delores, Dick's cousin, with whom he was brought up? The climate of the East did not agree with her, therefore I provided a home for her in San Diego, California, where she could attend school. Dick has learned that she is ill and in trouble. He wants me to go to her at once."

"What will you do?" asked Hodge.

"I must go," said Frank quietly.

Frank mounted the steps of a modern residence, standing on a palm-lined street in San Diego, and rang the bell. He was compelled to ring twice more before the door was opened by a sleepy-looking Mongolian.

"I wish to see Mr. Staples at once," said Merry. "Is he home?"

"Mistal Staple not home," was the serene answer, as the Chinaman moved to close the door.

Frank promptly blocked this movement with a foot and leg.

"Don't be so hasty," he said sharply. "If Mr. Staples is not home, where can I find him?"

"No tellee. Velly solly."

"Then I must see Mrs. Staples," persisted Merry.

"She velly sick. Velly solly. She can't slee anyblody."

"Well, you take her my card," directed Merry, as he took out a card-case and tendered his card to the yellow-skinned servant.

"No take cald. She tellee me no bothal her. Go 'way. Come bimeby—to-mollow."

"Now, look here, you son of the Flowery Kingdom," exclaimed Merry, "I am going to see Mrs. Staples immediately, if she's in condition to see anyone. If you don't take her my card, you will simply compel me to intrude without being announced."

"Bold, blad man!" chattered the Chinaman, with growing fear.

"I callee police; have you 'lested."

"You're too thick-headed for the position you hold!" exasperatedly declared Merry. "Take my card to Mrs. Staples instantly, and she will see me as soon as she reads my name, Frank Merriwell, upon it."

"Flank Mellowell!" almost shouted the Celestial. "You Flank Mellowell? Clome light in, quickee! Mladam, she expectee you."

The door was flung open now, and Frank entered.

"Well, you have come to your senses at last!" he said.

"You no undelstand. Blad men velly thick. Blad men make velly glate tloubal. Little glil she glone; mladam she cly velly much, velly much!"

"Hustle yourself!" ordered Frank. "Don't stand there chattering like a monkey. Hurry up!"

"Hully velly flast," was the assurance, as the Mongolian turned and toddled away at a snail's pace, leaving Frank in the reception room.

A few moments later there was a rustle of skirts, and a middle-aged woman, whose face was pale and eyes red and who carried a handkerchief in her hand, came down the stairs and found him waiting.

"Oh, Mr. Merriwell!" she exclaimed, the moment she saw him. "So it's really you! So you have come! We didn't know where to reach you, and so we wired your brother. He wired back that he had dispatched you and that he thought you would come without delay."

Her agitation and distress were apparent.

"Felicia," questioned Frank huskily; "what of her?"

"Oh, I can't tell you—I can't tell you!" choked the woman, placing the handkerchief to her eyes. "It's so dreadful!"

"Tell me, Mrs. Staples, at once," said Frank, immediately cool and self-controlled. "Don't waste time, please. What has happened to Felicia? Where is she?"

"She's gone!" came in a muffled voice from behind the handkerchief.

"Gone—where?"

The agitated woman shook her head.

"No one knows. No one can tell! Oh, it's a terrible thing, Mr. Merriwell!"

"Where is Mr. Staples?" questioned Frank, thinking he might succeed far better in obtaining the facts from the woman's husband.

"That I don't know. He is searching for her. He, too, has been gone several days. I heard from him once. He was then in Warner, away up in the mountains."

Merry saw that he must learn the truth from the woman.

"Mrs. Staples," he said, "please tell me everything in connection with this singular affair. It's the only way that you can be of immediate assistance. You know I am quite in the dark, save for such information as I received from my brother's telegram. It informed me that Felicia was in trouble and in danger. What sort of trouble or what sort of danger threatens her, I was not told. In order for me to do anything I must know the facts immediately."

"It was nearly a month ago," said Mrs. Staples, "that we first discovered anything was wrong. Felicia had not been very well for some time. She's so frail and delicate! It has been my custom each night before retiring to look in upon her to see if she was comfortable and all right. One night, as I entered her room, light in hand, I was nearly frightened out of my senses to see a man standing near her bed. He saw me or heard me even before I saw him. Like a flash he whirled and sprang out of the window to the veranda roof, from which he easily escaped to the ground.

"I obtained barely a glimpse of him, and I was so frightened at the time that I could not tell how he looked. Felicia seemed to be sleeping soundly at the time, and didn't awake until I gave a cry that aroused her and the whole house as well. I never had a thought then that the man meant her harm. She was so innocent and helpless it seemed no one would dream of harming her. I took him for a burglar who had entered the house by the way of her window. After that we took pains to have her window opened only a short space, and tightly locked in that position, so that it could not be opened further from the outside without smashing it and alarming some one. I was thankful we had escaped so easily, and my husband felt sure there would be no further cause for worry. He said that, having been frightened off in such a manner, the burglar was not liable to return.

"Somehow it seemed to me that Felicia was still more nervous and pale after that. She seemed worried about something, but whenever I questioned her she protested she was not. The doctor came to see her several times, but he could give her nothing that benefited her. I continued my practice of looking in at her each night before retiring. One night, a week later, after going to bed, something—I don't know what—led me to rise again and go to her room. Outside her door I paused in astonishment, for I distinctly heard her voice, and she seemed to be in conversation with some one. I almost fancied I heard another voice, but was not certain about that. I pushed open the door and entered. Felicia was kneeling by her partly opened window, and she gave a great start when I came in so quickly. A moment later I fancied I heard a sound as of some one or something dropping from the roof upon the ground.

"I was so astonished that I scarcely knew what to say. 'Felicia!' I exclaimed. 'What were you doing at that window?'

"'Oh, I was getting a breath of the cool night air,' she answered. 'With my window partly closed it is almost stuffy in here. Sometimes I can't seem to breathe.'

"'But I heard you talking, child,' I declared. 'Who were you talking to?'

"'I talk to myself sometimes, auntie, you know,' she said, in her innocent way. She always called me auntie. I confess, Mr. Merriwell, that I was completely deceived. This came all the more natural because Felicia was such a frank, open-hearted little thing, and I'd never known her to deceive me in the slightest. I decided that my imagination had led me to believe I heard another voice than her own, and also had caused me to fancy that some one had dropped from the roof of the veranda. After that, however, I was uneasy. And my uneasiness was increased by the fact that the child seemed to grow steadily worse instead of better.

"Often I dreamed of her and of the man I had seen in her room. One night I dreamed that a terrible black shadow was hanging over her and had reached out huge clawlike hands to clutch her. That dream awoke me in the middle of the night, and I could not shake off the impression that some danger menaced her. With this feeling on me I slipped out of bed, lighted a candle, and again proceeded to her room. This time I was astonished once more to hear her talking as if in conversation with some one. But now I knew that, unless I was dreaming or bewitched, I also heard another voice than her own—that of a man. My bewilderment was so great that I forgot caution and flung her door wide open. The light of the candle showed her sitting up in bed, while leaning on the footboard was a dark-faced man with a black-pointed mustache. I screamed, and, in my excitement, dropped the candle, which was extinguished. I think I fainted, for Mr. Staples found me in a dazed condition just outside Felicia's door. She was bending over me, but when I told her of the man I had seen and when she was questioned, she behaved in a most singular manner. Not a word would she answer. Had she denied everything I might have fancied it all a grewsome dream. I might have fancied I'd walked in my sleep and dreamed of seeing a man there, for he was gone when my husband reached the spot.

"She would deny nothing, however, and what convinced us beyond question that some one had been in her room was the fact that the window was standing wide open. After that we changed her room to another part of the house and watched her closely. Although we persisted in urging her to tell everything, not a word could we get from her. Then it was that Mr. Staples wired Richard, your brother.

"Three days later Felicia disappeared. She vanished in the daytime, when every one supposed her to be safe in the house. No one saw her go out. She must have slipped out without being observed. Of course we notified the police as soon as we were sure she was gone, and the city was searched for her. Oh! it is a terrible thing, Mr. Merriwell; but she has not been found! Mr. Staples believes he has found traces of her, and that's why he is now away from home. That's all I can tell you. I hope you will not think we were careless or neglected her. She was the last child in the world to do such a thing. I can't understand it. I think she must have been bewitched."

Frank had listened quietly to this story, drinking in every word, the expression on his face failing to show how much it affected him.

"I am sure it was no fault of yours, Mrs. Staples," he said.

"But what do you think has happened to her? She was too young to be led into an intrigue with a man. Still, I——"

"You mustn't suspect her of that, Mrs. Staples!" exclaimed Merry. "Whatever has happened, I believe it was not the child's fault. When I placed her in your hands, you remember, I hinted to you of the fact that there was a mystery connected with her father's life, and that he was an outcast nobleman of Spain. Where he is now I cannot say. I last saw him in Fardale. He was then hunted by enemies, and he disappeared and has never been heard from since. I believe it was his intention to seek some spot where he would be safe from annoyance and could lead his enemies to believe he was dead. I believe this mystery which hung like a shadow over him has fallen at last on little Felicia. I would that I had known something of this before, that I might have arrived here sooner. I think Felicia would have trusted me—I am sure of it!"

"But now—now?"

"Now," said Frank grimly, shaking his head, "now I must find her. You say you heard from your husband, who was then in a place called Warner?"

"Yes."

"Then he may have tracked her thus far. It's a start on the trail."

Mrs. Staples placed a trembling hand on Frank's sleeve.

"If you find her—the moment you find her," she pleaded, "let me know. Remember I shall be in constant suspense until I hear from you."

"Depend upon me to let you know," assured Frank.

A moment later he was descending the steps. He walked swiftly along the palm-lined streets, revolving in his mind the perplexing problem with which he was confronted. Seemingly he was buried in deep thought and quite oblivious of his surroundings. As he passed around a corner into another street he glanced back without turning his head. Already he had noted that another man was walking rapidly in the same direction, and this sidelong glance gave him a glimpse of the man.

Three corners he turned, coming at length to the main street of the city. There he turned about a moment later and was face to face with the man who had been following him. This chap would have passed on, but Frank promptly stepped out and confronted him. He saw a small, wiry, dark-skinned individual, on whose right cheek there was a triangular scar.

"I beg your pardon," said Merry.

"Si, señor," returned the man with the scar, lifting his eyebrows in apparent surprise.

"You seem very interested in me," said Merry quietly. "But I wish to tell you something for your own benefit. It is dangerous for you to follow me, and you had better quit it. That's all. Adios!"

"Carramba!" muttered the man, glaring at Frank's back as Merriwell again strode away.

CHAPTER VIII.

FELIPE DULZURA.

Frank did not find Rufus Staples at Warner. He had been there, however, and gone; but no one seemed to know where. The afternoon of a sunny day found Merry mounted on a fine horse, emerging from the mountains into a black valley that was shut in on either side by savage peaks. Through this valley lay a faint trail winding over the sand and through the forests of hideous cactus and yucca trees.

He had not journeyed many miles along this trail ere he drew up. Turning his horse about, he took a powerful pair of field glasses from a case and adjusted them over his eyes. With their aid he surveyed the trail behind him as far as it could be seen.

"I thought I was not mistaken," he muttered, as his glasses showed him a mounted man coming steadily along from the foothills of the mountains. "I wonder if he is the gentleman with the scarred cheek. I think I will wait and see."

He dismounted and waited beside the trail for the horseman to approach. The man came on steadily and unhesitatingly and finally discovered Frank lingering there. Like Merry, the stranger was well mounted, and his appearance seemed to indicate that there was Spanish blood in his veins. He had a dark, carefully trimmed Van Dyke beard and was carelessly rolling a cigarette when he appeared in plain view. His clothing was plain and serviceable.

Merry stood beside his horse and watched the stranger draw near. Frank's hand rested lightly on his hip close to the butt of his holstered revolver, but the unknown made no offensive move. Instead of that he called, in a pleasant, musical voice:

"Good-day, sir. I have overtaken you at last. I saw you in advance, and I hastened somewhat."

"Did you, indeed?" retorted Merry, with a faint smile. "I fancied you were coming after me in a most leisurely manner. But, then, I suppose that's what you call hurrying in this country."

"Oh, we never rush and exhaust ourselves after the manner of the East," was the smiling declaration, as the handsome stranger struck a match and lighted the cigarette.

Although Frank was confident the man was a Spaniard, he spoke with scarcely a hint of an accent. In his speech, if not in his manner, he was more like an American.

"Seems rather singular," questioned Frank, "that you should be traveling alone through this desolate region."

"The same question in reference to you has been troubling me, sir," retorted the stranger, puffing lightly at his cigarette. "To me it seems altogether remarkable to find you here."

"In that case, we are something of a mystery to each other."

"Very true. As far as I am concerned, the mystery is easily solved. My name is Felipe Dulzura. I am from Santa Barbara. I own some vineyards there."

Having made this apparently frank explanation, the man paused and looked inquiringly at Merry, as if expecting at least as much in return.

Frank did not hesitate.

"My name is Frank Merriwell," he said, "and I am a miner."

"A miner?"

"Yes, sir."

"You can't have any mines in this vicinity."

"Possibly I am looking the country over for an investment."

"It's possible," nodded Dulzura. "But from your intelligent appearance, I should fancy it hardly probable."

"Thanks for the compliment. In regard to you, being a planter, it seems quite unlikely that you should be surveying this region in search of a vineyard. It seems to me that I have been fully as frank, sir, as you have."

Felipe Dulzura lifted an objecting hand.

"I have not finished," he protested. "I didn't mean to give you the impression that I was seeking vineyards here. Far from it. On the contrary, having a little leisure, I am visiting the old missions in this part of the country. They interest me greatly. There was a time, long ago, you know, when this land belonged to my ancestors. My grandfather owned a vast tract of it. That was before gold was discovered and the great rush of 'forty-nine occurred.

"I presume it is needless to state that my grandfather's title to his lands was regarded as worthless after that and he lost everything. He died a poor man. My father was always very bitter about it, and he retired to Old Mexico where he spent his last days. I am

71

happy to say that he did not transfer his bitterness toward the people of this country to me, and I have found it to my advantage to return here and engage in my present occupation. You should see my vineyard, Mr. Merriwell. I think I have one of the finest in the State."

The manner in which this statement was made seemed frankly open and aboveboard. To all appearances, Felipe Dulzura had nothing to conceal and was unhesitating in telling his business.

"I, too," declared Merry, "am interested in the old Spanish missions. They remind me of the days of romance, which seem so far removed."

"Ah!" cried Dulzura, "then it may happen that we can journey a while in company. That will be agreeable to me. I confess that the trail has been lonely."

The planter was most agreeable and friendly in his manner, and his smile was exceedingly pleasant. In every way he seemed a most harmless individual, but experience had taught Merry the danger of always trusting to outward appearances.

"Company of the right sort will not be disagreeable to me," assured Frank.

"Good!" laughed Dulzura. "I am sick of talking to myself, to my horse, or to the landscape. I am a sociable chap, and I like some one to whom I can talk. Do you smoke, Mr. Merriwell? I have tobacco and papers."

"Thank you; I don't smoke."

"Ah, you miss one of the soothing friends of life. When I have no other company, my cigarette serves as one. This beastly valley is hot enough! The mountains shut it in and cut off all the cool breezes. However, ere nightfall we should get safely out of it and come to San Monica Mission. It lies yonder near the old Indian reservation. I have heard my father tell of it, and it has long been my object to see it."

For some little time they chatted, Dulzura seeming to be in the most communicative mood, but finally they prepared to go on together. When they were ready Frank suggested that his companion lead the way, as it was far more likely that he knew the trail better.

"No, no, Mr. Merriwell," was the protest. "There is but one trail here. Like you, I have never passed over it. You were in advance; it would scarcely be polite for me to take the lead."

Frank, however, had no thought of placing himself with his back turned on the self-styled planter, and, therefore, he insisted that Dulzura should proceed in advance, to which the latter acquiesced. As they rode on through the somewhat stifling heat of the valley, the Spaniard continued to talk profusely, now and then turning his head and smiling back at Merry.

"Next year," he said, "I mean to visit Spain. I have never been there, you know. Years and years ago my ancestors lived there. I trust you will pardon the seeming egotism, Mr. Merriwell, if I say it's not poor blood that runs in my veins. My ancestors far back were grandees. Did you ever hear of the Costolas? It's likely not. There were three branches of the family. I am a descendant of one branch."

"Costola?" murmured Frank. "The name seems familiar to me, but I presume there are many who bear it."

"Quite true. As for our family, however, an old feud has nearly wiped it out. It started in politics, and it divided the Costolas against themselves. A divided house, you know, cannot stand. My grandmother was a Costola. She was compelled to leave Spain. At that time another branch of the family was in power. Since then things have changed. Since then that powerful branch of the family has declined and fallen. It was not so many years ago that the sole surviving member was compelled, like my grandmother, to escape secretly from Spain. He came to this country and here lived under another name, taking that of his mother's family. I don't even remember the name he assumed after reaching America; but I did know that the surviving Costolas hunted him persistently, although he managed to evade and avoid them. What has become of him now is likewise a mystery. Perhaps he is dead."

The speaker suddenly turned so that he could look fairly into Frank's face, smiling a little, and said:

"It's not likely this interests you, sir."

"On the contrary," Merry smiled back, "I find it quite interesting. To me Spain is a land of romance. Being a plain American, the tales of those deadly feuds are fascinating to me. I presume the Costolas must have possessed large estates in Spain?"

"Once they did."

"And the one you speak of—the one who was compelled to flee from the country—was he wealthy?"

"I believe he was reckoned so at one time."

"And now," said Frank, "if this feud were ended, if any offense of his were pardoned, could he not claim his property?"

"That I don't know," declared Dulzura, shaking his head.

"Well, then, if he has any descendants, surely they must be the rightful heirs to his estate."

"I doubt, sir, if they could ever possess it. It must eventually be divided among his living relatives."

"Ah!" cried Merry. "I understand, Mr. Dulzura, why you must have a particular interest in visiting Spain. It seems probable that you, being distantly related to this exiled nobleman, may finally come into possession of a portion of his property."

"It's not impossible," was the confession, as the man in advance rolled a fresh cigarette. "But I am not counting on such uncertainties. Although my grandfather and my father both died poor, I am not a pauper myself. To be sure, I am not immensely rich, but my vineyards support me well. I have lived in this country and in Mexico all my life. In fact, I feel that I am more American than anything else. My father could not understand the democracy of the Americans. He could not understand their disregard of title and royalty."

Frank laughed.

"Had he lived in these days," he said, "and associated with a certain class of degenerate Americans, he would have discovered that they are the greatest worshipers of titles and royal blood in the whole world."

"I think that may be true," agreed the Spaniard, puffing at his cigarette. "I have seen some of it. I know that many of your rich American girls sell themselves for the sake of titles to broken-down and rakish noblemen of other countries. I think most Americans are ashamed of this."

"Indeed they are," seriously agreed Merry. "It makes them blush when a rich American girl is led to the altar by some broken-down old roué with a title, who has spent his manhood and wrecked his constitution in dissipation and licentiousness. Almost every week we read in the papers of some titled foreigner who is coming to America in search of a rich wife. We don't hear of the scores and scores of American girls with wealthy parents who go abroad in search of titles. But we have forgotten the Costolas. Can you tell me anything more of them?"

"You seem strangely interested in them," said Dulzura, again glancing back. "It almost seems as if you had heard of them before."

"And it almost seems so to me," confessed Frank. "I think I must have heard of them before. Sometime I shall remember when it was and what I have heard."

But, although they continued to talk, the Spaniard told Merry nothing more of interest in that line. Finally they relapsed into silence and rode on thus.

Frank's thoughts were busy when his tongue became silent. He remembered well that the most malignant and persistent enemy of little Felicia's father was a man who called himself Felipe Costola. This man had made repeated efforts to get possession of Felicia, but had been baffled by Delores and had finally lost his life in Fardale. Beyond question, Felipe Costola was dead, and what had become of Juan Delores no man seemed to know. Putting two and two together, Frank began to wonder if Delores might not be a Costola who had assumed the name of his mother's family while living in Spain, thus arousing the everlasting enmity of all the Costolas, and who had finally been compelled to flee to America. In many respects the history of this man agreed with that told by Juan Delores himself. He had once told Frank the name and title by which he was known in Spain, but never had he explained the fierce enmity of Felipe Costola. Now Merry was speculating over the possibility that Delores must have once been a Costola.

If this was true, then little Felicia was, by the statement of Dulzura, the rightful heir to the estate in Spain. Meditating on this possibility, Frank fancied he obtained a peep behind the curtain which hid the mystery of Felicia's disappearance. With the child out of the way, a false heir might be substituted, and the schemers behind the plot would reap their reward.

The shadows of evening were thickening in the mountain when Merry and his companion passed from the valley and reached the abrupt foothills. Here the trail was more clearly defined, and soon they were startled to see standing beside it an aged Indian, who regarded them with the stony gaze of the Sphinx. Dulzura drew up and asked the Indian in Spanish if the San Monica Mission was near. The reply was that it was less than half a mile in advance.

They came to it, sitting on a little plateau, silent and sad in the purple twilight. It was worn and battered by the storms of years. On its ancient tower the cross stood tremblingly. A great crack showed in its wall, running from base to apex. In the dark opening of the tower a huge bell hung, silent and soundless.

Merry drew up and sat regarding the ancient pile in almost speechless awe and reverence. It was a monument of other days in that sunny land. Here, long before the coming of the gold seekers, the Spanish priest had taught the Indian to bow his knee to the one true God. Here they had lived their calm and peaceful lives, which were devoted to the holy cause.

"Come," urged Dulzura, "let's get a peep within ere it becomes quite dark. There must be an Indian village somewhere near, and there, after looking into the mission, we may find accommodations."

Frank did not say that he was doubtful if such accommodations as they might find in an Indian village could satisfy him; but he followed his companion to the stone gate of the old mission, where Dulzura hastily dismounted. Even as Frank sprang from his horse he saw a dark figure slowly and sedately approaching the gate. It proved to be a bare-headed old monk in brown robes, who supported his trembling limbs with a short, stout staff.

Dulzura saluted the aged guardian of the mission in a manner of mingled worship and respect.

"What do ye here, my son?" asked the father, in a voice no less unsteady than his aged limbs.

"We have come, father, to see the mission," answered the Spaniard. "We have journeyed for that purpose."

"It's now too late, my son, to see it to-night. On the morrow I will take you through it."

"You live here alone, father?"

"All alone since the passing of Father Junipero," was the sad answer, as the aged monk made the sign of the cross.

Frank was deeply touched by the melancholy in the old man's voice and in the lonely life he led there in the ruined mission.

"What is the mission's income?" questioned Merry.

"Our lands are gone. We have very little," was the reply. "Still Father Perez has promised to join me, and I have been looking for him. When I heard your horse approaching I thought it might be he. It was but another disappointment. Still, it matters not."

"Let us take a peep inside," urged Dulzura. "Just one peep to-night, father."

"You can see nothing but shadows, my son; but you shall look, if you wish."

He turned and moved slowly along the path, aided by the staff. They followed him through the gate and into the long stone corridor, where even then the twilight was thick with shadows. In the yard the foliage grew luxuriantly, but in sad neglect and much need of trimming and attention.

At the mission door they paused.

"Let's go in," urged Dulzura.

"To-morrow will be time enough," answered Frank, a sudden sensation of uneasiness and uneasiness upon him.

At this refusal Dulzura uttered a sudden low exclamation and took a swift step as if to pass Merry. Frank instantly turned in such a manner that he placed his back against the wall, with the door on his left and the old monk close at hand at his right.

Suddenly, from beyond the shadows of the foliage in the yard, dark forms sprang up and came bounding into the corridor. Out from the door rushed another figure. Dulzura uttered a cry in Spanish and pointed at Frank. They leaped toward him.

Merry's hand dropped toward the holster on his hip, but with a gasp he discovered that it was empty. Instead of grasping the butt of his pistol, he found no weapon there with which to defend himself.

For all of the shadows he saw the glint of steel in the hands of those men as they leaped toward him, and he knew his life was in frightful peril.

How his pistol had escaped from the holster, whether it had slipped out by accident, or had in some inexplicable manner been removed by human hands, Frank could not say. It was gone, however, and he seemed defenseless against his murderous assailants.

In times of danger Frank's brain moved swiftly, and on this occasion it did not fail him. With one sudden side-step, he snatched from the old monk's hand the heavy staff. With a swift blow from this he was barely in time to send the nearest assailant reeling backward. The others did not pause, and during the next few moments Frank was given the liveliest battle of his career.

"Cut him down! Cut him down!" cried Dulzura, in Spanish.

They responded by making every effort to sink their knives in Frank. They were wiry, catlike little men, and in the gloom their eyes seemed to gleam fiercely, while their lips curled back from their white teeth.

Merriwell's skill as a swordsman stood him in good stead now. He took care not to be driven against the wall. He whirled, and cut, and struck in every direction, seeking ample room for evolutions. He knew full well that to be pressed close against the wall would put him at a disadvantage, for then he would not have room for his leaps, and swings, and thrusts, and jabs.

The fighting American bewildered and astounded them. He seemed to have eyes in the back of his head. When one leaped at him from behind to sink a knife between his shoulders Frank suddenly whirled like lightning and smote the fellow across the wrist, sending the steel flying from his fingers to clang upon the stones. The old monk lifted his trembling hands in prayer and tottered away. What had happened seemed to him most astounding and appalling.

"Come on, you dogs!" rang Frank's clear voice. "Come on yourself, Felipe Dulzura, you treacherous cur! Why do you keep out of reach and urge your little beasts on?"

The Spaniard uttered an oath in his own language.

"Close in! Close in!" he directed. "Press him from all sides! Don't let one man beat you off like that!"

"You seem to be taking good care of your own precious hide," half laughed Frank. Then, as the opportunity presented, he made a sudden rush and reached Dulzura with a crack of the staff that caused the fellow to howl and stagger.

It did not seem, however, that, armed only with that stick, Merry could long contend against such odds. Soon something must happen. Soon one of those little wretches would find the opportunity to come in and strike swift and sure with a glittering knife.

The racket and uproar of the conflict startled the echoes of the mission building, and in that peaceful, dreamy spot such sounds seemed most appalling. Frank knew the end must come. Had he possessed a pistol he might have triumphed over them all in spite of the odds.

Suddenly in the distance, from far down the trail toward the valley, came the sound of singing. As it reached Merry's ears he started in the utmost amazement, for he knew that tune. Many a time had he joined in singing it in the old days. Although the words were not distinguishable at first, he could follow them by the sound of the tune. This is the stanza the unseen singers voiced:

"Deep in our hearts we hold the love
Of one dear spot by vale and hill;
We'll not forget while life may last
Where first we learned the soldier's skill;
The green, the field, the barracks grim,
The years that come shall not avail
To blot from us the mem'ry dear
Of Fardale—fair Fardale."

"Fair Fardale!"—that was the song. How often Frank had joined in singing it when a boy at Fardale Military Academy. No wonder Frank knew it well! By the time the stanza was finished the singers were much nearer, and their words could be plainly distinguished. Dulzura and his tools were astounded, but the man urged them still more fiercely to accomplish their task before the singers could arrive.

The singing of that song, however, seemed to redouble Merry's wonderful strength and skill. He was now like a flashing phantom as he leaped, and dodged, and swung, and thrust with the heavy staff. His heart was beating high, and he felt that he could not be defeated then.

Finally the baffled and wondering assailants seemed to pause and draw back. Frank retreated toward the wall and stood waiting, his stick poised. The musical voices of the unseen singers broke into the chorus, and involuntarily Frank joined them, his own clear voice floating through the evening air:

"Then sing of Fardale, fair Fardale!
Your voices raise in joyous praise
Of Fardale—fair Fardale!
Forevermore 'twixt hill and shore,
Oh, may she stand with open hand
To welcome those who come to her—
Our Fardale—fair Fardale!"

It was plain that, for some reason, Dulzura and his band of assassins had not wished to use firearms in their dreadful work. Now, however, the leader seemed to feel that there was but one course left for him. Merry saw him reach into a pocket and felt certain the scoundrel was in search of a pistol.

He was right. Even as Dulzura brought the weapon forth, Frank made two pantherish bounds, knocking the others aside, and smote the chief rascal a terrible blow over the ear. Dulzura was sent whirling out between two of the heavy pillars to crash down into the shrubbery of the yard.

That blow seemed to settle everything, for with the fall of their master the wretches who had been urged on by him took flight. Like frightened deer they scudded, disappearing silently. Merry stood there unharmed, left alone with the old monk, who was still breathing his agitated prayers. From beyond the gate came a call, and the sound of that voice made Frank laugh softly with satisfaction.

He leaped down from the corridor and ran along the path to the gate, outside which, in the shadows, were two young horsemen.

"Dick—my brother!" exclaimed Merry.

"Frank!" was the cry, as one of the two leaped from the horse and sprang to meet him.

CHAPTER IX.

WHAT THE MONK TOLD THEM.

"By all that's wonderful!" exclaimed Merry, as he beheld his brother. "I thought I must be dreaming when I heard you singing. Dick, how did you come here?"

"I heard nothing from you, Frank," was the reply. "I didn't know for sure that you had received my message. I did know that Felicia was in trouble and in danger, and so I resolved to hasten to her at once. When I reached San Diego I found she was gone and that you had been there ahead of me. I have been seeking to overtake you ever since. This afternoon we saw you far away in the valley, although we could not be certain it was you. You had a companion. We thought it might be Bart Hodge."

Dick had made this explanation hastily, after the affectionate meeting between the brothers.

"It was not Hodge," said Frank; "far from it! It was a man I fell in with on the trail, and a most treacherous individual he proved to be."

Then he told of the encounter with Dulzura's ruffianly crew, upon hearing which Dick's companion of the trail uttered a cry.

"Whoop!" he shouted. "That certain was a hot old scrimmage. Great tarantulas! Why didn't we come up in time to get into the fracas! Howling tomcats! but that certain would have been the real stuff! And you beat the whole bunch off, did you, Mr. Merriwell? That's the kind of timber the Merriwells are made of! You hear me gently warble!"

"Hello, Buckhart!" exclaimed Frank, as the chap swung down from the saddle. Brad Buckhart and Dick Merriwell were chums at the Fardale Military Academy, and Frank knew him for one of the pluckiest young fellows he had ever met. Buckhart was a Texan through and through.

"Put her there, Mr. Merriwell," said Brad, as he extended his hand—"put her there for ninety days! It does my optics a heap of good to rest them on your phiz. But I'll never get over our late arrival on the scene of action."

"We knew you were here somewhere, Frank, when we heard you join in 'Fair Fardale,'" said Dick.

"And by that sound the greasers knew I had friends coming," added Merry. "It stopped them and sent them scurrying off in a hurry."

"Where are they now?" asked Brad. "Why don't they sail right out here and light into us? Oh, great horn spoon! I haven't taken in a red-hot fight for so long that I am all rusty in the joints."

"Where is Felicia, Frank?" anxiously asked Dick.

Merry shook his head.

"I can't answer that question yet," he confessed. "I have followed her thus far; of that I am satisfied, for otherwise I don't believe these men would have attacked me."

Through the shadows a dark figure came slowly toward them from the direction of the mission building.

"Whoever is this yere?" exclaimed Buckhart.

"It's the old priest," said Merry, as he saw the cloaked and hooded figure.

The old man was once more leaning on his crooked staff, which Merry had dropped as he hastened to meet his brother. Even in the gathering darkness there was about him an air of agitation and excitement.

"My son," he said, in a trembling voice, still speaking in Spanish, "I hope you are not harmed."

"Whatever is this he is shooting at you?" inquired Buckhart. "Is it Choctaw or Chinese?"

Paying no attention to Brad, Merry questioned the monk, also speaking in Spanish.

"Father," he said, "who were those men, and how came they to be here?"

"My son, I knew not that there were so many of them. Two came to me to pray in the mission. The others, who were hidden outside, I saw not until they appeared. Why did they attack you?"

"Because they are wicked men, father, who have stolen from her home a little girl. I am seeking her, hoping to restore her to her friends."

"This is a strange story you tell me, my son. Who is the child, and why did they take her from her home?"

"There's much mystery about it, father. She's the daughter of a Spanish gentleman, who became an exile from his own country. There are reasons to suppose she may be an heiress. Indeed,

81

that seems the only explanation of her singular abduction. I have traced her hither, father. Can you tell me anything to assist in my search?"

The old man shook his hooded head, his face hidden by deep shadows.

"Nothing, my son—nothing," he declared, drawing a little nearer, as if to lay his hand upon Frank. "I would I could aid you."

Suddenly, to the astonishment of both Dick and Brad, Merry flung himself upon the monk, grasping his wrist and dropping him in a twinkling. He hurled the agitated recluse flat upon his back and knelt upon his chest.

"Frank! Frank!" palpitated Dick. "What are you doing? Don't hurt him!"

"Strike a match, one of you," commanded Merry. "Give us a look at his face."

The man struggled violently, but Frank's strength was too much for him, and he was pinned fast.

Dick quickly struck a match and bent over, shading it with his hands, flinging the light downward upon the face of the man Merry held.

"Just as I thought!" Merry exclaimed, in satisfaction, as the light showed him, not the features of the old monk, but those of a much younger man, with dark complexion and a prominent triangular scar on his right cheek. "This is not the holy father. He couldn't deceive me with his attempt to imitate the father's voice. I have seen this gentleman on a previous occasion. He dogged my steps in San Diego after I left Rufus Staples' house."

It was, in truth, the same man Merry had warned on the street corner in San Diego. The little wretch swore savagely in Spanish and glared at his captors.

"Spare your breath, my fine fellow," said Frank. "Profanity will not help you."

"Well, whatever was the varmint trying to do?" cried Buckhart. "I certain thought he was going to bless you."

"He would have blessed me with a knife between my ribs had I been deceived by him," asserted Merriwell. "In my saddlebags you will find some stout cord. Give it to me."

A few moments later, in spite of his occasional struggles, the captured rascal was securely bound.

"There," said Merry, "I think that will hold you for a while. Now, boys, I am going to see what has become of the holy father. This is his cloak."

"You're not going back there alone," protested Dick, at once.

"Not on your life!" agreed Buckhart. "We are with you, Frank."

They followed him into the yard, where the darkness was now deep, and came together to the entrance of the mission, but without discovering anything of the aged monk. Standing in the corridor, they peered in at the yawning door, but could see or hear nothing. Frank called to the monk, but only echoes answered him from the black interior of the mission.

"Here's where you may get all the fight you want, Buckhart," he said grimly. "Be ready for anything, boys."

"I am a heap ready, you bet your boots!" answered the Texan, who had a pistol in his hand.

"Same here," said Dick.

Frank struck a match on the cemented wall. A cold wind from the interior of the building came rushing through the open door and blew it out. It was like the breath of some dangerous, unseen monster hidden within the mission. Merry promptly struck another match. This time he shaded it with his hands and protected it until it sprang into a strong glow. Then, with his hands concaved behind it, he advanced through the doorway, throwing its light forward. Almost immediately an exclamation escaped his lips, for a few feet within, lying on the cold floor, he discovered a human form. As he bent over the figure, he saw to his dismay it was the monk from whose body the brown cloak had been stripped.

Then the match went out.

"Is he dead, Frank?" whispered Dick.

"I can't tell," answered Merry. "I didn't get a fair look at him. We will know in a moment."

He lighted another match and bent over the prostrate man. The light showed him the eyes of the monk fixed stonily on his face. It also showed him that a gag had been forced between the old man's teeth and fastened there. The father was bound securely with a lariat.

"He is far from dead!" exclaimed Merry, in satisfaction. "Here, Dick, cut this rope and set him free. Get that gag out of his mouth, while I hold matches for you to do so."

Soon the rope was cut, the gag removed, and together they lifted the old man to his feet. Frank then picked him up and carried him out into the open air.

"You seem to have met with misfortune, father," he said. "I sincerely hope you are not harmed much."

"My son," quavered the agitated monk, "it is not my body that is harmed; it is my spirit. Against no living creature in all the world would I raise my hand. Why should any one seize me and choke me in such a manner? Much less, why should any who profess to be of the holy faith do such a thing?"

"They were frauds, father—frauds and rascals of the blackest dye."

"But two of them came here to pray," murmured the priest, as if he could not believe such a thing possible. "Have we not suffered indignities enough? Our lands have been taken from us and we have been stripped of everything."

"They were infidels, father. You may be sure of that."

"Infidels and impostors!" exclaimed the old man, with a slight show of spirit. "But I couldn't think men who spoke the language of old Spain and who prayed to Heaven could be such base creatures."

"What they certain deserve," growled Buckhart, unable to repress his indignation longer, "is to be shot up a whole lot, and I'd sure like the job of doing it."

"I don't understand it—I cannot understand it!" muttered the monk. "It's far beyond me to comprehend. Why did they set upon me, my son?" he questioned, his unsteady hand touching Frank's arm. "Why did they seek to slay you?"

"Wait a minute, father, and I will explain," said Merry.

He then told briefly of the abduction of Felicia and his pursuit of her captors. As he spoke, the aged listener betrayed some signs of excitement.

"My son, is all this true?" he solemnly questioned. "You are not one of our faith, yet your words ring true."

"I swear it, father."

"Then I have been twice deceived!" cried the old man, with surprising energy, shaking his hands in the empty air. "Yesterday there came here two men and a sweet-faced child. They told me they were taking her home. I believed them. With her they knelt at the shrine to pray. I blessed them, and they went on their way."

"At last!" burst from Merry's lips. "Now there's no question. Now we know we're on the right trail! Father, that little girl is a cousin of my half-brother here. He will tell you if I have spoken the truth."

"Every word of it is true," affirmed Dick, who spoke Spanish as fluently as Frank. "If you can tell us whither they were taking her, father, you may aid us greatly in our search for her."

"Alas! it is not possible for me to tell you! I know that they were bound eastward. Beyond these mountains are the great San Bernardino plains, a mighty and trackless desert. Where they could go in that direction I cannot say."

"Is it possible to cross the desert?" questioned Dick.

"It is a waste of burning sand. Who tries to cross it on foot or mounted is almost certain to leave his bones somewhere in that desert."

"Then if they kept straight on——"

"If they kept straight on," said the old monk, "I fear greatly you will never again behold the child you seek."

"They are not fools!" exclaimed Frank. "It is not likely they will try to cross the desert. The fact that they have taken so much trouble to endeavor to check pursuit here is proof they felt hard pushed. Is there no town, no human habitation beyond these mountains?"

"No town," declared the father. "Straight over to the east you will come to the El Diablo Valley. It is deep and wild, and in it are some ruined buildings of stone and cement. Tradition says they were built long ago by Joaquin Murietta, a Californian outlaw, who waged war on all Americans. He expected to retreat there some day and defend himself against all assailants. At least, so the legend runs, although I much doubt if he built the castle which is now called Castle Hidalgo. Of late it has another occupant, who has taken the name of Joaquin—Black Joaquin he is called."

"Well, this is somewhat interesting, too," declared Merry. "Is this new Joaquin endeavoring to follow in the footsteps of his predecessor?"

"I believe there is a price upon his head."

Merry turned to Dick with sudden conviction.

"Our trail leads to Castle Hidalgo," he asserted. "I am satisfied of that. I am also satisfied that I have here encountered some of Black Joaquin's satellites."

"And I will wager something," Dick added, "that we have one of them this minute, bound hand and foot, a short distance away."

"That's right," said Frank, "and we may be able to squeeze a little information from him. Father, the man who has your cloak is outside the gate. Perhaps you may know him. Come and look at him."

Together they left the yard and came to the spot where the man with the scar was supposed to be. On the ground lay the old monk's cloak, but the man was gone. Undoubtedly he had been set free by some of his comrades.

CHAPTER X.

THREE IN A TRAP.

The day was declining when Frank, Dick, and Brad came down into El Diablo Valley. It was, indeed, a dark, wild place, and for some time it seemed almost impossible of access. No plain trail led into it. On an elevation in the valley they had seen a ruined pile that bore a strong resemblance to a crumbling castle. The very appearance of these buildings belied the tale that Joaquin Murietta had built them there. Had they been so recently constructed their ruined condition was unaccountable. It seemed certain that at least a hundred years had passed since their erection. About the valley and the castle appeared hanging an air of mystery and romance.

That any one should choose such a remote and desolate spot to rear those buildings was beyond comprehension to the three young Americans who now beheld the ruins for the first time. Somehow those crumbling stones reminded them of the march of Cortez and his conquering treasure hunters. What Spaniard of that day, left behind in Mexico and supposed to be dead, had enriched himself with the treasures of the Aztecs and had escaped northward, only to find himself imprisoned in the new land, and to finally use a part of his treasures to erect this castle?

During the middle hours of the day alone did the southern sunshine fall soft and golden in El Diablo Valley. Therefore, they descended into the shadows and approached the castle, which seemed to lie silent and deserted in the midst of the valley.

"It's a whole lot strange we never heard of this place before," observed Buckhart. "Of course, others have seen it."

There was a cloud on Dick's face.

"Do you think, Frank," he questioned, "that there is any hope of finding Felicia here? Since leaving the mission we have seen nothing to indicate that we were still on the right trail."

"It's a good deal like hunting for a needle in a hay-stack," confessed Merry.

"Maybe those galoots who have her doubled back on us," suggested Brad. "Maybe they turned on us there at the mission."

"It's not impossible," was Merry's regretful admission. "However, we are here, and we will find what there is to find."

There were no echoes in the valley. It seemed a place of silence and gloom. As they approached the ruins they surveyed them with increasing wonder. There were old turrets and towers, crumbling and cracked, as if shaken by many earthquakes. The black windows glared at them like grim eyes.

"I will bet my boots that there is no one around this yere ranch," muttered Buckhart. "Perhaps that old priest fooled us a whole lot."

Merry shook his head.

"I am sure not," he said.

They mounted the rise on which the castle was built and passed through a huge gate and dark passage, coming into a courtyard, with the crumbling ruins all around them. Here they paused. Suddenly at one of the narrow, upper windows of the old turret a face appeared. Some one was there looking out at them. Frank's keen eyes were the first to discover it. Then to their ears came the cry of a voice electrifying them. The face at the window pressed nearer, and, together with the voice, it was recognized.

Dick gave a shout of joy.

"Felicia!" he exclaimed. "There she is, Frank. Can you see her in that window up there? Felicia! Felicia!"

But even as he called to her thus she suddenly vanished. As they stared at the window, another face showed for a moment and another pair of eyes looked down at them.

Then these also disappeared.

"Waugh!" exploded Brad Buckhart. "Here's where we get into action."

"She's there," declared Frank. "She's there—a captive!"

"It's sure to be a red-hot scrimmage," said Buckhart, looking at his revolver. "Take care that your guns are ready for action."

They leaped from their horses and swiftly approached the ruins, leaving the animals to wander where they might in the valley, well knowing they would not leave it.

Up the stone steps they bounded, coming to the deepset door, which by its own weight or by the working of time had fallen from its hinges. Nothing barred them there, and they entered. As they dashed in, there was a sudden whirring sound, and they felt themselves struck and beaten upon as by phantom hands. This was startling enough, but Frank immediately comprehended that they were bats and the creatures were fluttering wildly about them. From one dark room to another they wandered, seeking the stairs that should lead them up into the turret.

"We need a light," said Merry.

"That certain is correct, pardner," agreed Buckhart. "We are a heap likely to break our necks here in the dark."

"But we have no light," panted Dick, "and no time to secure a torch. If we waste time for that we may lose her."

"Where are those pesky stairs?" growled the Texan.

Their search led them into a huge echoing room that seemed windowless. Frank was exasperated by the aimlessness of their search. Had they not seen Felicia's face at the window and heard her voice, the silence and desolation of the place must have convinced them that it was in truth deserted. But now, of a sudden, there was a sound behind them. It was a creak on the rusty stairs. It was followed by a heavy thud and absolute silence.

"What was that?" asked Dick.

"It sounded to me," muttered Merry, "like the closing of a massive door."

A moment later he struck a match, and by its light they looked around. Holding it above his head, it served to illumine the chamber dimly.

"Wherever did we get into this hole?" asked Brad. "I fail to see any door."

The repeated lighting of matches seemed to show them only four bare walls. At last Frank found the door, but he discovered it was closed. More than that, he discovered that it was immovable.

"Boys," he said grimly, as the match in his fingers fluttered out and fell into a little glowing, coal at his feet, "we are trapped. It's plain now that we did a foolish thing in rushing in here without a light. That glimpse of Felicia lured us into the snare, and it will be no easy thing to escape."

"Let me get at that door!" growled Buckhart.

He flung himself against it with all his strength, but it stood immovable. They joined in using their united strength upon it, but still it did not stir.

"Well, this certain is a right bad scrape," admitted the Texan. "I don't mind any a good hot fight with the odds on the other side, but I admit this staggers me."

"What are we to do, Frank?" whispered Dick.

"Easier asked than answered," confessed Merry. "It's up to us to find some means of escape, but how we can do so I am not ready

88

to say."

"Pards," said the Texan, "it seems to me that we are going to get a-plenty hungry before we leave this corral. We are some likely to starve here. The joke is on us."

"Hush!" cautioned Merry. "Listen!"

As they stood still in the dense darkness of that chamber they heard a muffled voice speaking in English. It seemed to be calling to them derisively.

"You're very courageous, Frank Merriwell," mocked the voice; "but see what your courage has brought you to. Here you are trapped, and here you will die!"

"Hello!" muttered Merry. "So my friend, Felipe Dulzura, is near at hand!"

The situation was one to appall the stoutest heart, but Frank Merriwell was not the one to give up as long as there was the slightest gleam of hope. Indeed, in that darkness there seemed no gleam. It is not wonderful that even stout-hearted Brad Buckhart began to feel that "the jig was up."

In most times of danger, perplexity, or peril, Dick relied solely on himself and his own resources; now, however, having Frank at hand, he turned to him.

"Is there any chance for us to escape?"

"Boys," said Merry, "we must not think of giving up until we have made every effort in our power. The first thing to be done is to sound the walls. You can help me in this. Go around the walls, rapping on them and listening. See if you can find a hollow place. This is not the donjon, and it may have been originally intended for something different from a prison room."

Directed by him, they set about their task, sounding the walls. Hopeless enough it seemed as they went knocking, knocking through the darkness. When the room had been circled once and no discovery made, Buckhart seemed quite ready to give up the effort in that direction. Frank was not satisfied, but continued feeling his way along the walls, rapping and listening as he went. Finally he remained a long time in one place, which aroused the curiosity of his boy comrades.

"Have you discovered anything?" asked Dick.

Before replying Merry struck a match.

"Here, boys," he said, "you will see there is a crack in the wall. That may be the cause of the hollow sound I fancied it gave. But, look!" he added, holding the match high above his head, "see how the crack widens as it rises toward the ceiling. By Jove, boys! it's almost wide enough up there for a cat to get through."

Then the match burned too short to be held longer, and he dropped it. Several moments he stood in silence, paying no heed to the words of Dick or Brad. His mind was busy. Finally he said:

"Get up here, boys, both of you. Face this wall and stand close together. I want to climb on your shoulders. I am going to examine that crack. It may be our only hope of salvation."

They followed instructions, and Merry mounted to their shoulders, on which he stood. In this manner he was high enough to reach some distance into the crack in the wall. He found nothing but crumbling bits of cement and stone, which was a disappointment to him.

"Keep your heads down," he said. "I am going to see if I can loosen some of this outer coat of cement here. It may rattle down about your ears."

He pulled away at the cement, cleaving it off easily and exposing the fact that the wall was somewhat shabbily built above a distance of eight feet from the floor. An earthquake or convulsion of nature, or whatever had caused the crack in the wall, had seriously affected it, and it seemed very shaky and unstable indeed.

Several times he shifted about on the boys' shoulders to give them rest, as his heavy boots were rather painful after remaining in one position a few moments. They were eager to know what progress he was making.

"I can't tell what it amounts to, boys," he declared. "This crack may lead nowhere, even if I can make an opening large enough to enter."

At length he was compelled to descend in order to give them a chance to rest. Three times he mounted on their shoulders and worked at the cement and stones until the skin of his fingers was torn and his hands bleeding. He was making progress, nevertheless, and it seemed more and more apparent that, if given time enough, an opening might be made there at that height in the wall. In his final efforts he loosened a mass of the stuff, that suddenly gave way and went rattling and rumbling down into the wall somewhere. To his intense satisfaction, this left a hole large enough for a human being to creep into.

"Brace hard, boys," he whispered. "I am going to make a venture here. I am going to crawl into this place."

"Be careful, Frank!" palpitated Dick. "What if you get in there and the old wall crumbles on you! You will be buried alive! You will be smothered, and killed!"

"Better that than starvation in this wretched hole," he half laughed. "We will have to take chances if we ever escape at all.

Steady now."

They stiffened their bodies, and he gave a little spring, diving into the opening as far as he could and slowly wiggling and dragging himself forward. In this manner he gradually crept into it, although it was no simple matter. There was barely room enough for him to accomplish this feat, and when it was done he lay still a few moments to rest. As he lay thus he heard some of the stones and cement rattling and falling beneath him, and felt the whole wall seem to settle. His heart leaped into his throat, for it seemed, indeed, that he was about to be smothered and crushed to death in that place. Still he did not retreat. Instead of that, he squirmed and crawled forward as fast as possible. Suddenly a mass of the wall came down upon his back and shoulders, and he was pinned fast.

Trying to squirm forward still farther, he found himself held as if in the jaws of a vise, and never in his adventurous career had his position seemed more desperate and helpless. Dust filled his eyes and nostrils, and he seemed smothered.

Summoning all his wonderful strength, Merry made a mighty effort. Suddenly, as he did so, the wall beneath him seemed to give way, and downward he fell, amid showers of stones and cement, which rained upon him. He had fallen into some sort of open space, and, although somewhat dazed and stunned, he quickly crept forward to escape the falling mass of stuff. In this he was successful, and, although the air of the place seemed dense and stifling, he was practically uninjured.

As soon as possible, he sought to learn what kind of a place he had dropped into so unexpectedly. There were yet a few matches left in his match safe, and one of these he lighted. Its light showed him a small, narrow passage, leading away he knew not where. Behind him there was a mass of fallen debris where the top of the passage had caved in. Even then still more was threatening to fall, and he quickly moved away.

"I have heard of secret passages in old castles and mansions," Frank muttered, "and this must be one of them. Where will it lead me? It must take me somewhere, and this is better than remaining in the chamber where we were trapped."

For a long time he felt his way cautiously onward along the passage. He came in time to its end. His hand could feel nothing but the bare stones, and it seemed that the passage terminated there. Once more he struck a match, the light of which revealed to him nothing of an encouraging nature.

"Well," he said, "I seem to be in a trap still. It can't be possible this was simply a blind passage. Why was it constructed? There must be some way of getting out of it."

Again at the end of the passage he fell to sounding the wall and listening. His hands roamed over it, feeling every protrusion or irregularity. Finally he touched something that was loose. Immediately he pressed it with considerable vigor, upon which there was a faint muffled click, and a heavy door that had been skillfully covered by cement swung slowly against his hands.

Frank's wonderful command of his nerves kept him from uttering an exclamation of satisfaction. He quickly seized the edge of the door and pulled it wide open. Fresh air rushed in upon him, and he filled his lungs with a sensation of satisfaction and relief.

He now thought of returning and seeking to assist Dick and Brad in following him, but after a few moments he decided to investigate still further. Soon he found himself on a high terrace, which opened into an inclosed courtyard of the ruins. As he leaned there, looking down, the ring of ironshod hoofs came through the arched gate, reaching his ears. A moment later two horsemen rode into the courtyard, leading behind them three animals. The clank and clang of the horses' feet upon the flagstones echoed in the inclosure. Merry drew back, watching and listening.

"Three fine beasts," said a voice in Spanish. "And they are ours, comrade. The chief said we were to have them if we captured them."

"Why not?" sullenly returned the other man. "Are we to have nothing? Is the chief to get it all?"

"Hush, Jimenez!" hastily warned the first speaker. "Better not let him hear you utter such words."

"At least one can think, Monte," retorted Jimenez. "We take all the risks, and what do we get? Not even when we faced that young devil Americano at the mission did the chief put himself in peril. He urged us on, but he took good care of his precious self, I noticed."

"If you talk more in this manner, Jimenez," exclaimed Monte, "with you I will have nothing whatever to do!"

"Bah! You are a coward," snarled the other. "Now, be not hasty in your movements, for I, too, am armed."

"Fly at it!" whispered Frank, in satisfaction. "Go at each other, and do your prettiest. Cut each other's throats, and I will applaud you, you rascals!"

But the two scoundrels did not engage in an encounter. After growling a little at each other, they proceeded with the horses to a part of the courtyard where the stables seemed to be, and there disappeared. Merry did not have to watch long for their return. They again crossed the open space below and disappeared; but, listening where he stood, he heard their voices, and they seemed ascending stairs not far away.

His curiosity now fully aroused, with a pistol in his hand, Frank stole onward as swiftly as possible in an attempt to keep track of them. He left the terrace and came to the stairs by which they ascended. Even as he stole like a panther up those stairs, he caught the hum of voices and the flash of a light.

Thus it was that the daring young man at last reached a dark nook, from which sheltered spot he could peer through an open door into a lighted room where several men were gathered. Beyond doubt these were the members of Black Joaquin's band, several of whom had set upon him at San Monica Mission.

disappeared. Merry did not have to watch long for their return.
They again crossed the open space below and disappeared, but
listening where he stood, he heard their voices and they seemed
ascending stairs not far away.

His curiosity now fully aroused and the lamp in his hand, Frank
stole onward as swiftly as possible in an attempt to keep track of
them. He left the terrace and came to the stairs by which they ascended. Even as he stole like a panther up those stairs, he caught
the purr of voices once more high above him.

Thus it was that the daring young student had reached a dark
nook, from which sheltered spot he could peer through an open
door into a lighted room where several men were gathered. Be-

CHAPTER XI.

RUFFIANS AT ODDS.

Some of the men were idly lounging about as they
smoked, while others were playing cards. The card
players were gambling, and money clinked on the table
before them. A picturesque and desperate-looking group they
were, yet Merriwell felt and knew by experience that they
were far more dangerous in appearance than in actual fact.
He had met a number of them face to face, and succeeded in
holding them in check with no more than the crooked staff of
the old monk for his weapon of defense. They were the kind
to strike at a man's back and cower before his face.

The card players did not always get along amicably. At times
they quarreled excitedly, over their game. Finally one of them lost
everything and flew into a passion, roundly berating his more
lucky companions. They laughed at him as they puffed their cig-
arettes.

"What matters it, Pachuca?" cried one. "It is only a little. Soon
you will have more."

"Oh, yes, much more!" smiled another. "The chief has promised
you plenty when he shall get the girl safely away."

"I much prefer money to promises," solemnly retorted Pachuca.
"It's an honest game I play. Why should I win with you?"

"Now, it's best that you have a care with your tongue," rather
hotly returned one of the winners. "Yesterday it was your luck to
win; now it is mine."

"Is it luck you call it?" sneered Pachuca. "Ha! ha!"

"Yes, luck. What was it when you won?"

"It was my skill," declared Pachuca loftily. "But even skill is no
match for some methods."

At this the little fellow who had won the most sprang up and
struck the table with his fist, glaring across at Pachuca.

"Do you dare say to my face that I cheat?" he sharply cried.

"Speak it out, if you do!"

Merry was quite satisfied by the course events seemed to be taking, for he felt that it might be much to his advantage if a quarrel between these two men followed.

Pachuca, however, shrugged his shoulders and showed his teeth, as he rolled a cigarette.

"You have won, Ramon," he returned. "Keep the money. My turn comes."

"Any time you like," was the defiant challenge. "When I lose it is not like a stuck pig that I squeal."

Then Ramon sat down as if quite satisfied, and the game proceeded without Pachuca participating further.

Merry was disappointed. Still he saw there was bad blood among the men, and he felt that what he had heard in the courtyard and since indicated dissension and dissatisfaction.

As the gamblers continued they again fell to speaking of "the girl."

Suddenly behind him, toward the stairs, Merry heard a soft footfall. He pressed himself closer into the darkness of his niche and scarcely breathed as a man brushed past. This man halted in the door, hearing something of the words of the gamblers. Suddenly he stepped forward.

"What is this?" he demanded angrily. "Again you are talking too much. I have warned you before. You are not to speak at all of the girl. You know she's here; let that be enough, and hold your tongues!"

"Hello, my fine friend!" whispered Frank to himself, as the light fell on the face of the newcomer and he saw that there was a scar on the man's cheek. "So it's you?" Sudden silence fell upon the men. The man with the the scar singled out Ramon, at whom he pointed.

"You are always talking too much," he declared. "When will you learn better?"

As he stood behind the table, Ramon's hand slipped down to his sash, where it touched the hilt of a knife, and the look on his face was far from pleasant.

"It's me you always single out, Carlos!" he exclaimed. "Why do you never talk thus to the others?"

"Because it is you who make trouble. It is you I have been compelled to caution. What think you the chief would say should he hear you?"

"The chief!" cried Ramon. "Where is he? It is easy to make promises, Carlos. How know we that we are to receive all that is promised?"

"Have you not been satisfied in the past?"

"Not always," was the bold retort. "I am not the only one; there are others here who have not been satisfied. It is time to speak plainly. When all danger is over——"

"It is already," was the assertion.

"How so?"

"You know the three dogs who followed the trail have been trapped. They are secure, and never from this place will they go forth."

"But there may be others. There was another who followed us far."

"What of him?" sneered Carlos, snapping his fingers. "He has long lost the scent. It is only these three fellows who tracked us here, and better for them had they never come. Here their bones will rot!"

"If that is true, there is now nothing to prevent the chief from carrying the girl whither he likes. Who is she? That you have not told us, Carlos."

"That is nothing to you. It is a matter to concern the chief alone."

"Ah! we know she must be of great value to him, else he would have never taken so many chances. Why was she deceived with the tale that she was to be carried to her father?"

"How know you so much?" grimly demanded Carlos.

Then suddenly he wheeled on Jimenez.

"It's you who talk a great deal likewise!" he snarled.

Up to this point Jimenez had been silent. Now, like a flash, he sprang up and advanced to the side of Ramon.

"My tongue is my own," he harshly said. "On it no one has placed a lock. What harm has the child done that she should be deceived? We are the men who did the work; why should not we be trusted? Answer that—if you can. I know that she was told that she should find her father here. I know, too, that he is a fugitive and has long hidden from his enemies. However, I know that she was led to believe that he had sent for her. Where is this man?"

"You fool!" burst from Carlos. "I knew that it was a mistake when you were placed to guard her. I knew it was unsafe that she should tell you too much. Wait until the chief learns of this."

"Let him pay us what he has promised," said Ramon. "We will take it and be silent. He may then go where he pleases and carry the girl. Carlos, we are not the only ones here who demand to see this money and to hear it clink in our hands. Comrades, it is time we show our colors. Let those who are with me stand forth."

At this there was a stir. Some of the men seemed to hesitate, but a moment later two more men came over to the side of Ramon and Jimenez.

"This is not all," Ramon declared. "There are still others who are not satisfied with bare promises. Let the chief satisfy us. Where is he?"

Merry had been so deeply interested that he failed to hear a step behind him, and had not he been cautiously pressed in the shadows of his nook he might have been observed. The approaching man, however, had heard sounds of a quarrel in that room, and he strode past Frank and entered by the door.

"Who calls for me?" he demanded, in a clear, steady voice. "Why all this uproar?"

"Joaquin!" muttered one, while others exclaimed, "The chief!"

And Frank recognized Felipe Dulzura!

Sudden silence fell upon them. Dulzura, whom Frank now knew to be Black Joaquin, stood boldly looking them over. Despite the assertion made by one of the men that the chief was one who avoided danger, his bearing now seemed that of utter fearlessness and command.

"Speak!" he exclaimed. "What is the meaning of this?"

"Ask Ramon," said Carlos. "He will tell you—perhaps."

Ramon drew himself up. The time had come that he must face the matter unflinchingly.

"It is this," he said; "we have been promised much and have received little. Some of us are not satisfied."

"Indeed!" exclaimed Black Joaquin. "And you are one of the dissatisfied, I see."

"I am," was the admission; "but I am not alone. You will find that there are many more. Ask them. You will find nearly all are dissatisfied."

The chief glanced them over, and what he saw in their faces convinced him that Ramon spoke truly. Suddenly he smiled on them in that pleasant manner of his, and his voice was soft and musical as he spoke again.

"I would not have any of my faithful fellows dissatisfied," he declared. "If there is anything I can do in justice, let them name it."

Carlos seemed disappointed by this unexpected manner of their leader.

"It is that you have promised us a great deal we have not received," said Ramon.

"And is it yet time?" was the placid question.

"Why not? You said the time would come when the girl was safely yours, with no danger of pursuit. To me it seems that time has come. The three Americans who pursued you are captured and cannot escape. The girl is now yours to do with as you like. Is it strange we suspect she is a prize of great value? If she were not, why should Black Joaquin put himself to so much trouble?"

"You are right," smiled the man Merry knew as Dulzura. "But you are hasty. It is only lately the pursuers I most feared have fallen into my hands. Had you waited a little it might have given me more satisfaction. You were always too hasty, Ramon."

The rebuke was of the mildest sort, and Ramon accepted it without a show of anger.

"However," continued the chief, "I can pardon you this once, but you shall be satisfied. I have not at hand all I have promised you, but it is where I can soon secure it. Nevertheless, I have something here, and it shall be divided among you."

As he said this, he drew forth a leather pouch, which he flung with a careless gesture upon the table. It struck with a heavy thud and a slight clanking sound.

"I call upon you," he said, "to see that it is divided equally and fairly. The rest shall be paid you soon. Carlos, I would speak with you."

He then turned toward the door, and Carlos followed him. Outside, in the shadows, they halted not fifteen feet from Frank.

"Carlos," said Joaquin, "not one coin more will those dogs get. I have no further use for them. You and I must abandon them and get away before the coming of another day. It is no longer well for us to remain in this land. As Black Joaquin my work is done. Can we reach Spain in safety with the girl, our fortunes are made. But those snarling curs will object if they suspect we are contemplating leaving them behind. You I depend on. You know where the wine is kept. Take this which I give you and with it drug the wine. When you have done so, bring it for them to drink. Make merry with them, and encourage them to drink deeply. They will sleep soundly after that, and we shall have no trouble. I will get the girl ready. Before those fools awaken I shall be far from here, and we can laugh at them."

"Good!" said Carlos, having accepted from Joaquin's hand the bottle proffered him. "It shall be done. Leave it to me."

The chief clapped his trusted comrade upon the shoulder.

"Faithful Carlos!" he said. "With me you shall share the reward. Lose no time, for time is precious now."

"The Americans," questioned Carlos, "what of them?"

"Leave them where they are. Let them starve there."

Little did they dream when they turned away that they were followed by Frank Merriwell, who observed the greatest possible caution. They separated, and it was Black Joaquin whose footsteps led Frank through many winding ways and up long flights of stairs into one of the turrets. When Joaquin unbarred the door and entered the little room up there Frank was near at hand. Merry stole forward and peered into that room, from which the light shone forth.

"She's there!" he told himself, in deep satisfaction, as he beheld Felicia.

The captive girl had been weeping. When Joaquin saw this he spoke to her in a voice that seemed full of tenderness and compassion.

"My dear child," he said, "why do you shed these foolish tears?"

"Oh, sir!" exclaimed Felicia, "where are the friends I saw from the window? Why are they not permitted to come to me?"

"They are near and you shall see them soon," was the treacherous promise.

"How am I to believe you?" cried the girl. "You told me I should find my father here. You told me he was hiding here to escape his enemies. You told me he had sent for me to come to him, longing to see my face once more. I believed you. I trusted you. At your command I even deceived the good friends I knew in San Diego. Now I fear it was wrong and wicked for me to do so. Now I know it was wrong! But what was I to do? You told me, over and over, that my father would be placed in awful peril if I breathed a word of the truth."

"Which clears up that part of the mystery," thought Frank, as he listened outside.

"I told you nothing but the truth," declared Joaquin. "Your father sent that message to you by me."

"But he is not here—he is not here!" panted the distressed child. "You said I should find him here. If you deceive me in that, why not in everything?"

"Your father was here, but ere we could reach this place he found it necessary to depart. Enemies were searching for him, and he was forced to flee; but he left a message for me, telling me whither he went and directing me to bring you. Trust me, Felicia, and you shall soon see him."

Frank quivered a little with rage as he listened to the lying wretch.

Felicia drew a little nearer and looked earnestly into the face of the man.

"Oh, I can't believe you are deceiving me!" she said. "You do not seem so terribly wicked."

He laughed pleasantly.

"I know it must seem suspicious to you, child; but trust me a little longer."

"If you had only let my friends come to me!"

"Within two hours you shall be with them. Some of my men, I regret to say, I cannot trust, and so I hastened to send your friends away. They are not far from here, and we will join them. Are you ready to go, child?"

"Quite ready," she answered.

"Then give me your hand and trust me in everything."

She placed her hand confidingly in his, and they turned toward the door. Then Black Joaquin found himself face to face with a great surprise, for in that doorway stood Frank Merriwell, a cocked pistol leveled straight toward the scoundrel's heart.

"Up with your hands, Joaquin!" commanded Merry sharply. "One moment of hesitation on your part and I shall pull the trigger. I will send your black soul to the bar of judgment as true as my name is Frank Merriwell!"

The villain paled and was utterly dumfounded by the marvelous appearance of the man he believed secure in the dungeon.

"Put up your hands!" palpitated Frank, and in that second command there was something that caused Black Joaquin to quickly lift his hands above his head.

"One cry, one sound, even a murmur from your lips, will cause me to shoot you on the spot," declared the young American.

Felicia had been spellbound, but now she started forward, uttering a cry.

"Be careful," warned Frank, not taking his eyes off Joaquin for an instant. "Don't touch me! Keep out of the way!"

She paused and hastened to say:

"You must not hurt him, Frank. He is taking me to my father."

"He has lied to you from start to finish, like the treacherous snake he is," asserted Merry. "He doesn't mean to take you to your father."

Then he advanced two steps, and another command came from his lips.

"Face about, Joaquin," he said, "and walk straight toward that wall. Be quick about it, too."

Now, for all of the complaints of his followers that he seldom placed himself in danger, Black Joaquin was not a coward. Nevertheless, in those terrible, gleaming eyes of the American youth he had seen something that robbed him of his usual nerve and convinced him beyond doubt that unless he obeyed to the letter he would be shot on the spot. This being the case, he turned as directed and advanced until his face was against the wall.

"Stand thus," said Frank, "and don't move for your very life."

One glance around showed him a blanket upon a couch. Behind Joaquin's back he quickly took out and opened a knife.

"Here, Felicia, take this and cut that blanket into narrow strips. Hasten as much as possible."

She was, however, too trembling and excited to make the needed haste. Seeing this, Frank lost no time in searching Joaquin's person and disarming him, removing every dangerous weapon he found upon the man.

When this was done, he directed Felicia to bring the blanket, and, holding his pistol ready in his left hand, he gave her directions and assistance in cutting and tearing it into strips. As soon as one good, strong strip had been removed from the blanket Frank took it, seized Joaquin's hands, twisting them downward and backward behind his back, and tied them thus. After this he was able to remove from the blanket further strips he needed, although as he worked his pistol was ready for instant use. All the while he kept Joaquin with his face toward the wall, three times cautioning the man against turning his head in the slightest.

With the strips removed from the blanket Joaquin's ankles were securely tied. Then Frank unceremoniously kicked the fellow's feet from beneath him and lowered him to the floor upon his back. The rage, fury, and hatred in the conquered fellow's eyes was terrible to behold, but Merriwell heeded it not in the least. Deftly he rolled a wad of the blanket and forced it between Joaquin's teeth. With another piece of the torn blanket he fastened it there, knotting a strip behind the man's head. He took pains to make this as secure as possible, so that it would require no simple effort to remove it.

"Now, Black Joaquin, otherwise known as Felipe Dulzura," said Frank, standing over the man and looking down on him, "we will bid you good-night. You can rest easy here until your comrades recover on the morrow and release you. Perhaps they will find you. I hope, for your sake, that you do not smother before they awaken and come here. You have my best wishes for a short life and a speedy hanging."

With Felicia he left the chamber, closing and barring the door behind them.

Thus far Frank's success had been enough to astonish himself, but now he thought with dismay of Dick and Brad still confined in the chamber from which he had escaped. As with Felicia he descended the stairs he paused, hearing in some distant portion of the ruins the sound of singing.

"Carlos is doing his work," he thought. "He has brought them the wine. Thanks, Carlos; you have given me great assistance."

Merry decided that it would be necessary to conceal Felicia somewhere while he sought to return to Dick and Brad by means of the secret passage.

He found his way back to the terrace from which he had first looked down into the courtyard after his escape. As they reached that place, Merry heard beneath him some slight sound that caused him to again look downward. He was surprised to see a dark figure coming from the direction of the stables and leading three horses. His surprise increased when the feet of the horses gave forth no more than a faint, muffled sound on the courtyard flagging.

"What's up now?" he asked himself. "That must be Carlos preparing for flight. Whoever it is, he has muffled the feet of those horses. More than that, I believe they are our horses."

The human being and the horses crossed the courtyard and disappeared into the arched passage that led outward.

"Keep close behind me, Felicia," whispered Merry. "Be courageous. I may have to leave you for a short time; but I will return as soon as possible."

He had decided to conceal her in the secret passage while he endeavored to return to the prison chamber. The door of the passage he found to be slightly ajar. Swinging it open, he entered, with Felicia at his heels. Barely had he advanced ten feet into the passage before he felt himself suddenly clutched by a pair of strong hands.

"Keep still, Felicia!" called Frank, knowing she would be greatly frightened by the struggle.

Instantly the hold of these hands slackened and a joyous voice exclaimed in his ear:

"Frank! Frank! my brother, is it you?"

"Dick!" gasped Frank; "how did you get here?"

"We managed to pry open a hidden door which was disclosed when a part of the wall fell after you crept into that opening," said Dick.

"Where is Brad?"

"That's what I'd like to know. We separated to search for you.

He was to meet me here. We agreed on a signal. When you entered the passage without giving the signal I thought you must be an enemy."

"It's up to us now," said Merry, "to find Brad and get away from here in a hurry. We have a fine chance to do so. I can't explain everything, but I will tell you later. Here is Felicia."

"Felicia!" gasped Dick.

She uttered a low cry of joy, and the cousins were clasped in each other's arms.

"Come," said Merry. "Moments are precious."

"But Brad——"

"We will hope that luck may lead us to him."

But it was something more than luck, for Brad Buckhart was returning to meet Dick as he had promised when they encountered him. He heard them, and, thinking it might be Dick, whistled the soft signal agreed upon. Immediately Dick answered, and when the Texan found them all together, he came very near throwing up his hat and giving a cowboy yell.

"Oh, great jumping horned toads!" he whispered. "If this don't beat the record you can have my horse, saddle, and the whole blamed outfit! Talk about your miracles! So help me Davy Crockett, this is the greatest on record. You hear me gurgle!"

"There is yet danger in the air," said Merry. "As we were seeking the passage I saw a man, leading three horses with muffled feet, crossing the courtyard below. It must have been Carlos, Black Joaquin's lieutenant, for they planned a flight to-night, and Joaquin's wretched gang has been drugged."

"Guess again," advised the Texan, chuckling. "The gent you observed was yours truly, Bradley Buckhart."

"You?" gasped Frank, astonished.

"Precisely, pard—precisely. I was it. In my perambulations I discovered our horses, and it struck me as being something a whole lot proper to get them outside and have them where we could straddle them in a hurry when we took to our heels. I muffled their feet with the aid of blankets, and I can lead the way straight to them."

"Brad, you're a dandy!" laughed Frank softly. "Watch out for Carlos and lead on, you son of the Lone Star State."

They had come down into the courtyard when somewhere above, amid the ruins, there was a sudden sound of high-pitched voices, followed by a single pistol shot. Then came silence.

"If fortune is still with us," said Merry, "the bullet from that pistol lodged in the carcass of Carlos. Evidently he has kicked up

103

some sort of trouble, and I fancy a little chap by the name of Ramon fired that shot."

Outside the ruins they came upon the horses where Buckhart had concealed them. They were not long in mounting. Frank took up Felicia behind him, and away they rode into the night, with no hand raised to stay them.

CHAPTER XII.

A LIVELY FISTIC BOUT.

Three days later they arrived in San Diego, where Felicia was returned to the home of Mr. and Mrs. Staples, the former having given up the search in despair.

It was Frank who led a party of Americans to the Castle Hidalgo, in El Diablo Valley. The only human being found there was a man who had been shot and left where he fell in one of the chambers of the ruins. As Merry looked at the body, he grimly said:

"Retribution, swift and terrible, overtook you, Carlos, on that dark night. Who can say the hand of Providence was not in it? You were the only one who might have given us trouble, for your chief was bound and gagged, and your mates were drugged by your own hands. It is likely that Black Joaquin yet lives; but it is certain he must in time meet his just deserts."

Fearing that Black Joaquin would not give up his scheming to get possession of the girl, Frank decided that it was unsafe to leave her in San Diego. Therefore, when he started on his return to Arizona, accompanied by Dick and Brad, he took Felicia along.

The railroad journey to Prescott was made without any incident worth recording. Having arrived there, Merry secured accommodations at the best hotel, for he expected to remain in the place a day or more before setting out for his new mines in the Enchanted Valley, where he had left Wiley and Hodge.

Little Abe was found safe in Prescott, where he had been left by Merry. But for the fact that what she had passed through had shaken Felicia's nerves and left her in a very excited frame of mind, the whole party would have been in high spirits. Dick was anxious to visit the mines, and the prospect was also attractive to Buckhart.

Imagine Frank's surprise, on leaving the hotel an hour after his arrival, to encounter Cap'n Wiley on the street. The sailor looked somewhat battered and weather-worn, and there was an unnatural flush in his cheeks and a suspicious odor upon his breath. The moment his eyes fell on Merry he stopped short and made a profound salute.

"Mate Merriwell!" he cried, "it is with a sensation of the most profound satisfaction that my eyes again behold your unexpected reappearance."

"Cap'n," said Frank soberly, shaking his head, "I fear you have been looking on the corn juice. There is something suspicious about your breath and your heightened color."

"Hush!" said the marine marvel. "The dreadful ordeal through which I have lately promulgated myself made it necessary for me to take something in the way of medicine. Mr. Merriwell, there have been riotous doings since you departed."

"Any trouble in regard to the new mine?" asked Merry, somewhat anxiously.

"Oh, no; nothing of that sort. I have been tending strictly to business. At the suggestion of Mate Hodge, I gathered up in Cottonwood, Central Butte, Stoddard, Bigbug, Cherry and elsewhere a score of hale and hearty laborers and piloted them safely to the valley, where they now are. He then sent me hither for supplies and other needed articles. I have secured half a dozen more good men, who will journey with us to the valley."

"Now, Wiley," said Frank, "tell me about these men you say you have engaged. What sort of men are they?"

"They are charming," assured the sailor. "You remember your Terrible Thirty."

"Yes."

"Well, they are men of the same class. They are the real thing."

"But I am afraid such men are not just what we want, cap'n."

The sailor looked surprised.

"Why not?" he questioned.

"What we need are miners, not fighting men. It happened that I was able to control the Thirty, and they proved valuable to me at that time. You remember that as miners I couldn't retain one of them. You say you have picked up some more men here?"

"Sure, sure."

"I'd like to look them over, cap'n. Where are they?"

"If you will perambulate with me, I will present you to the bunch. I have them corralled not far away."

"Lead on," said Frank. "I will look them over."

Wiley led the way straight to a saloon, which they entered. As they walked in, several men were drinking at the bar, and Merry distinctly heard one of them, a huge, pockmarked fellow, say:

"It sure is ten chances to one the gent loses his mine afore he ever sets eyes on it again."

Frank recognized the fellow at a glance. He was a desperado with a bad reputation, and was known as Spotted Dan.

"There they are," said Wiley. "Those fine boys I have collected. You can see at a glance that they are the real thing."

"Altogether too real!" muttered Frank.

He was confident that the words of Spotted Dan referred to him, and in a twinkling his mind was made up.

"Mates," said Wiley, calling the attention of the ruffians, "it gives me untold pleasure to introduce you to Mr. Merriwell, the owner of the mines I told you about."

They turned and looked Frank over. His youthful appearance seemed to surprise them, and it was evident that they regarded him as a tenderfoot.

Frank lost no time.

"It's my duty to inform you, gentlemen," he said, "that Cap'n Wiley has made a slight mistake. I shall not need you."

This seemed to astonish them.

"What's that?" cried Spotted Dan hoarsely. "Whatever is this you says, mister?"

Frank quietly repeated his words, upon which one of the ruffians swore.

"I reckons you is the one mistaken," said Spotted Dan, stepping out. "I opines, sir, that you does need us."

"Then you opine wrong."

"We has been engaged all fair and square, and we sticks by it. We proposes to see that you sticks by it, too."

"Cap'n Wiley had no authority from me to engage anybody," declared Merry. "That being the case, you can see at once that no agreement made with him counts for anything."

"Say you so?" sneered Dan. "Well, now, we thinks a heap different."

"What you think is a matter of indifference to me," said Merry, looking the ruffian straight in the eyes.

"Whatever does you take us fer?" snarled the pox-marked fellow. "We're no kids to be fooled with this yere way. You shakes us none whatever. If you tries it——"

"What then?" asked Merry, in a low tone.

"What then? Well, by the everlasting, I chaws you up! I flattens you out! There will be a funeral in Prescott to-morrow!"

"There may be," said Frank; "but, if there is, you will be highly interested, and yet you will know nothing about it."

Spotted Dan glared at Merry in his fiercest manner. It seemed to astonish him that the smooth-faced young man was not in the least awed by this fierceness.

"Look a here, Mr. Merriwell," he said, "do yer know who yer dealing with in this yere piece of business?"

"From all appearances, I should say that I am dealing with a thoroughbred ruffian," was the serene answer.

"Yer dealing with a bad man with a record, and don't yer forget it," snarled Dan. "My record is as long as my arm. And whar I goes I leaves graves in my footsteps. I adds to the population of the cemeteries."

"You're plainly a big bluffer and a blowhard," said Frank.

Then, as Spotted Dan made a suspicious movement, quick as a flash of light a pistol appeared in Merriwell's hand.

"Don't try to pull a gun on me, you big duffer!" exclaimed the youth. "If you do, I will run a couple of tunnels in you."

"Correct in the most minute particular," chipped in Cap'n Wiley. "He will do it scientifically and skillfully. When it comes to shooting, he is a shooter from Shooterville. Say, you oughter see him shoot out a pigeon's eye at four thousand yards! Why, he can shoot with his feet better than any man in this bunch! At the same time I happen to be provided with a couple of large-bore fowling pieces, and I shall feel it my duty to shed real gore in case any of you other gents take a notion to chip in to this little circus."

While speaking the sailor had produced a pair of Colt's revolvers, which he now flourished with reckless abandon.

"Oh, that is the way yer does it, is it?" sneered Spotted Dan. "Mebbe yer thinks this settles it. Well, wait and see. You has the drop now; but our turn comes. It's a good thing fer you, young feller," he declared, still glaring at Frank, "that I don't git my paws on yer. Ef I'd ever hit yer a crack with my maul you would sprout wings instanter. Sometimes I gits at yer, tenderfoot, and I hammers yer all up."

"You think you will," retorted Merry. "You might find yourself up against a snag."

"Waal, ef I can't knock you stiff in less than one minute, I'll take to my hole and stay thar for a year."

"I presume you would consider this engagement ended in case you fail to put me down and out in short order?" said Merry. "If you were the one whipped, you would call all dealings off?"

"Sartin sure. I'd be so ashamed of myself I'd never look a dog in the face again."

"Give your weapons to one of your pards there," directed Merry. "I will pass mine to Wiley, and I'll agree to take off my coat and give you a chance to do me up right here."

"I think I smell smoke," murmured the sailor, sniffing the air. "I think I smell fire and brimstone. I think there will be doings around here directly."

"Whoop!" cried Spotted Dan. "It's a go! Say, I makes you look like a piece of fresh beefsteak in just about two shakes."

Then he turned to one of his companions and handed over a pistol and knife. He wore no coat, and when he had cast his old hat on the floor and thrust back his sleeves, exposing his brawny, hairy arms, he declared he was ready.

The barkeeper had remonstrated. Merry was known in Prescott, and to the man behind the bar he said:

"Whatever damage is done I will pay for. I will set 'em up for every one who comes in for the next hour besides."

Then he placed his revolver on the bar and coolly drew off his coat, which he lay beside the pistol.

"Keep your ellipticals parabolically peeled," warned Cap'n Wiley. "The gent with the dented countenance looks like a Peruvian dog. I don't know as there is a Peruvian dog, but I judge so, because I have heard of Peruvian bark."

Merry said nothing. His face was calm and grim as he thrust back the sleeves of his woolen shirt. He had a handsome forearm, finely developed and finely moulded, with the flesh firm and hard and the supple muscles showing beneath the silken skin.

"Come on!" cried Spotted Dan eagerly. "Step right out yere and git yer medicine."

The ruffian's friends were chuckling and muttering among themselves.

"Dan paralyzes him the first time he hits him," declared one.

"You bet your boots he does!" put in another.

"I seen him break Bill Goddard's neck with a blow down in Buckeye," said a third.

Frank removed his wide-brimmed hat and laid it on the bar, tossing back his head with a slight shaking motion to fling a lock of hair out of his eyes. Then he suddenly advanced to meet his antagonist, his arms hanging straight at his sides and his hands open. It seemed as if he invited annihilation, and Spotted Dan improved the occasion by making a strong swinging blow with his huge fist, aiming straight at the face of the fearless youth.

Quick as a flash of light, Merry ducked just the slightest and tipped his head to one side.

Dan's fist shot over Frank's shoulder. With a quick movement of his foot, Merriwell struck the ruffian's feet from beneath him, and the giant crashed to the floor so heavily that the glasses and bottles rattled on the shelves behind the bar.

With a roar of surprise, Spotted Dan made a spring and landed on his feet. Before him stood Merriwell, still with his hands hanging at his sides, regarding him with just the faintest suggestion of an amused smile. That smile was enough to infuriate the bruiser beyond description.

"Dodges, does yer!" snarled the man. "Well, dodge this if yer ken!"

Again he struck, and again Merry escaped by simply tipping his head like a flash over upon his shoulder and crouching the least bit. He did not lift a hand to ward off the blow. Like a panther he leaped to one side, and his outstretched toe caught his enemy's ankle as the force of that blow, wasted on the empty air, sent Dan staggering forward. A second time the fellow went crashing to the floor. A second time he sprang up with amazing agility for one so huge and ponderous.

"Whatever kind of fighting does yer call this?" he shouted, in a rage. "Why don't yer stand up like a man and fight? Is that all yer can do? Does yer know nothing else but jest ter dodge?"

"You're too easy," declared Frank. "I hate to hurt you—really I do. It seems a shame."

"Yah!" shouted the infuriated man. "You would hurt nobody if yer hit um."

"I beg you to pause a moment, Daniel," put in Wiley. "Have you made your will? If not, I entreat you to do so. If he ever hits you—oh, luddy, luddy! you'll think you've been kicked by a can of dynamite."

The ruffian's companions had been astonished by the ease with which Merriwell escaped Dan's blows; but they, too, believed the fight would quickly end if Merry stood up and met his enemy.

Spotted Dan slyly edged around Frank, seeking to force him into a corner. Apparently without suspecting the fellow's object, Merry permitted himself to be driven back just as Dan seemed to desire. Getting the young mine owner cornered, as he thought, the bruiser quickly advanced, seeking now to seize him with one hand, while the other hand was drawn back and clinched, ready for another terrible blow.

With a snapping movement, Frank clutched the wrist of Dan's outstretched arm. There was a sudden twist and a whirl, and although the ruffian struck with all his force, he felt his shoulder wrenched in the socket and knew he had missed even as he delivered the blow. That twisting movement turned the fellow about and brought his arm up behind him on his back. Then Merry sent him forward with a well-directed and vigorous kick.

"It is too easy!" sighed Cap'n Wiley, sadly shaking his head. "It isn't even interesting. I fancied possibly there might be some excitement in the affair, but I am growing sleepy, and I fear I shall miss the finish while I take a nap."

Spotted Dan was astonished now. Never had he encountered any one who fought in such a singular manner, and he could not understand it. Just when he felt certain that he had the youth where he wanted him, Merry would thwart his design and trip him, or, with the utmost ease, send him staggering.

"Dern yer! What makes yer fight with yer feet?" rasped the ruffian. "That ain't no way whatever ter fight. Fight with yer fists on the squar, and I will annihilate yer."

"I don't believe that anything was said about the style of fighting," retorted Merry pleasantly. "However, if you don't like my methods I will agree not to use my feet any more."

"That settles it!" roared Dan. "I will fix yer in thirty seconds now."

"Dear, dear!" yawned Wiley, leaning on the bar. "How sleepy I am! I think this bout should have been pulled off under Marquis of Deusenbury rules. I, too, am against the use of feet. Cut it out, mates, and come down to real business."

"Very well," said Frank.

"You kick no more?" questioned the ruffian.

"Not to-day."

"Then I thumps the head off you right away."

Spotted Dan sailed into it then, and for a few moments the fight was rather lively, although the ruffian was doing all the hitting. That is, he was trying to do all the hitting, but he was wasting his blows on the air, for Frank parried them all or ducked and dodged and escaped by such cleverness as none of Dan's comrades had ever before witnessed. Still the bruiser was the aggressor, and they were confident he would soon weary the youth, when a single blow would bring about the finish of the encounter.

Indeed, one thing that led Dan on and made him force the fight harder and harder was the fact that Merry seemed to be panting heavily and betrayed signs of great exhaustion. The desperado was sure the youth was giving out, and so, although he was likewise somewhat winded, he continued to follow Merry up. At length, quick as a flash, Frank's manner changed. He no longer retreated. He no longer sought to escape his enemy. He made Dan parry two heavy blows aimed at him. Then he countered, and the big fellow was sent reeling. Like a wolf Frank followed the bruis-

111

er up, hitting him again and again until he went down.

Cap'n Wiley roused up a little at this and observed:

"That's somewhat better. Now it grows slightly interesting. But he hasn't oiled his machinery and started in earnest yet. Wait a few moments, gents, and see him cut parabolical circles through the diametrical space around Daniel's dizzy cranium."

Spotted Dan sat up, astonished beyond measure at what had happened. He saw Frank standing at a little distance, with his hands on his hips, smiling down at him and showing not the least sign of exhaustion. The man who had seemed winded a few moments before and ready to drop was now as fresh and unwearied as if nothing had happened.

Through the bruiser's dull brain crept a suspicion that he had been deceived by this handsome, smooth-faced young man. He knew now that Merriwell could fight in the most astounding manner. This, however, enraged him to such an extent that he banished reason and coolness and rose to charge on Merry, with a roar like that of a mad bull. Frank avoided the rush, but hit the ruffian a staggering blow on the ear as he went past. Dan turned quickly and charged again.

Four times the big bruiser charged, and four times Merry avoided him and sent him reeling. The fourth time Frank followed him up. He gave Spotted Dan no chance to recover. Blow after blow rained on the man's face and body. Dan was driven back until he was close upon the card table that sat in the rear of the room. Then, with a swinging upward blow, Merriwell's fist hit the fellow on the point of the jaw, and the ruffian was actually lifted off his feet and hurled clean over the table against the wall. He fell to the floor and lay there in a huddled, senseless heap, literally knocked out.

Frank turned toward the bar, rolling down his sleeves.

"Watch his pards like a hawk, Wiley," he said. "Now is the time they may try treachery, if ever."

"Depend on me," nodded the sailor.

Frank quickly slipped on his coat and placed his hat upon his head. Then he turned to the amazed ruffians, saying, quietly:

"Gents, you heard the agreement between us. If I whipped that fellow, the engagement which he claims to have made for himself and for you through Cap'n Wiley was off. I think you will acknowledge that he is whipped. That settles it."

He backed toward the door of the saloon, followed by the sailor, also backing in the same manner and keeping his pistols ready. When the door was reached Merry turned and disappeared, and Wiley followed him.

CHAPTER XIII.

MACKLYN MORGAN APPEARS.

ate," said Cap'n Wiley, as they hurried along the street on their way back to the hotel, "you are in every minute particular the finest specimen of exuberant manhood that it has ever been my fortune to associate with. Of course, I felt sure you would do up that fellow, but you came through the seething and turgid fray without so much as a scar. I don't believe he even touched you once."

"Yes, he did," said Merry, "a couple of times. He hit me on the shoulder, but the blow was spent, and he caught me a fair one over the heart. I leaped away just in time to spoil the effectiveness of that."

"But you are certainly the supreme fighter of this period of scrappers. If you chose to enter the ring, you might be champion of the world. It would delight my soul to be able to put up a real fight like that."

"It disgusts me," returned Merry.

"Wha-a-at?" gasped the sailor. "I think I fail to catch your meaning."

"It disgusts me," repeated Merry. "If there is anything that makes me feel degraded, it is being compelled to take part in a fight of that sort. I was practically forced into it on this occasion. I saw those fellows meant mischief, and I felt that the only way to settle the affair was to give that big duffer a thumping. It's about the only reasoning a man can use on men of his calibre. Words and arguments fail to affect them, and a good thrashing moves them to respect."

"But do you mean to tell me," said Wiley, "that you are not an admirer of the manly art of self-defense? Do you mean to tell me that you take no interest in the prize ring and the glorious heroes of it?"

"If there is anything for which I have absolutely no use," said

Merry, "it is a professional prize fighter. To me prize fighting is the most degrading of all the so-called sports."

"This is more than passing strange," said the sailor. "If such can be the case, will you elucidate to me how it happened that you ever learned to use your little dukes in such a marvelously scientific manner?"

"I think it is the duty of every American youth to learn to defend himself with his fists. No matter how peacefully inclined he is, no matter how much of a gentleman he is, no matter how much forbearance he may have, there is bound to come a time in his life when he will be forced to fight or suffer insults or bodily injury. As a rule, I never fight if I can avoid it. In this instance I might have avoided it for the time being, but I was certain that if I did so the matter would culminate in something more serious than a fistic encounter. Had I escaped from that saloon without meeting Spotted Dan, he and all his partners would have regarded me as afraid of them, and you know very well that they would have sought to force trouble on me at every opportunity. The easiest way to settle the whole matter was to fight then and there, and therefore I did so."

"Well, you oughter feel proud of the job you did!"

"Instead of that, I feel as if I had lowered and degraded myself. I'll not throw off the feeling for some time. To make the matter still worse, it was a saloon fight. However, I do not go there to drink. Out in this country the man who does business with the men he finds here is sometimes compelled to enter a saloon."

"That's true—quite true," sighed Wiley. "I sometimes find it necessary to enter one myself."

By this time they had reached the hotel, and as they entered the office Merry suddenly paused in surprise, his eyes fastened on a man who stood before the desk.

This man was tall and well dressed, with a somewhat ministerial face and flowing grayish side whiskers. He was speaking to the clerk.

"I see here the name of Mr. Frank Merriwell on the register," he was saying. "Can you tell me where to find him?"

"Mr. Merriwell!" called the clerk. "Here is a gentleman inquiring for you."

The man at the desk turned and faced Frank.

"Is that so?" muttered Frank. "It is Macklyn Morgan!"

Morgan, one of the money kings of the great Consolidated Mining Association of America, looked Merriwell over with a glance as cold as ice.

"How do you do, sir?" he said, in a calm, low voice. "It seems that I have found you at last."

"From your words," returned Merry, "I should fancy you had been looking for me for some time?"

"I have."

"Indeed?"

"Yes, I have looked for you in Denver, in Holbrook, and at your Queen Mystery Mine."

"It appears that I have given you considerable trouble?"

"Not a little; but I was determined to find you."

"You have done so."

"Yes; you can't hide from me."

"I have not the least desire in the world to hide from you, Mr. Morgan."

"You say so," returned the man, with a cold sneer; "but I am certain you have taken pains to keep out of my way for the last two weeks."

"You are utterly mistaken. I would not take pains to keep out of your way for two minutes. What do you want of me?"

"I have a little matter to talk over with you—some private business."

"I was not aware that there could be business dealings of any sort between us, Macklyn Morgan."

"Be careful!" warned Morgan, lifting a thin finger. "You are putting on a very bold face."

"And is there any reason why I should not? I know, Mr. Morgan, of your methods at the time of my affair with the C. M. A. of A."

"I have not forgotten that."

"Nor I. Nor do I regret that, although the C. M. A. of A. was compelled to give up its unlawful efforts to rob me, you entered into a combination with another moneyed rascal to accomplish the work."

"Be careful!" again warned Morgan. "I am not the man to whom you can talk in such a manner."

"Like any other man, you are one to whom I can tell the truth. If the truth cuts, so much the worse for you, sir."

"Don't get on your high horse, young man; it will be better for you if you refrain. Don't be so free with your accusations, for you will soon find that there is an accusation against you of a most serious nature."

"What new game are you up to, Mr. Morgan? It seems to me that the failures of the past should teach you the folly of your plots and schemes."

"I have told you that I wish to have a private talk with you, young man. Perhaps you had better grant me the privilege."

"As far as I am concerned, there is no necessity of doing so; but really I am curious to know just what you're up to. This being the case, I will not object. I have a room, and we may go there."

"Your record indicates that you are a desperate character, Merriwell. I should hesitate to place myself alone with you in any room unless you were first disarmed. If you will leave your weapons here at the desk we will go to your room."

"I am quite willing in case you leave your own revolver, sir."

"I never carry a revolver, Merriwell."

"But you have one in your pocket now," declared Frank positively.

He seemed to know this to be a fact, and, after a moment's hesitation, Morgan took out a small revolver, which he laid upon the desk.

"I thought it best to provide myself with such an article while in this part of the country," he said. "There it is. I will leave it here."

Immediately Frank walked to the desk and placed his own pistol upon it.

"Come," he said. "You may follow me to my room."

In Frank's room, with the door closed behind them, Merry motioned to a chair.

"Sit down, Mr. Morgan," he said, "and make whatever statement you choose. I will listen."

Morgan took the chair.

"First," observed Morgan, "I wish to speak of Milton Sukes."

"I thought likely."

"You know the interests of Mr. Sukes and myself were closely allied."

Frank laughed.

"Yes; although Sukes was at the head of the concern, I know that you conspired with him to defraud me."

"Have a care!" again warned Morgan. "You are now dealing with a man of power and influence."

"I have dealt with such men before. As a bugaboo, the mere fact that you have money does not frighten me in the least, Mr. Morgan. If, like Sukes, you fancy that money gives you power to commit any fraud, like Sukes, you are to learn your mistake."

"I know all about your scandalous attack on Mr. Sukes in Denver. I know of your attempted blackmailing of him, Merriwell. You did try to blackmail him, and you can't deny it."

"You lie, Morgan!" retorted Frank, with perfect control of himself.

"Then what was the meaning of your threat to expose his mining operations?"

"Morgan, Milton Sukes pitted himself against me and attempted to rob me of my mine. When he did so he aroused my fighting blood. He was defeated in every effort he made against me, and the decision against him in the courts of the Territory was the final blow that upset his plans. In the meantime I had learned that his Great Northwest Territory Mining Company was a swindle of the most outrageous sort. I had threatened to expose him, and, when he found himself whipped to a standstill, he sought to enter into a compact with me, by which I was to remain silent and let him go on with his dishonest work.

"He sent one of his tools to me with a contract for me to sign. I tore it up. As I say, my blood had been aroused, and I warned him then that neither cajolery nor money could silence me. I warned him that I would expose and disgrace him, so that every honest man in the country would regard him with scorn and aversion. Had it been mere blackmail, Sukes could have silenced me with money. He sought to do so, but found he was barking up the wrong tree. He threatened libel suits and all that; but I kept on at my work. As a last desperate resort he paid an employee of mine to fire my office in Denver, and the result of that affair was that the treacherous fellow who betrayed me fancied I had perished in the fire. It drove him insane. He pursued Sukes relentlessly, and it is certain that Sukes was finally killed by that man's hand."

"So you say, Merriwell; but I hold quite a different opinion— quite a different opinion."

"Whatever your opinion may be, Morgan, it is a matter of absolute indifference to me."

Macklyn Morgan showed his teeth.

"You may think so just now, young man, but you will change your mind. I have been investigating this matter thoroughly. I have followed it up faithfully. I know how and where Sukes was shot. I have taken pains to secure all the evidence possible. You were present at the time. You were there in disguise. Why did you pursue and hunt him in disguise? It looks black for you, Mr. Merriwell—it looks black. These things will count against you at the day of reckoning, which is surely coming. How will you explain your behavior to the satisfaction of the law?"

"That's no matter to worry you, Macklyn Morgan," calmly returned Merriwell. "If there is anything of explanation, I shall have the explaining to do. Don't trouble yourself over it."

"You have a great deal of nerve just now, young man; but it will weaken—it will weaken. Wait until you are arrested on the charge of murder. Had you killed an ordinary man it might have been different; but Milton Sukes was a man of money, a man of power, a man of influence. All his money, if necessary, will be used to convict you. You cannot escape. Just as true as this case is put into the hands of the law you will eventually be hanged."

In his cold, calm, accusing way, Morgan was doing everything in his power to unsettle Frank's nerves. As he spoke, he watched the youth as a hawk watches its prey.

"I fail to see your object in coming to me with this," said Merry. "It seems most remarkable. If you intend to push such a charge against me, why don't you go ahead and do it? Why do you tell me what you contemplate doing? The proper method is to secure every scrap of evidence and then have me arrested without warning and thrown into jail."

"I have all the evidence I need," asserted the money king. "Merriwell, I have men who will swear that you fired that shot."

"Did they see me do it?"

"They did."

"Most amazing, Morgan! Are you aware of the fact that Sukes was shot in the dark? Are you aware that every light in the place had first been extinguished by other shots? Will you explain to me how any one could have seen me shoot him under such circumstances?"

"One of the men was standing within two feet of you. He saw the flash of your weapon, as did the other man, who was a little farther away."

Frank smiled derisively.

"Wonderful evidence!" he said. "I doubt a great deal if a jury anywhere in this country would convict a man on such proof. At the time, as I think you will acknowledge, there was another man who did some shooting. I deny that I fired the shot. But even had I done so, who could say that it was not I who shot out the lights and the other man who killed Milton Sukes?"

"Did you know that you left a pistol with your name upon it in a hotel where you stopped in Snowflake?"

"I did nothing of the sort."

"You did, Merriwell! The bullet that killed Sukes is in my possession. It is a bullet such as would have been fired from that pistol. The pistol is in my possession, Merriwell! I have the evidence against you, and you can't escape!"

"Although you are lying in every particular, Morgan, I am curious to know what your game may be. What is behind this singular procedure of yours?"

Macklyn Morgan seemed to hesitate for a few moments, and then, leaning forward on the edge of his chair and holding up one finger, he suddenly exclaimed:

"There is only one escape for you!"

"And that is——"

"If I abandon the case you may escape. If I drop it there will be no one to push it."

"And you will drop it?" questioned Merry, with pretended anxiety. "On what inducements?"

"Now you're coming to your senses," nodded the man. "Now I fancy you comprehend just where you are. You possess several mines, and they are of considerable value. I have spent some money to get possession of one of those mines, having, as both Milton Sukes and I believed, a good claim to it. I speak of the Queen Mystery. Frank Merriwell, the day you deed over to me the Queen Mystery and give me possession of it I will abandon my determination to prosecute you for murder. I will even place such proofs as I have in your hands and you may destroy them. Of course there will remain the two men who are ready to swear they saw you fire the shot, but they may be easily silenced. That's my proposition. And it is by that method alone you can save your neck. Now give me your answer."

"I will!" exclaimed Merriwell suddenly.

And then, with a spring, he seized Macklyn Morgan by the collar. Immediately he ran the man to the door, which he hurled open.

"That is my answer!" he cried, as he kicked Morgan out of the room.

CHAPTER XIV.

THE MESSENGER.

s Morgan was hurled headlong from Merry's room he collided with a man outside, who was very nearly upset. This young man caught a glimpse of Frank in the act of violently ejecting the man of money, and what immediately happened to Morgan was the result of this discovery.

"What's the meaning of this great agitation by which you seek to overthrow my corporosity?" savagely demanded Cap'n Wiley, for it was he. "This insult to my indignity is several degrees beyond my comprehension, and without waste of verbosity or the expenditure of violent language, I feel called upon to precipitate your corporosity on its journey."

Saying which, he sprang, catlike, on the millionaire, seized him, ran him swiftly along the corridor and flung him head over heels down the stairs. As Morgan crashed to the bottom, Wiley stood at the head of the stairs, his arms akimbo, nodding with satisfaction, and remarked:

"Possibly that jarred you some."

Morgan was not seriously hurt, but he arose in a terrible fury.

"I will land you both where you belong for this outrage!" he declared, white to the lips. "I will place you both behind iron bars!"

Then he limped away. Merriwell had followed, and his hand fell on the sailor's shoulder.

"Why do you mix up in this, Wiley?" he demanded sternly. "It was not your quarrel."

"If I have offended by my impulsive and impetuous demeanor, I entreat pardon," said the sailor. "When the gent bumped me and I saw that he had been scientifically ejected by you, I couldn't resist the temptation to give him another gentle boost."

"And by doing so you may find yourself in a peck of trouble," said Frank. "That man has power and influence, and he will try to make good his threat, which you heard. He is a money king."

"What is money?" loftily returned Wiley. "I scorn the filthy stuff. But, regardless of his money, it seems to me that you unhesitatingly elevated his anatomy with the toe of your boot."

"It was my quarrel, Wiley; and there is no reason why you should pitch in."

"My dear comrade, I ever feel it my duty to stand by my friends, and your quarrel in some degree must be mine. I inferred that in some manner he offended you most copiously."

"He did arouse my ire," admitted Merry, as he walked back to his room, followed by the sailor. "But he is the sort of a man who will seek to make good his threat and place us behind bars."

"It will not be the first time your humble servant has lingered in endurance vile. In connection with that, I might mention another little nannygoat. On the last occasion when I indulged too freely in Western jag juice I was living in regal splendor in one of those hotels where they have lots of furniture and little to eat. I started out to put a red stripe on the city, and somewhere during my cruise I lost my bearings. I didn't seem to remember much of anything after that until I awoke with my throat feeling as dry as the desert of Sahara and my head splitting.

"Just where I was I couldn't tell. I had some vague remembrance of whooping things up in glorious style, and knew I had been hitting the redeye. In a somewhat dormant condition I stretched my hands above my head, and, to my horror, they encountered iron bars. This aroused me slightly, and I looked in that direction and beheld before me, to my unutterable dismay, the bars I had touched. 'Cap'n,' says I, 'you have again collided with the blue-coated guardians of the peace, and you are pinched.'

"I noted, however, that these iron bars seemed somewhat frail and slender, and it struck me that my colossal strength might be able to bend them. With the thought of escape, I wrenched the bars apart and thrust my head between them. By vigorous pushing I injected my shoulders, but there I stuck. In spite of all my desperate efforts, I could not crawl through, and I finally discovered that I couldn't get back. I floundered and kicked a while and then gave it up and yelled for help. My cries finally brought some one, who entered the place and dragged me from the trap, at the same time nearly shaving off my left ear with one of the bars. My rescuer proved to be a hotel attendant, who asked me, in no small astonishment, what I was trying to do. Then, to my inexpressible relief, on sitting up and looking round, I found that I was in my own room at the hotel, where I had somehow landed, and that my delusion had led me to endeavor to escape from limbo by crawling through the bars at the head of my iron bedstead. I gave the attendant who had dragged me out seven thousand dollars and pledged him to eternal silence. This is the first time my lips have ever betrayed the tale to mortal ears."

In spite of the humor of the sailor's whimsical story, Merry did not laugh. This convinced Wiley that the affair with Macklyn Morgan was far more serious than he had at first apprehended.

"Cap'n," said Frank, "I wish you would find Dick and send him here. After that, if you can get track of Morgan and keep watch of his movements it will be a good thing. I'd like to know just what he means to do."

"Depend upon me," nodded the sailor. "I will shadow him with all the skill of those heroes about whom I used to read in the yellow-backed literature."

Saying which, he hastily left the room. Within ten minutes Dick appeared and found Merry walking up and down.

"What's the matter, Frank?" he asked. "From Wiley's words I inferred there was trouble in the air."

"There is," Merry nodded; and he proceeded to tell his brother the whole story.

Dick's indignation burst forth.

"The unmitigated scoundrel!" he cried. "Tried to force you to give up the Queen Mystery, did he?"

"That was his game."

"Well, you didn't give him half what he deserves. And he threatened to have you arrested for murder—you, Frank, arrested for murder!"

Merry smiled grimly.

"That was the threat he made."

"But it was a bluff, Frank—a bluff pure and simple. He will never try that game."

"You can't tell what a man like Morgan may try. Sukes was desperate and dangerous, but I regard Macklyn Morgan as even more so. As a rule, he is quiet, cold, and calculating, and he lays his plans well. He would not have started in on this thing had he not been convinced that there was a good prospect of succeeding."

"Why, he can't succeed! It is impossible!"

"I don't propose to let him succeed, but I feel certain I am going to have a hot time with him. I am ready for it; let it come."

Again Frank's fighting blood was aroused, and Dick saw it in the sternness of his handsome face and the gleam of his flashing eyes.

"That's the talk, Frank!" cried the boy, thrilled by the spirit of his brother. "They can't down you. They've tried it and failed too many times. But what are your plans now? You intend to start for the new mines early to-morrow?"

"I may alter my plans. I may remain here for a while to face Macklyn Morgan. For all of his power and his money, I think I have a few friends and some influence in Prescott. There is one, at least, whom I can depend upon, and that is Frank Mansfield. He is white to the bone, and he always stands by his friends."

"But you cannot depend upon your friends alone in an emergency like this," said Dick. "You will have to rely on yourself. Of course, Brad and I will stand by you, no matter what happens."

While they were talking Wiley came rushing in.

"The gent who lately descended the stairs with such graceful impetuosity is now in consultation with the city marshal," he declared. "I traced him thither, and I have left one Bradley Buckhart to linger near and keep an eagle eye upon his movements."

"By Jove!" exclaimed Dick; "I believe he does mean to have you arrested, Frank."

"His movement seems to indicate something of the sort," was Frank's cool confession. "I suppose he will make a charge of personal assault, with the idea of putting me to inconvenience and detaining me until he can again try the effect of his threats of arrest on a more serious charge. Were I sure things are all right at the Enchanted Valley, I would not mind. I am afraid you have made a mess of it, cap'n, in sending those men there."

"It seems that I have a clever little way of putting my foot into it," retorted the sailor. "When I seek to do what I supremely consider to be for the best I make a bobble."

"Yet we will not worry over that now," said Merry. "However, in case of emergency, Dick, I wish you to have my horse constantly ready for me. If anything happens that I decide to get out in a hurry, you, and Brad, and Wiley are to take care of Felicia and little Abe."

"All right," nodded Dick. "I will see to it at once."

Ten minutes later Frank was standing alone upon the steps of the hotel, when a man on horseback came riding furiously down the street. He was covered with dust, and his horse was so spent that it was only by the most savage urging that the beast was forced into a gallop. Behind the man, at a distance, came two more horsemen, who were likewise spurring their mounts mercilessly. Plainly they were in pursuit of the man in advance.

As Merry was wondering what it meant, the horse of the fugi-

tive went down, as if shot, directly in front of the hotel, flinging
the rider, who seemed stunned.

With a great clatter of hoofs, the pursuers came up and stopped
short, leaping from their saddles. As one of them dismounted, he
whipped out a wicked-looking knife. Both seemed to be desperadoes, and it was evident that their intention toward the fugitive
was anything but friendly.

Now, it was not Frank's nature to stand idly by and see two men
jump on a third who was helpless and do him up. Without a moment's hesitation, Merry leaped from the steps and rushed upon
those men. A heavy blow sent one of them to the ground.

The other had stooped above the fallen man when Frank's toe
precipitated him headlong and caused him to roll over and over
in the dust.

At the same time Merriwell drew a pistol.

"Get up and sneak, both of you!" he ordered. "If you linger, I
will blow a window in each of you!"

Muttering oaths, the ruffians rose, but the look they saw in
Frank's face caused them to decide that the best thing they could
do would be to obey.

"It's none of your funeral!" cried one, as he grasped the bridle
rein of his horse.

"But it will be yours if you linger here ten seconds!" retorted
Merry. "Git! If you value your skins, don't even turn to look back
until you are out of shooting distance."

As the baffled ruffians were retreating, the fugitive sat up, slowly recovering from his shock.

"Thank you, pard," he said. "It was mighty lucky for me you
pitched in just as you did. But for you, they had me dead to rights,
and I opine they would have finished me."

"What is it all about?" questioned Merry.

"Got a message," answered the man. "Got to send it without
fail. They meant to stop me. It has been a hot run. They headed
me off from Bigbug, and I had to strike for this town. They've
wasted lots of lead on me; but they were riding too fast to shoot
well. And I didn't hold up to give them an easy chance at me."

As the man was speaking, Merry assisted him to his feet. His
horse had likewise risen, but stood with hanging head, completely pegged out.

"Poor devil!" said the man, sympathetically patting the creature's neck. "It's a wonder I didn't kill you. But even if I did, I
was going to send the message to Frank Merriwell, if possible."

"What's that?" shouted Frank, in astonishment. "A message to

Frank Merriwell! Man, I am Frank Merriwell!"

"You?" was the almost incredulous answer. "Why, Hodge told me to wire to San Diego. He said it might reach you there."

"I am just back from San Diego. Give me the message."

The man fumbled in his pocket and brought forth a crumpled piece of paper, which he placed in Merriwell's hand.

Opening the paper, this was what Merry read:

"If possible, come at once. Trouble at the mines. Plot to seize them. —Hodge."

"Come into the hotel," said Frank, turning to the man who had brought this message. "We will send some one to take charge of your horse."

The man followed him. Having asked that the horse be cared for, Merry instructed his companion to follow, and he proceeded to his room.

"What's your name?" he asked.

"It's Colvin—Dash Colvin."

"Well, Colvin, you are from the Enchanted Valley?"

"Yes, sir."

"You were one of the men engaged by Wiley, I presume?"

"Yes, sir."

"It seems that Hodge trusts you?"

"He did, sir."

"What's the trouble there?"

"Those men are plotting a heap to take the mines, sir. Hodge discovered it."

"How did he make the discovery?"

"That I don't know. He discovers it, somehow, and he sends me with this yere message. He picks me out and asks me could he trust me a whole lot. I tells him he could, and he chances it. I plans with him to git out in the night, and I does so."

"But you were followed?"

"Yes. One of the crew sees me a-talking with Mr. Hodge, and they suspects me. Arter that they watches me mighty close. That makes it plenty hard for me to git away. I don't opine I am much more than out of the valley afore they finds out I am gone. I didn't think they'd git on so quick, and so I fails to push as hard as I might at first. Shortly after sun-up I sees two horsemen coming miles behind me. Even then I'm not dead sure they're arter me. But they was, sir—they was. I had a hard run for it, but I have made good by getting the message to you."

"And you shan't lose by it, Colvin. Be sure of that. Did you know about this plot to seize the mines—before Hodge discovered it?"

125

"I knows there was something up, sir; but the rest of the gang they don't trust me complete, and so I don't find out just what was a-doing. I sees them whispering and acting queer, and I thinks there's trouble brewing before Hodge speaks to me about it."

"What sort of men are they?"

"A right tough lot, Mr. Merriwell. They has liquor, too. Somehow it's brought to them, but the head one of the bunch, Texas Bland, he don't ladle it out free at once. He seems to keep it for some occasion later."

Merry's face wore a serious expression.

"How many men do you think there are in this plot?"

"Fifteen or twenty, sir."

"All armed?"

"Every mother's son of them."

"If I had my Thirty!" muttered Frank.

But he was not prepared with an organized force to meet the plotting ruffians, and he felt that it would require precious time in order to get together a band of fighting men.

"Whatever do you propose to do, Mr. Merriwell?" asked Colvin.

"I see it is necessary for me to lose no time in reaching the mines."

"But you don't go alone, I judge? You takes some good men with you?"

"If possible."

"Better do it, sir. That gang is a heap tough, and it takes twice as many men to down 'em."

"Not twice as many of the right sort. I have two or three comrades I can depend upon."

"But two or three are no good, Mr. Merriwell; you hears me."

"Perhaps not; but if I can get the move on those rascals it will count in my favor."

"Now, don't you reckon any on holding those mines with the aid of two or three backers," warned Dash Colvin. "You will never do it."

At this juncture Dick came in.

"Your horse is ready, Frank," he said. "I have given orders to have it saddled and held prepared for you."

"I may have to use it within an hour."

Dick immediately perceived that some new development had transpired, and he glanced from his brother to the stranger in the room.

"What is now, Frank?" he anxiously questioned.

"Read that," said Merry, thrusting the message into his hand.

"By Jove!" exclaimed Dick, "this is bad business, Frank—bad

business! How did you get this?"

"It was brought by Mr. Colvin here. He was pursued and barely reached me with his life."

"Which I allows I would not have done but for Mr. Merriwell himself," said Colvin. "My horse throws me unexpected, and the two galoots arter me has me down and is about to silence me some when Mr. Merriwell takes a hand."

"Are you sure this is straight goods?" questioned Dick.

"That's Bart's writing," declared Merry. "I'd know it anywhere."

"Then there can be no mistake."

"Certainly not. Colvin tells me that there are fifteen or more ruffians in this plot."

"Do you believe, Frank, that it is their scheme?"

"I can't say."

"Perhaps this Macklyn Morgan is behind it."

"He may be."

"I believe he is!" cried Dick. "Somehow I am confident of it, Frank. If he detains you here in Prescott, you will lose those mines. You must get out of this place without delay."

"It certainly looks that way. I shall do so, Dick."

"But we must go with you."

"Have you thought of Felicia? She is here. Some one must remain to look after her."

"But, good gracious, Frank! I can't stay here, knowing that you are in such difficulties. It is impossible!"

"It may seem impossible to you, Dick, but you know the peril through which Felicia has lately passed. You also know that Black Joaquin is at liberty and may find her again."

"But can't we take her?"

"Do you think she is prepared to endure the hardships she would be compelled to face? No, Dick, it can't be done. You will have to stay with her."

"I will be crazy, Frank. When I think of you pitting yourself against such odds I will literally explode."

Dick's cheeks were flushed and he was panting with excitement. It seemed that even then the scent of battle was in his nostrils and he longed for the fray.

"Don't let your hot blood run away with your judgment, boy," half smiled Merriwell. "Colvin, do you know anybody in Prescott?"

"I reckons not, sir."

"You don't know a man you can depend upon—a good fighter who will stick by us if paid well?"

"Nary a one, sir."

"Then that's not to be reckoned on."

Merriwell frowned as he walked the floor. Of a sudden there came a sound of heavy feet outside and the door burst open. Into the room strode Brad Buckhart, color in his cheeks and fire in his eyes.

"Waugh!" he cried. "Get out your artillery and prepare for action!"

"What's up now, Brad?" demanded Frank.

"I certain judge they're after you in earnest," said the Texan. "Cap'n Wiley left me to watch a fine gent named Morgan. I did the trick, and I'll bet my shooting irons that Morgan has a warrant sworn out for you this minute, and he is on his way here with officers. They mean to jug you, pard, sure as shooting. You hear me gently murmur!"

"Then," said Frank calmly, "it's about time for me to make myself scarce in Prescott."

"If you're going, you want to get a move on," declared Brad. "I am not a whole lot ahead of old Morgan and the officers."

Even as he spoke there reached their ears the sound of many feet outside.

"Here they come!" said Dick.

With a leap, the Texan reached the door and pressed himself against it. A hand fell on the knob of the door, but the powerful shoulder of Buckhart prevented any one from entering. Immediately there was a heavy knock.

"Open this door!" commanded a voice.

"Who is there? and what do you want?" demanded Buckhart.

"We want Frank Merriwell. Open this door!"

"Perhaps you will wait some," retorted Brad.

Then another voice was heard outside, and it was that of Morgan himself.

"Break down the door!" he commanded. "Merriwell is in there! Break it down!"

"Remember my instructions, Dick," said Frank, as he coolly turned and opened a window. "Just hold this window a moment."

On the door there fell a crashing blow.

"That's right!" growled Buckhart, who remained immovable. "I hope you don't damage yourself in doing it."

Frank balanced himself on the window ledge, glancing downward.

"Remember, Dick," he said again.

Crash, crash! fell the blows upon the door. It could not withstand such shocks, and the hinges began to break clear.

"I am good for four seconds more!" grated Brad, maintaining his position.

Frank made a light spring outward and dropped. It was more than fifteen feet to the ground, but he landed like a cat upon his feet, turned to wave his hand to Dick, and disappeared round the corner.

Dick quietly lowered the window.

"Let them in, Brad," he said.

The Texan sprang away from the door and two men came plunging into the room as it fell. Behind them was a third, and behind him was Macklyn Morgan.

Dick faced them, his eyes flashing.

"What is the meaning of this?" he demanded.

"Where is Frank Merriwell?" questioned one of the officers.

"He is here! He is here!" asserted Morgan, in the doorway. "I know he is here!"

"You're a whole lot wise," sneered Buckhart. "You certain could have given old Solomon a few points! I admire you a great deal—not!"

"He is hiding somewhere in this room," asserted Morgan, paying no attention to the Texan.

"If that is so, he may as well come out," said the leading officer. "We will have him in a minute."

"Go ahead," said Dick, beginning to laugh. "Pull him out."

Dick's laughter was tantalizing, and one of the officers became enraged and threatened him.

"Why, you're real amusing!" said Dick. "Ha! ha! ha! Oh! ha! ha! ha! Some one has a door to pay for. There is a joke on somebody here."

"Who are you?" demanded Morgan.

Dick took a step nearer, his dark eyes fixing on the man's face.

"Who am I? I will tell you who I am. I am Frank Merriwell's brother."

"His brother? I have heard of you."

"Not for the last time, Macklyn Morgan; nor have you heard of Frank for the last time. Your plot will fizzle. Your infamous schemes will fail. You know what the plotting of your partner, Milton Sukes, brought him to. Look out, Mr. Morgan—look out for yourself!"

"Don't you dare threaten me, you impudent young whelp!" raged Morgan.

"You will find, sir, that I dare tell you just what you are. Your money and your power do not alarm me in the least. You're an unscrupulous scoundrel! You have trumped up a charge against my brother. He will fool you, and he will show you up, just as he did Milton Sukes. Where is Sukes now? Look out, Macklyn Morgan!"

Although usually able to command his passions and appear cold as ice, the words of this fearless, dark-eyed lad were too much for Morgan, and he lifted his clinched fist.

Quick as thought, his wrist was seized by Buckhart, who growled in his ear:

"If you ever hit my pard, you will take a trip instanter to join Milton Sukes down below!"

Then he thrust Morgan aside. In the meantime the officers had been searching the room. They opened the closet, looked under the bed, and inspected every place where a person could hide.

"You're mistaken," said one of them. "Your man is not here."

"He must be!" asserted Morgan. "I know it!"

"You can see for yourself he is not here."

"Then where is he?"

As this question fell from Morgan's lips there was a clatter of hoofs outside. Morgan himself glanced from the window and quickly uttered a cry of baffled rage.

"There he is now!" he shouted. "There he goes on a horse! He is getting away! After him!"

"And may the Old Nick give you the luck you deserve!" laughed Dick.

CHAPTER XV.

A DESPERATE SITUATION.

orning in the Enchanted Valley. Bart Hodge was standing in front of a newly constructed cabin. His ear was turned to listen for sounds of labor from the lower end of the valley, where a crew of men was supposed to be at work building other cabins. The valley was strangely still.

"They're not working," muttered Hodge, a dark frown on his face. "They have quit. What will this day bring? Oh, if Frank were only here!"

Finally, as he stood there, to his ears from far down the valley came a faint sound of hoarse voices singing.

"I know the meaning of that!" he declared. "They're drinking. At last Bland has given them the liquor. They're getting ready for their work."

He turned back into the cabin, the door of which stood open. From a peg on the wall he took down a Winchester rifle and carefully examined it, making sure the magazine was filled and the weapon in perfect working order. He also looked over a brace of revolvers, which he carried ready for use.

Tossing the rifle in the hollow of his left arm, he left the cabin and turned toward the end of the valley where the men were engaged. He observed some caution in approaching that portion of the valley. At last he reached a point amid some bowlders from which he could look down into a slight hollow, where stood some half-constructed cabins upon which the men had been working.

Not one of them was at work now. They were lying around carelessly, or sitting in such shade as they could find, smoking and drinking. Several bottles were being passed from hand to hand. Already two or three of them seemed much under the influence of liquor, and one bowlegged fellow greatly amused the others by an irregular, unsteady dance, during which he kicked out first with one foot and then with the other, like a skirt dancer. At intervals some of them sang a melancholy sort of song.

"The miserable dogs!" grated Bart. "They're ready to defy me now and carry out their treacherous plans."

A tall man, with a black mustache and imperial, stepped among the others, saying a word now and then and seeming to be their leader.

"You're the one, Texas Bland!" whispered Hodge. "You have led them into this!"

As he thought of this his fingers suddenly gripped the rifle, and he longed to lean over the bowlder before him, steady his aim, and send a bullet through Texas Bland. Bart was unaware that two men were approaching until they were close upon him. This compelled him, if he wished to escape observation, to draw back somewhat, and he did so. He did not crouch or make any great effort at hiding, for such a thing he disdained to do. He was not observed, however, although the men stopped within a short distance.

"Well, what do yer think o' this game, Dug?" said one of them, who was squat and sandy.

"I reckons the boss has it all his own way, Bight," retorted the other, a leathery-faced chap with tobacco-stained beard.

"The boss!" exclaimed Bight. "Mebbe you tells me who is the boss?"

"Why, Bland, of course," said Dug. "He is the boss."

"Mebbe he is, and then—mebbe again," returned the sandy one.

"Well, we takes our orders from him."

"Sartin; but I reckons he takes his orders from some one else."

Bight pulled out a bottle.

"Now," he said, "he furnished plenty o' this. My neck is getting dry. How is yourn, Dug?"

"Ready to squeak," returned Dug, grasping the bottle his comrade extended.

When they had lowered its contents until very little was left, Bight observed:

"I s'pose Bland he's going to chaw up this yere chap, Hodge?"

"Sure thing," nodded Dug. "Pretty soon he calls Hodge down yere on a pretense o' business or something, and then he kicks up a fuss with him. He has it all fixed for several of the boys to plug him as soon as the fuss starts. That settles his hash."

The eyes of Bart Hodge gleamed savagely.

"I wonder how he gits onter it that anything's up?" questioned Dug. "Mebbe that sneak, Colvin, tells him."

"Mebbe so," nodded Bight. "Anyhow, nobody trusts Colvin none, and I opines he'd been polished off here ef he'd stayed."

"And he'll sartin never git very fur," declared Dug. "Them boys arter him will sure run him down and make buzzard bait o' him."

Hearing this, Hodge knew for the first time that there were men in pursuit of Colvin, his messenger, who had slipped out of the valley the previous night. Colvin had sworn, if he lived, to carry the message for Frank to the nearest telegraph station and send it. But he was pursued by ruffians who meant to slay him. It was doubtful if he reached a telegraph office. If he failed, of course Merriwell would remain uninformed as to the situation in the Enchanted Valley and would not hurry about returning there.

Even if Colvin succeeded, it might be too late. Bart believed it probable that Merry was in San Diego or that vicinity, and therefore it would take him some time to reach Prescott and travel by horse from Prescott to the valley. Long before he could make such a journey the mutineers would be able to accomplish their evil design.

"Who do you s'pose is back of this yere business, Dug?" said Bight. "You thinks Bland is not behind it, does yer?"

"Dead sartin. Bland he never does this fer hisself. He wouldn't dare. It wouldn't do him no good."

"Why not?"

"Because he can't hold this yere mine and work it. Somebody locates him, and he has to evaporate, for his record counts agin' him. Howsomever, he can jump the mine for some other gent and git paid fer doing the trick, arter which he ambles into the distance and gently disappears. This is his little game, and I will bet on it."

"I wonders some who the gent is behind it."

"That's nothing much ter us as long as we gits our coin."

"Does we git it sure?"

"You bet I gits mine. Ef I don't, there'll be blazes a-roaring around yere."

"Why, you don't buck up agin' Bland none?" half laughed the other. "You knows better than ter do that."

"I don't do it by my lonesome; but if I raises a holler there is others does the same thing. But I will git my dust, all right. Don't you worry about that."

At this point several of the men in the vicinity of the unfinished cabins set up a wild yell of laughter. One of their number had attempted to imitate the awkward motions of the former dancer and had fallen sprawling on his stomach. Immediately after this burst of laughter the men began to sing again.

"That oughter bring this yere Hodge over this way," said Dug, with a hoarse laugh. "Ordinarily he comes a-whooping to see what is up, and he raises thunder. He sets himself up as a boss what is to be obeyed, and I reckons so far he has had the boys jumping when he gives orders."

"If he comes over now," observed Bight, "he gits his medicine in a hurry. I don't care any about shooting him up, so I am for staying away from the rest of the bunch."

"Oh! what ails yer?" growled Dug.

"It's murder!" said Bight.

"Well, I opines you has cooked yer man afore this?"

"Ef I ever has," retorted Bight, "it certain was in self-defense."

"I reckon you're something of a squealer, pard," sneered Dug. "You wants to git your share o' the dust without taking no part in the danger. You tells how you raises a roar if you don't git your coin, but what does yer do to earn it?"

"Well, I fights some when I has to," returned Bight, rather savagely. "Mebbe you talks too much to me, Dug, and you gits yourself into some trouble."

Bight was ugly now, and his companion involuntarily retreated a step, for the squat chap had a reputation as a fighter.

"Go slow, pard!" exclaimed Dug. "I am not a-picking trouble with you."

"All right, all right," nodded Bight, "Only just be a little keerful—a little keerful. Don't think just because a gent don't keer about shooting another gent down promiscuous-like that he is soft and easy. There's Texas Bland out yander. He has a reputation as a bad man. Well, partner, I picks no quarrels with him, but if he stomps on my tail he gets my claws."

"What's that?" exclaimed Dug, in astonishment. "You ain't a-giving it ter me that you bucks up agin' Bland, are yer?"

"I am a-giving it ter yer that I does in case I has to. I don't propose any ter have ter do it. I jines in with this yer move because it seems popular with the gang, and I am none anxious ter work myself. This yere is a nice bunch o' miners, now, ain't it? Why, the gent what hires this outfit and brings it yere had a whole lot better stick to his sailoring business! He may know how to pick out seamen, but it's right certain he makes a mess of it when it comes to engaging miners."

"That's right," agreed Dug. "And he certain is the biggest liar it ever were my pleasure to harken unto. The way he can tell things to make a galoot's eyes bug out is a whole lot remarkable. Whither he gits his lively imagination I cannot surmise. Let's see, whatever was his name?"

"Wiley—Cap'n Wiley he calls himself."

"Well, however does he happen to be hiring men for this yere mine? I don't judge any that he is interested in it."

"Not a whole lot. The mine is owned by a gent named Merriwell, and by this yere Hodge. Them two locates it."

"Relocates it, you mean. I onderstand it were located original by another gent what is dead now. And I reckons some that it is through this other gent's action that the man that is back o' this yere jumping movement is going to stake his claim to the mine. I hears one o' the boys say that if Bland ain't back o' the game, it sartin is a gent with heaps o' money—one o' them yere money kings we hears about."

This conversation was of no simple interest to Hodge, for, although it did not reveal the instigator of the movement, it satisfied him that the plot did not originate among the men themselves. Some enemy of Frank Merriwell must be behind it all. As Sukes was dead, it was not easy for Bart to conjecture who this new enemy was.

After a few moments more the two ruffians finished the contents of the bottle and moved slowly away. This gave Hodge an opportunity to turn back toward his cabin, and he hastened to get away from that dangerous locality.

"It's well for me that I suspected what was up," he muttered, as he hurried along. "Under ordinary circumstances, failing to hear the men at work and hearing their singing and shouts, I should have hastened over and demanded to know the meaning of it. As a result they would have finished me in short order. Now I am prepared for them. But what can I do? What can I do alone?"

The situation seemed desperate and hopeless.

Another fellow in Bart's position, and realizing his desperate peril, might have lost no time in getting out of the valley. Even though he happened to be a courageous person, his judgment might have led him to pursue such a course, for certainly it seemed a wild and hopeless plan to think of remaining there alone and contending against those ruffians.

Bart, however, was an obstinate chap and one in whom fear was an emotion seldom experienced. Not that he had always been fearless, for as a boy he had sometimes felt the thrill of terror; but his iron will had conquered, and time after time he had refused to submit to the approach of the slightest timidity, until at last fear seemed banished from his heart. Now, as he hastened back to the cabin, he revolved in his mind certain thoughts in regard to the situation; but not once did he entertain the idea of leaving the valley and abandoning it to those desperadoes.

"I will stay," he muttered. "I will stay as long as I am able to shoot. While I live they will never gain full possession of the valley. Merry left me here to guard this property, and I will do it with my life. But for Wiley's carelessness——"

He stopped, suddenly struck by a startling suspicion.

"Was it carelessness?" he asked himself.

An instant later he was ashamed of the suspicion, for he remembered how on other occasions he had suspected Wiley, and each time had found himself wrong.

"No, no," murmured Hodge; "it was simply a blunder, on Wiley's part. He remembered Merriwell's thirty, and thought he was doing the right thing in engaging men of similar calibre. The cap'n is on the level."

Still troubled and perplexed by his thoughts, he grew, if possible, more fixed in his determination to defend the mines single-handed. He approached the cabin, the door of which was still standing open as he left it. Hurrying in, he stopped, suddenly turned to stone as he saw sitting on the floor, with his back against the wall, a human being, who was calmly smoking a long pipe.

A moment later the muzzle of Bart's revolver covered this figure, which, however, did not stir or lift a hand. Coming, as he did, from the bright light outside into the shadows within the cabin, Hodge failed at first to note more than that the smoker who sat thus was wrapped in an old blanket. After a moment or two, however, he finally saw that he was face to face with an aged, wrinkled, leathery-skinned Indian. The little sharp eyes of the old savage were fixed steadily on Bart's face, and he betrayed not a symptom of alarm as Hodge brought the rifle to bear upon him. With stoical calmness he deliberately pulled at his pipe.

"What in thunder are you doing here?" demanded Hodge, in astonishment.

"Ugh!" was the only reply vouchsafed.

Somehow that grunt seemed familiar. Bart had heard it before, but it simply increased his amazement. Lowering the rifle, he stared wonderingly.

"Great Scott!" he breathed. "Is it possible? Are you old Joe?"

"Heap same," was the curt answer.

In a twinkling Bart dropped the rifle on the table and strode forward to shake the hand of an old friend.

"Old Joe Crowfoot!" he shouted. "Where under the stars did

you drop from?"

"Joe he come visit. How, how!"

"Why, you amazing old Nomad!" cried Bart, in delight. "You're always turning up just when you're wanted the most, and if ever you were wanted it is now."

"Frank him not here?"

"No."

"Joe he want see Frank."

"If that's the case, you will have to wait a while."

"Strong Heart he better be here," declared the aged redskin. "Heap lot o' trouble pretty soon."

"That's right, Joe. But how do you know anything about it?"

"Joe he know. Him no fool. Him find out."

Bart had extended his hand, and now he assisted the old man to his feet. Although old Joe tried to conceal the fact, he seemed rather stiff in his joints just then.

"What's the matter, Crowfoot?" questioned Bart. "Rheumatism troubles you again?"

"Debble got old Joe in his bones," indignantly returned the savage. "Old Joe him no good any more. Make old Joe mad when him think he no good."

Under other circumstances the indignation of the redskin over his infirmities might have been somewhat amusing.

"But tell me—tell me how you came to be here at this time," questioned Hodge. "We last saw you away up in Wyoming. You said then that you'd never travel south again."

"Heap think so then. When winter he come Joe have debble ache in his bones plenty bad. Sabe?"

"And so the rheumatism and cold weather drove you south, eh?"

"One time," said the redskin, drawing his blanket about his shoulders with an air of dignity, "Joe him face cold and never feel um. One time him no care how cold. One time he laugh at snow and ice. Then all him bones be good. Then old Joe a heap strong to hunt. Now it ain't the same. Once Joe him hunt the grizzly bear for game; now he hunt poker."

In spite of himself, Bart was forced to smile. He knew something of the skill of old Joe at the white man's game of poker, and the thought of the old Indian who had once tracked the grizzly now turned to gambling was both amusing and remarkable.

"So that is what brought you south. You turned this way to escape the cold and to find at the same time the kind of game you were after?"

"Heap so," nodded Crowfoot, as he produced from beneath his blanket a greasy pack of cards. "I came to play some. Mebbe I find um good players here."

"I don't know where, Joe," said Hodge.

"Mebbe over yon," suggested the Indian, waving his hand toward the southern end of the valley.

"See here, Joe," said Bart, "those men down there are my enemies. They have betrayed me. There are valuable mines in this valley, and they belong to Frank Merriwell and myself. These ruffians mean to seize them. Even now they are ready to shoot me on sight, and intend to drop Frank when he appears."

"Heap bad," observed Joe, without betraying the slightest emotion.

"Bad!" cried Hodge. "I should say so!"

"Too many for you, Black Eyes," asserted the redskin. "Mebbe you pull up stake and lope?"

"Not by a blamed sight!" grated Hodge. "I will stay here and defend these mines as long as I am able to lift a weapon."

The Indian shook his head.

"Heap young, heap young," he declared, as if speaking to himself. "Blood hot. Joe him know. Once him blood hot."

"Well, you don't suppose I'd let them drive me out, do you?" indignantly demanded Hodge. "You don't think I'd betray Frank like that! He left me here in charge of the property, and here I will remain. I want you to stick by me, Joe."

"Ugh!" grunted the old fellow noncommittally. "Mebbe not much difference to old Joe. I may croak pretty soon now. Mebbe only make it some quicker."

"Perhaps that's right," said Hodge slowly. "I have no right to ask you to lose your life in helping me fight against overwhelming odds. It's not your quarrel, Joe. You can do as you please."

"Joe him think it over," said the Indian. "No like to see Frank lose um mines, but him have plenty more."

Bart turned away, not without a feeling of disappointment. As he did so, through the still open door he caught a glimpse of a man who was advancing toward the cabin. Instantly he strode toward the door, and his eyes rested on Texas Bland, who was several rods away.

"Oh, Mr. Hodge!" Bland called at once. "I want yer ter come over yon. The men has quit work, and they refuse to strike another stroke."

Trying to repress and conceal his indignation, Bart asked, as if wholly unsuspicious of the real situation:

"What's the matter, Bland?"

"I dunno," lied the scoundrel. "I can't make 'em work; perhaps you can, sir."

Suddenly, almost without being aware of what was happening, Bart permitted his hot indignation to get the best of his judgment. Instantly, as he stepped out of the cabin, he blazed:

"You're lying, Bland, and I know it! I am on to the whole dastardly game! You're at the bottom of it, too! You have incited the men to mutiny. I know your plot, you treacherous whelp! I know you meant to get me over there for the purpose of assassinating me. The end of this business will be a rope for you, Bland. Go back and tell your dogs I am onto their game. Go back and bring them here. They will meet a hot reception!"

Texas Bland had been astonished, but now, quick as a flash, he whipped out a revolver for the purpose of taking a shot at Hodge, whose hands were empty. Rapid though he was in his movements, he was not quick enough, for within the cabin sounded the loud report of a rifle, and the bullet knocked Bland's pistol from his hand, smashing two of his fingers.

CHAPTER XVI.

CROWFOOT MAKES MEDICINE.

Although taken by surprise, the man looked at his benumbed and bleeding hand a moment, then pulled from his neck a handkerchief tied there and wrapped it around the mutilated member. By this time Hodge had his own pistol out, and Bland was covered.

"You're lucky to get off with your life, you treacherous cur!" he cried. "Now make tracks, and hurry about it, too."

"All right," said the leader of the ruffians, still with amazing coolness. "But you pays dear for this hand—you and the gent inside who fires the shot."

With that he turned his back and hastily strode away, the handkerchief already dripping with blood and leaving a red trail behind him.

Hodge watched until the hurrying man disappeared down the valley. Reentering the cabin, he found old Joe standing near the table on which still lay Bart's Winchester. The Indian had refilled his pipe and was smoking again in his most imperturbable manner.

"Crowfoot," said Hodge, with sincere gratitude, "I owe you my life. It's lucky for me you fired just when you did. An instant more and Bland would have shot me down. How did you happen to be so quick with the shot?"

"Look um rifle over," grunted the old man. "Pick um rifle up. When Black Eyes him go out, Joe think mebbe white man act crooked. Joe watch him white man. When white man tries to shoot, Joe him shoot."

"You're a jewel, Crowfoot!" declared Bart; "but this thing will bring trouble to the cabin in a hurry. As soon as Bland can have his hand cared for, he will lead those ruffians over here to wipe us out. Now is your chance to get away."

"Oh, no great hurry," returned Crowfoot. "Plenty time, plenty time."

"On the contrary, there may be very little time. If you're going, you had better go at once."

"Plenty time," persisted the old man placidly. "Joe too old to hurry. They no come right away. Mebbe Joe him look around a little."

As the old fellow was leaving the cabin, Bart called:

"Here's your own rifle, Joe, standing in the corner. Don't you want to take it?"

"Leave him there now," returned the redskin. "Take him bime-by."

Outside the door, leaning against the wall, were a pick and spade. To Bart's surprise, the old man picked these implements up and shouldered them; after which he found Bland's revolver where it had fallen on being knocked from the man's hand by the bullet, and took that along. Crowfoot turned northward toward a tangled wild thicket, into which Bart saw him disappear.

"Well, of all peculiar things for him to do!" muttered Hodge, completely puzzled. "What the dickens is he up to?"

This question bothered Bart not a little, and, after a time, having made sure none of the ruffians were yet approaching from the south, Bart caught up his rifle and ran swiftly toward the thicket. On entering the tangled underbrush, he soon came in sight of Crowfoot, who, although he must have heard the other approaching, paid no attention whatever. The defender of the mines paused in amazement as he noted the Indian's occupation, for old Joe was busily at work, engaged with pick and shovel, digging in the ground.

"What in the name of all mysteries are you doing, Crowfoot?" asked Hodge, as he approached and stood nearer.

"Dig a little," returned the old man, with something like a joking twinkle in his keen black eyes. "Mebbe get some exercise. Strong Heart him great on exercise. Crowfoot hear Strong Heart tell exercise much big thing."

Now, Hodge knew well enough that the aged redskin was not expending so much energy and labor in mere exercise, and he lingered to watch a while longer. Pretty soon old Joe unearthed a long root that ran beneath the ground, which he immediately seized and dragged forth with considerable grunting. Hodge noted then that he had one or two similar roots lying near.

"Mebbe him be 'nuf," observed Crowfoot, as he severed the last root unearthed and placed it with the others. "Think him be. Joe he get plenty exercise for to-day."

Then, abandoning the pick and shovel where he had dropped

them, the old man gathered up the roots and started to retrace his steps to the cabin. Still wondering at Crowfoot's strange actions, Hodge followed.

The sunshine lay warm on the valley, which seemed deserted save for themselves.

"Man git hand hurt, him no hurry back much," observed Crowfoot.

"Not yet," said Hodge. "But he will come and bring his dogs with him soon enough."

When the cabin was reached Crowfoot stood some moments looking at a little pile of wood lying in a corner near the open fireplace.

"You build a fire, Black Eyes," he said. "Joe him cold—him cold."

"Well, your blood must be getting thin," declared Hodge. "You can bake out in the sun to-day if you want to."

"No like sun bake," was the retort. "Too slow; not right kind. Want fire bake."

"Oh, all right," said Bart, ready to humor the old man. "I will have a fire directly."

To his surprise, while he was starting the fire, old Joe brought in more wood that had been gathered in a little pile outside and threw it down in the corner. Several times he came with an armful of wood, but finally, seemed satisfied.

"There's a good hot fire for you, Joe," said Hodge. "Now toast yourself, if you want to."

"Ugh!" grunted the Indian. "You keep watch. Keep eye open wide. Mebbe bad palefaces come soon."

Bart knew this was a good suggestion, and he proceeded to watch for the possible approach of the enemy. At the same time, he occasionally turned from the open doorway to observe what Crowfoot was about. The old Indian did not seem very anxious to warm himself at the fire. Instead of that, he took the roots he had dug and held them toward the fireplace, turning them over and over and warming them thoroughly, after which he beat off the particles of dirt that clung to them. While he was beating one of the roots by holding it toward the fire, he had the others arranged on the flat stones of the hearth quite near the blaze, where they also would receive warmth from the flames.

At last, his curiosity reaching a point where he could repress it no longer, Hodge again asked old Joe what he was doing.

For some minutes the Indian did not reply. Once or twice he grunted to himself, but finally said:

"Joe him make medicine. Sometime him big medicine maker."

"Oh, so that's it," said Hodge. "You are making medicine for your rheumatism?"

"Ugh!" was the answer to this.

Bart was surprised and almost annoyed as the day dragged on and the ruffians failed to appear. It seemed remarkable that they should delay the attack so long; still, he was confident that it must come sooner or later. All through the day after securing his roots old Joe worked over them patiently by the fire. He dried them and turned them over and over. And, while he was handling one of them and turning it before the heat like a thing he was toasting, the others remained in a long mound of hot ashes. The patience of the Indian over such a trifling task was something to wonder at.

As night came on Crowfoot paused to say:

"Now, Black Eyes, keep sharp watch. Bad white men come to-night. Mebbe they try to ketch um sleeping."

The first half of the night, however, passed without alarm. During these hours the old redskin continued to putter with his roots, which he carefully scraped with a keen knife. At midnight he buried them in the ashes, on which hot coals were heaped, and then directed Bart to lie down and sleep.

"Joe him watch now," said the old fellow.

Trusting everything to the redskin, Hodge rolled himself in a blanket and slept soundly for two hours. He was awakened by Joe, who stirred him with a moccasin foot.

"Get up, Black Eyes," said the old fellow, in a whisper. "Pretty soon we fight."

"Those ruffians?" questioned Bart, as he leaped to his feet.

"They coming," declared Crowfoot.

He was right. Bland and his desperadoes were creeping on the cabin, hoping to take its defenders by surprise. Crowfoot pointed them out, and when they were near enough, Hodge called from the window for them to halt. Realizing they were discovered, they sprang up and charged.

Instantly Bart and the redskin opened fire on them, Hodge working his repeater swiftly and accurately, while the clear spang of Crowfoot's rifle was heard at irregular intervals. The ruffians were unprepared for such a defense, and, as they saw several of their number fall and others were wounded, they halted, wavered, then turned and fled. Looking from the window, the starlight showed the defenders a few wounded men dragging themselves away.

"Pretty good," said Joe. "No more bother to-night."

With which he turned from the window, uncovered his roots, and replanted them in a fresh pile of hot ashes.

CHAPTER XVII.

HOW THE MEDICINE WORKED.

aving left their horses picketed in a secluded spot, four men came stealing down the steep and narrow fissure that was the one entrance into the Enchanted Valley. Three days had passed since Dash Colvin stole out of that valley in his desperate attempt to carry the message to Frank. The third night had fallen.

Frank had arrived, and with him were Pete Curry, of Cottonwood, an officer who knew him well and liked him, and two deputies whom Curry had called into service. Frank had picked these men up at Cottonwood after his flight from Prescott. The promise of a liberal reward under any circumstances, and possibly of a big capture, had led them to accompany him. Before seeking to descend into the valley they had seen from the heights above, far away to the southern end, the glow of two or three bright fires, and had heard at intervals something like singing.

Frank feared the entrance to the valley might be in the hands of the enemy and guarded. He was relieved on discovering that this was not so, and his satisfaction was great when, with his companions, he found himself in the valley with no one to block the way.

"What next, Mr. Merriwell?" asked Curry, in a low tone.

"I am for finding out what is going on down there to the south," said Frank.

"All right, sir. Lead on. We're with you."

In time they approached near enough to look down upon that portion of the valley where the unfinished cabins were, and saw two or three fires burning there. Men were lying around on the ground in the light of these fires. Others were staggering about in a peculiar manner. Now and then one of them would utter a wild yell and dance about like a crazy man, sometimes keeping it up until, apparently exhausted, he ended by flinging himself on the ground and seemed immediately to fall asleep.

As Frank and his companions watched these singular movements they saw three men join hands and execute a singular dance in the firelight.

"Cæsar's ghost!" muttered Merry, "am I dreaming?"

"What's the matter, pard?" asked Curry.

"Look at those three men—look at them closely. One of them is an Indian."

"Sure thing," said Curry.

"And I know him!" palpitated Merry. "If my eyes don't fail me, it is old Joe Crowfoot."

"Who is old Joe Crowfoot?"

"A redskin I have believed to be my friend."

"Waugh!" ejaculated Curry, in disgust. "There never was a red whelp as could be trusted."

"But you don't know Crowfoot."

"I know 'em all. Here is this yere Crowfoot a-whooping her up with your enemies, Mr. Merriwell. What do you think of that?"

"It's mighty singular," confessed Merry. "Look! look! they are drinking!"

It was true. The dance had stopped and one of the three had flung himself on the ground. Crowfoot bent over this fellow and offered him a bottle, which he eagerly seized. The Indian snatched it from the man's lips, refusing to let him drink all he seemed to desire. It was then given to the other men, and afterward the old redskin passed from one to another of the reclining men, rousing those he could and offering them the bottle. Some drank, but others seemed too nerveless to hold the bottle in their hands.

"Well, this yere is lucky for us," declared Curry. "The whole bunch is paralyzed drunk. We oughter be able to scoop 'em in without any great trouble."

"I wonder where Hodge is," speculated Merry. "I wonder if they have killed him."

This possibility so aroused Frank that he was determined to seek Bart without delay. Curry was opposed to this; but Frank had his way, and they stole off leaving Crowfoot and his newly chosen companions to continue their carousal. As they approached Bart's cabin, there came from the window a sharp command for them to halt. Merry recognized the voice and uttered a cry of satisfaction.

"Hodge!" he called. "It is I—Frank."

From within the cabin there was another cry of joy, and a moment later the door flew open and Hodge came running toward them.

"Merry, thank Heaven you're here!" he exclaimed,

"Thank Heaven you're still alive!" returned Frank. "I was afraid I might arrive too late. Tell me what has happened. How have you managed to stand those ruffians off?"

"They attacked the cabin twice," said Hodge; "but we were ready for them both times."

"We? But aren't you alone?"

"I am now; but old Joe Crowfoot——"

"Crowfoot—what of him?"

"He was with me. I don't know what has become of the old man now. He left to-night as soon as darkness fell, saying he was going to take a look at the ruffians down yonder. The old man is pretty well used up; he is nearly dead with rheumatism. He spent the greater part of the time after coming here in digging roots and making them into medicine by drying them at the fire, scraping them, then grinding them into powder between stones, finally preparing a decoction with water and the powder of the roots."

Frank then told Bart what he had lately seen, and Hodge was greatly astonished.

"Old Joe down there with those men?" he muttered. "Why, I don't see——"

"Ugh!" grunted a voice near at hand, and out of the shadows slipped another shadow that unhesitatingly approached. It was Crowfoot himself, as they immediately perceived.

"How, how, Strong Heart!" said the old man, extending his hand to Frank. "Heap glad to see um."

"Why, you old wretch!" cried Merry. "We saw you a short time ago down there with that bunch of claim jumpers drinking and whooping things up. What do you mean by such conduct?"

"Old Joe him got very bad rheumatism," returned the redskin. "Him make medicine. Him think mebbe um white men down there got bad rheumatism, too. He give um white men some medicine. He find um white man drinking a heap. Joe he mix um medicine with drink. They like medicine pretty good. One white man, who lead um, him get shot up a great lot. Him in no shape to lead um some more. So white men they wait for more men to come. Now they very much tired. They sleep a lot. Come down see um sleep. You like it."

Of a sudden the truth dawned on Frank.

"Why, you clever old rascal!" he laughed. "Hanged if I don't believe you've drugged them some way!"

"Joe he give um medicine, that all," protested the redskin. "Sometimes medicine make um sleep. Come see."

"Come on," said Frank, "we will follow this slick old rascal and

146

find out how hard they are sleeping."

As they approached the cabins at the lower end of the valley they saw the fires were dying down, while from that locality no longer came shouts and singing, and, in truth, all the ruffians seemed fast asleep on the ground, where they had fallen or flung themselves.

Unhesitatingly Crowfoot led them amid the mass of drugged men, and the sinking firelight revealed on his leathery face a ghost of a shriveled smile.

"Medicine heap good sometimes," he observed. "Strong Heart find him enemies sleeping. Mebbe he takes hatchet and chop um up? Joe he get many scalps."

"You're a dandy, Crowfoot!" laughed Frank. "Here they are, Curry, the whole bunch. You can gather them and escort them to Cottonwood, or anywhere you please."

"And a great haul it is, pard," nodded Curry. "I sees three gents now what has rewards offered for them. It's my opinion that they hangs. Get to work, boys, and we will tie up the whole bunch so they can't wiggle when they awake."

Old Joe looked on in apparent dissatisfaction and dismay.

"You no chop um up some?" he questioned. "You no kill um a heap. Then what Joe him get? He no have a scalp."

"What do you get, Joe?" exclaimed Merry. "You have saved my mines for me. You get anything you want—anything but scalps."

CHAPTER XVIII.

A BUNCH OF PRISONERS.

Pete Curry and his two deputies set off the next morning with their prisoners—thirteen in all. They were taking the ruffians direct to the nearest point where they could be confined and afterward delivered for trial into the hands of certain officers, who would take several of them to different parts of Arizona where they had committed crimes. At noon the second day they reached a point in a barren valley where the sun beat fiercely. Scorched mountains rose to the east and west. They came to a halt.

In the party of sixteen there were only three horses, ridden by the officers. The prisoners had been compelled to tramp over the desert, the mountains, and valleys. The wrists of each captive were bound behind his back.

A tough-looking, desperate lot they were, taken all together. There were Mexicans and men with Indian blood in their veins among them. They had weather-beaten, leathery, bearded faces. Many of them had a hangdog expression. Their eyes were shiftless and full of treachery.

It was a most important capture for Curry, as there were among those men desperate characters for whose apprehension rewards had been offered. In short, it was a round-up of criminals that would make Curry's name known as that of a wonderfully successful officer of the law. He was proud of his accomplishment, although he regretfully admitted to himself that he deserved very little credit for it. He and his two companions had already been well paid by Frank Merriwell.

Now, with his weapons ready, Curry was watching the prisoners, while his two companions sought for water in the bed of the creek.

"How are you hitting her, Bill?" he called.

"She's moist, Pete," answered one of the diggers. "There's water here."

"It takes a right good while for her to gather in the hole," said the other digger. "If we makes a hole big enough, we will have some in an hour or so."

Curry took a look at the sky, the mountains, and the westering sun.

"Well, I opines we stops here a while," he said. "We may as well."

A big, burly fellow among the captives carelessly stalked toward Curry, who watched him with a keen eye.

"I say, Pete," said the prisoner familiarly, "mebbe you tells me just how this yere thing happens. I am a whole lot bothered over it."

"Why, Bland, I has you—I has you foul," retorted Curry, with a grim smile.

"That I certain admits," nodded the other; "but how it was did is what puzzles me a-plenty."

"You has some bad habits, Bland," returned the captor. "You monkeys with firewater, and, for a man like you, with a price on him, it's a keerless thing to do."

"No firewater ever lays me out," proudly retorted he of the drooping black mustache. "I knows my capacity when it come to the real stuff. But what I gits against this yere time is different a whole lot."

The deputy sheriff smiled again.

"Mebbe you're right, Bland," he admitted. "You thinks yourself a heap clever, but this time you is fooled right slick."

Texas Bland frowned.

"I confess, Pete, that it cuts me deep to realize it, but it certain is a fact that I gits tripped up. However, how it happened is what I wants ter know. There sure was dope in that booze."

"Likely you're correct," nodded Curry.

"How does it git there?"

"Have you noticed a certain old Injun in this bunch sence we started out?" asked the officer.

"No," said Bland, shaking his head. "I looks fer him some, but he is not yere. Does yer mean to insinuate that the old varmint loaded this bunch with dope?"

"Well, how does it look to you?"

"Why, ding his old pelt!" exclaimed the captive indignantly. "Some of the boys knowed him. Some o' them had seen him afore. One or two had seen him to their sorrer. They say to me that he plays poker somewhat slick. When he comes ambling into our

149

camp, seeming a whole lot jagged hisself, I was a bit suspicious; but the boys what knowed him says he is all right, and so I takes a drink with him. Arter that I gits a heap sleepy and snoozes. Next I knows you is there, Pete, and you has us nailed solid."

"That's about the way of it," nodded Curry.

"And the old whelp dopes us, does he!" growled Texas Bland. "Whatever does he do that fer?"

"Why, Bland, that yere old redskin is a friend of Mr. Merriwell. He gives you the dope to help Merriwell. When we comes down into the valley there and finds you all sleeping sweetly, the old Injun proposes to scalp you up some. To be course, we objects, and then he seems mighty disappointed-like. He seems to think he is cheated. He seems to reckon that, having done the job so slick, your scalps belong to him."

Bland listened with a strange look on his face and a vengeful glare in his deepset eyes.

"So that's however it is!" he growled. "Well, I am some glad I finds it out."

"Mebbe it relieves your mind some of worry," returned the captor; "but it does you little good."

"Don't you think it!" returned Bland harshly. "I settles with that old Injun, you bet your boots!"

"First you settles with the law, Bland. You roams free a long time with a good price on your head. I am sorry fer you, but I reckons you are due to stretch hemp."

Texas Bland actually laughed.

"Pete," he said, "the rope ain't made yet what hangs me."

"Your nerve is good, but I opine you're wrong this yere time. I has you, Bland, and I keeps you. I deliver you to them what wants you bad."

"That's all right, Pete," was the cool retort. "No hard feelings on my account, you understand. I takes my medicine when I has to, and so I swallows this all pleasant and smiling. Just the same, you mark what I tells you, the rope ain't made what hangs Texas Bland. I goes back a-looking for that red skunk later, and I pots him. When I gits a chance, I starts a lead mine in his carcass. The idea of being fooled by a redskin galls me up a heap. But you don't tell me any how it happens you drops down thar and gathers us in just then."

"I am some acquainted with Frank Merriwell. I has done business for him before. When he comes sailing into Cottonwood and locates me, he says: 'Curry, I am up against it some, and I needs assistance.' 'I am yours to order,' says I. 'Whatever is a-doing?'

"Then he up and tells me that a gent with a whole lot of coin, what calls himself a money king, is trying to get possession of some new mines he has located. This gent, he says, has faked up a false charge against him and gives him a heap o' trouble. This gent's partner once tried mighty hard to get his paws on another mine belonging to Merriwell, and in the end he runs up against a bullet and lays down peaceful and calm. This gent's name were Sukes. The one what is a-bothering Merriwell now is Macklyn Morgan."

"You interest me a-plenty," nodded Bland. "Now, there were some gent behind this yere deal what says it pays us well if we seizes those mines. Just who it were that puts up the coin fer the job I didn't know for sure. All I knows is that it comes straight through a gent what I depends on, and the coin is in sight the minute we delivers the mines over. I reckons, Pete, the gent you speak of is the one what lays the job out fer us."

Curry nodded.

"Likely that's all correct, Bland. But he makes a big mistake if he thinks this yere Merriwell is easy. Merriwell is a fighter from 'Way Back."

"He is a whole lot young."

"In experience he is a whole lot old. Mebbe he don't grow whiskers much, but he gets there just the same. Whiskers don't always make the man, Bland. With all his money, this yere Sukes don't get ahead of Merriwell any. When Morgan he tackles the job he finds it just as hard or harder. It does him no good to fake a charge that Merriwell shoots up Sukes."

"Where did this yere shooting happen, Pete?"

"Over yon in Snowflake."

Bland shook his head.

"Then it's ten to one he gits disturbed none fer it. If he proves conclusive this yere Sukes bothers him, why, supposing he did do the shooting, it convicts him of nothing but self-defense down in this yere country!"

"Sukes was a whole lot wealthy, you understand."

"All the same, I reckons it is pretty hard to put murder on a gent yereabouts in case he is defending his rights."

"That's so," nodded Curry, at the same time lifting his eyes and watching with interest several horsemen who now appeared far up the valley, riding toward them through the heat haze.

Bland noticed Curry's look and turned in the same direction.

"Who does you allow is coming?" he questioned, with repressed eagerness.

Instead of answering, Curry called to the men who were laboring in the bed of the creek.

"Oh, Bill! Oh, Abe! Come up yere right away."

The inflection of his voice indicated that something was wrong, and the two men hastened to join him.

Curry motioned toward the approaching horsemen.

"Mebbe we is troubled some," he observed. "We needs to be ready."

The horsemen came on rapidly. There were seven of them in all. Like Curry and his two companions, the captives watched the approaching men with no small amount of anxiety. As the horsemen drew near, having told Bill and Abe to watch the prisoners closely, Curry rode forward.

"Howdy, gents!" he called.

"Howdy!" returned one of the men. "Is that you, Curry?"

"Surest thing you know," said the deputy sheriff. "Somehow I don't seem to recall you any."

"That's none strange," said the spokesman of the party. "I am Gad Hackett. No particular reason why you should know me."

"Whatever are you doing yere?" inquired the officer suspiciously.

"Just making a short cut, leaving all trails, from Fulton to Oxboro."

"Say you so? Seems ter me you're hitting in the wrong direction."

"I reckon I know my course," returned Hackett. "I have traveled this section a-plenty. There seems to be a good bunch of you gents. Whatever are you a-doing?"

"We're holding up for water now," answered Curry evasively. "Mebbe you hurries right along? Mebbe you has no great time to waste?"

"We look some for water ourselves," returned the other man.

"Well, you has to look mighty sharp yereabouts. We digs our own water hole, and unfortunately we can't share it any. If you goes down the valley a mile or two, mebbe you finds a locality where water is easier to reach."

"Seems ter me you're some anxious to hurry us on," laughed Hackett. "We're slightly tired, and I reckons we holds up for rest, water or no water."

"That being the case," said Curry, "let me give you some advice. Yander I has a few gents what are wanted for various little doings in different parts, and I am takin' pains careful-like to deliver them over. They're lawbreakers to the last galoot of the bunch.

Mebbe you bothers them none. I does my duty."

"Oh—ho!" retorted Hackett, "so that's how the wind blows! Why, certain, Curry, we interferes none whatever with your business. Instead o' that, we helps you any we can in running in your bunch of bad men."

"Thanks," returned the deputy sheriff coolly. "So long as I am not bothered with, I needs no help."

Hackett laughed again.

"I see, pard," he said, "you counts on gathering in the reward money yourself, and proposes to divide it none. All right; you're welcome."

Then, with his companions, he again rode forward. Curry looked them over critically. In his eyes, with one or two exceptions, they appeared little different from the collection of ruffians who were his prisoners. With them he recognized one man, at least, who had an unenviable reputation—a tall, pockmarked individual— no less a person than Spotted Dan.

There was in the party a man who seemed strangely out of place there. His every appearance was that of a tenderfoot, while his face, with his shaven lips and iron-gray beard, looked like that of a stern old church deacon. Somehow this person interested Curry more than all the others. He wondered not a little at the appearance of such a man in such a party.

"Who is the parsonish gentleman?" asked the deputy sheriff, as Hackett came up with him. He spoke in a low tone and jerked his hand slightly toward the tenderfoot.

"That?" said Hackett loudly. "Why, that is Mr. Felton Cleveland, a gentleman what is looking around some for mining property, and it is him we escorts to Oxboro. He engages us to see that he gets there all safe-like, and he is in a hurry."

The man indicated did not betray that these words had reached his ears, although he had not missed the statement.

"He looks more like a missionary than a mining man," declared Curry.

As the new arrivals reached the captives and their guards, Felton Cleveland was soon looking the captives over with an expression of interest, not to say of sympathy. He turned to the deputy sheriff and observed:

"It seems hardly possible, sir, that so many men could be law-breakers; still, their faces indicate that they are desperate characters."

"I reckon you're some unfamiliar with this part of the country," returned the officer. "We tries to keep our towns clean, but down along the Mexican border there are a few bad men. Sometimes they go in bunches."

"But it is remarkable that you should capture so many of them at one time. Do you mind telling how it happened?"

"I am not feeling a whole lot like talking just now," returned the deputy sheriff. "I opines you takes my word for it that they are just what I says."

"Oh, certainly, sir—certainly," nodded Cleveland. "I don't dispute you in the least. I assure you it is not mere idle curiosity on my part, for I have interests in this part of the country, and I wish to be well informed about it and its inhabitants. However, if you don't care to tell me what these men have been doing, we will let it drop."

"Well, I don't mind saying that they was caught redhanded trying to jump a claim. Mebbe that is the charge made agin' a few o' them, but I reckons the most of the bunch is to face things a heap more serious."

"Trying to jump a claim?" said Cleveland. "Where was this, if you don't mind giving that much information?"

"Over yon," answered Pete indefinitely, with a wave of his hand.

"Well, it's truly remarkable that you should be able to capture so many of them. They outnumber you, it appears. If they are such desperate men, it surely is a strange thing that you could take them all."

"We has a way of doing things sometimes, mister. Let me advise you to keep your own eyes open. Mebbe some o' that bunch you has is not to be trusted too far."

"There is no reason why they should betray me," was the assertion. "I have nothing on my person that could tempt them. They will be paid well when we reach our destination. That should be enough to guarantee their faithfulness to me."

"You're some wise in leaving your valuables behind," nodded Curry.

Some of the captives attempted to converse with the newcomers, but Curry's companions promptly put a stop to that. Between Spotted Dan and one or two of them passed significant looks. The horsemen dismounted, as if to take a brief rest and give their animals a breathing spell.

Gad Hackett lighted his pipe and engaged one of Curry's comrades in conversation. Seeing this, Curry approached them and quietly said:

"You talks a little, Bill—a very little."

Bill nodded.

"I knows my business, Pete," he assured.

Hackett laughed.

"Why does he seem so mighty suspicious?" he asked. "We don't bother him none."

After talking with Bill a few moments, however, he turned to Abe and engaged him in conversation. He seemed careless and indifferent in his manner, and occasionally a few low words passed between them. After a time, Abe examined the water hole and announced that water was rising in it. Bill joined him, and they were on their knees beside the hole when a startling thing happened. Curry suddenly felt something thrust against the back of his head and heard a harsh voice commanding him to stand still or be shot in his tracks.

The voice was that of Spotted Dan, who held the muzzle of a revolver touching the deputy sheriff's head. Curry knew on the instant that he was in for it. He knew better than to attempt the drawing of a weapon, although one hung ready in the holster at his side. Hackett, a pistol in his hand, appeared before the officer.

"We don't care to shoot you up, Curry," he said; "but we has to do it if you gits foolish. Put up your hands."

"Whatever is this game?" exclaimed the startled man. "You arrays yourself agin' the law. You gits yourself into a heap o' trouble."

"Put up your hands," repeated Hackett sharply. "If you delays any, the gent behind you blows off the top of your head."

Knowing the folly of refusing to obey, Curry lifted his empty hands. Hackett then removed the revolver from the officer's holster. Instinctively Curry turned his eyes toward the water hole to see what was happening to his assistants there. He found them on their feet, but covered by drawn weapons of several men. He saw them also disarmed. Then one of the newcomers went among the captives and rapidly cut their bonds and set them free.

Texas Bland turned to Curry and laughed in his face.

"Pete," he said, "I tells you a while ago that the rope is not made that hangs me."

CHAPTER XIX.

THE VALLEY OF DESOLATION.

Six persons, all mounted, sat on their horses and gazed down the valley. From that elevation they were able to see its full length. The six were Dick Merriwell, Brad Buckhart, Cap'n Wiley, Dash Colvin, little Abe, and Felicia Delores. Being aware that Macklyn Morgan had started with a number of desperate men in pursuit of Frank, in spite of Frank's admonition to stay in Prescott and care for Felicia, Dick found it impossible to remain quiet.

He knew his brother was in deadly danger, and he longed to be with him when the tug of war came. Feeling certain likewise that the men employed by Cap'n Wiley and taken to the Enchanted Valley as miners were desperate characters, it did not seem possible to Dick that Frank and Bart unaided could cope with so many and overcome them.

Dick had not worried long over the matter. Calling Brad, he said:

"Buckhart, I am going to follow Frank and the men who are in pursuit of him."

The eyes of the Texan gleamed.

"Pard," he said, "I observed that you were notified to stay hereabouts and guard your cousin. Frank told you to do that. Do you let on that you're going to disobey orders?"

"I can't stay here, Brad. I feel certain Frank needs me. His enemies are very powerful and desperate. What would I think of myself if anything serious happened to my brother? I should hate myself forever afterward."

The rancher's son nodded.

"I allow that's dead right, partner," he agreed. "I am feeling some that way myself. I certain smell smoke in the air, and I have an itching to be in the midst of the fray. But whatever are you going to do with Felicia?"

"Why, I did think of leaving her here with you. I thought of leaving you in charge of her."

"What, me?" squealed the Texan. "Leave me behind when there's a ruction brewing? Do you mean, pard, that you propose to cut me out of this yere scrimmage? Oh, say, Dick, you'd never treat me that low down! I came West to stick by you a heap close, and I am going to do it. Why don't you leave your cousin in the care of Cap'n Wiley?"

"I wouldn't dare," answered Dick. "Wiley is square enough; but he is careless. Besides that, how can I find my way to the Enchanted Valley unless guided by Wiley himself?"

"That's so. I never thought of that. You've got to take Wiley along—unless you can get hold of that man Colvin, who brought the message to Merry."

Dick frowned a little, seeming deep in serious thought.

"Then there's the hunchback boy," he finally muttered. "Possibly he might know the trail, but I doubt it."

"You can't depend on him none whatever," put in Buckhart. "He looks like a good wind would blow him away."

Dick rose to his feet.

"Brad," he said, "we will find Wiley and talk this matter over."

The sailor was found, and he turned an attentive ear to Dick's words.

"My young mate," he observed, resting a hand on Dick's shoulder, "I have been seriously meditating on the problematical problem of hoisting anchor and setting my course for the Enchanted Valley all by my lonesome. In my mouth danger leaves a sweet and pleasant taste. I love it with all my yearning heart. If you are bound to set sail for the Enchanted Valley, I am ready to ship with you as pilot. It may be well for me to do so. If I linger here I may dally with the delusive jag-juice. When there is no temptation I can be the most virtuous man in the world. Yes, my boy, we will pull out of Prescott and cut away toward the valley in question. You may depend on me."

"Then let's lose no time!" impatiently exclaimed Dick, feeling a powerful desire to hasten to his brother's side. "Let's make preparations without the least delay."

This was done. Dick found Felicia and little Abe together, for the two had become fast friends in a short time. Felicia settled the question in regard to herself by immediately declaring that she was ready to accompany them.

"It will do me good," she said. "The doctor in San Diego told me that what I most needed was more open-air exercise. I am feeling much better now. Oh, you will take me with you, won't you,

Dick? Please take me!"

"Me, too," urged little Abe. "You can't leave me behind."

It was found necessary to take them both, and when the time for starting came Cap'n Wiley appeared in company with Dash Colvin, the messenger. Colvin likewise was anxious to return to the Enchanted Valley, for he declared that there were two of his late companions in the valley with whom he had a score to settle. Although they had pursued him into the very heart of Prescott, on recovering from the effects of that desperate race he had sought them in vain. He learned, however, that they had joined Macklyn Morgan's party in the pursuit of Frank.

Thus it may be seen how it happened that Dick and his friends were watching to see what transpired in the barren valley amid the mountains at the time when Morgan's party released Texas Bland and his ruffians from the custody of Pete Curry, of Cottonwood. Wiley had pressed forward with such restless determination that they were close on the heels of Morgan and his men when this valley was reached, although this fact was not known by any of the men in advance. Provided with a powerful pair of field glasses, Dick watched what transpired, and saw Curry and his assistants held up while the captured desperadoes were set free.

Although he had only his eyes to observe what was taking place, Buckhart grew greatly excited and eagerly proposed a dash into the valley for the purpose of aiding Curry.

"Steady, Brad, old man!" warned Dick. "We're too far away for that. By the time we got there the whole thing would be over. The best we can do is to keep quiet and take care that we are not seen."

"Who do you suppose those men are?" asked Buckhart.

"It doesn't seem possible!" Dash Colvin was muttering to himself.

"What is it that doesn't seem possible?" questioned Dick.

"Let me take your glass a moment," requested Colvin.

Dick handed it over. The man took a hasty look through it.

"Well, of all things wonderful, this is the most remarkable!" he exclaimed.

"What is it?" questioned Dick impatiently.

"Yes, whatever is it you're driving at?" demanded Buckhart.

"Speak up, you, and keep us no longer in suspenders!" cried Wiley.

"Those men—those men who have been released——"

"What of them?" demanded Dick.

Colvin passed the glass quickly to Wiley.

"Take a look yourself, cap'n," he directed. "You oughter to know some of them."

After one glance, the sailor ejaculated:

"Dash my toplights! Shiver my timbers! May I be keelhauled if they ain't that sweet little aggregation I gathered for the purpose of operating the new mines! Why, there's Texas Bland! I recognize his sable mustache and flowing hair."

"That's it," nodded Colvin—"that's it exactly. They are the very men. What air they doin' here?"

"A short time ago they seemed to be in endurance vile. If I mistake not, three gentlemen in that party were escorting them as captives of war to some unknown port. Mates, I will stake my life there have been voluminous doings in the Enchanted Valley. Something of a critical nature surely happened there."

"But Frank is not in that party," said Dick. "Where can he be?"

"At this precise moment," confessed Wiley, "I am in no calm and placid frame of mind, therefore I am unable to answer the riddle. One thing, at least, is certain: Those gay boys have not seized your brother's property. That should relieve your agitated mental equilibrium to a conclusive susceptibility."

"We take chances of being seen here," said Dick. "Let's retire."

They did so, but from a point of partial concealment continued to watch everything that occurred in the valley. Within an hour Morgan's men, accompanied by the rescued ruffians, turned toward the south, which action assured the watchers that once more they were headed for the Enchanted Valley. They appropriated the horses of Curry and his two assistants, taking also the weapons of the three men, who were left a-foot and unarmed in that desolate region. The trio was warned not to follow and were further advised to make straight for Cottonwood or the nearest camp. Apparently Curry and his assistants decided this was the only course to pursue, for they turned to the north and hurried up the valley. Morgan and his men soon disappeared far away to the south.

Burning with eagerness to know the truth, Dick rode forward into the valley the moment the ruffians were beyond view. He was followed closely by Buckhart and Colvin. Cap'n Wiley remained long enough to caution Abe and Felicia to remain where they were, for, knowing nothing of Curry and his companions, Wiley fancied it possible there might be trouble of some sort.

"I will look out for Felicia," declared little Abe, whose violin was hung over his back by a cord. "I will take care of her."

"All right, my noble tar," said the sailor. And then he also rode forward into the valley.

Curry and his assistants halted in some alarm when they saw four horsemen dashing swiftly toward them. As they were unarmed, they could not think of offering resistance in case the quartette proved to be enemies. Being on foot, they could not escape, and, therefore, they did the only thing possible, which was to wait for the approaching riders.

Dick was the first to reach them.

"We have been watching this whole affair," he said. "We don't understand it."

"Well, we do!" growled Curry in disgust, while his companions growled likewise. "We understands that we have lost a bunch of valuable prisoners."

"But how did you happen to have such prisoners in the first place?" questioned Dick.

"That's our business, yonker. Why should we be for telling you any?"

"Because I am interested. Because those men are my brother's enemies."

"Who is your brother, kid?"

"Frank Merriwell."

"What?" shouted Curry. "Whatever are you giving us?"

"He is giving you the dead-level truth, stranger," put in Brad,

"That's right," agreed Dash Colvin, coming up. "Look here, Pete Curry, you knows me and I knows you. This boy is Frank Merriwell's brother."

"That being the case," said Curry, "he wants to get a hustle on and join his brother some lively. That fine bunch you saw hiking down the valley is bound for Frank Merriwell's new mines, which they propose seizing a heap violent. We counts ourselves some in luck to get off with whole skins from such a measly outfit. All the same, if we had played our hand proper I reckon they'd never set that lot of mavericks loose. I am a-plenty ashamed of myself."

"But tell me," urged Dick, "how you came to have those men as prisoners?"

Curry then briefly related the whole story, to which Dick and his friends listened with the greatest interest.

"That's how it were," finished Curry. "I allows to your brother I sure could take that gang to the nearest jail. He and his pard, Hodge, stays to guard their mines, leaving the job of disposing of those tough gents to we three. We makes a fizzle of it, and now the whole outfit is bound back for the Enchanted Valley. They are frothing to get at your brother and do him up. At the same time, they counts on salivating the old Injun what fools them a-plenty."

"Frank will fight to the last," said Dick. "We must help him some way. We're all armed, and I think we can furnish you with weapons. Are you with us, or are you ready to give up?"

"Pete Curry, of Cottonwood, gives up none at all," was the reply. "I counts on hiking somewhar to get weapons and horses and then hustling back for the purpose of doing whatever I can to help your brother."

"If you try to do that, you will be too late to render any assistance," declared Dick.

"Then give us some shooting irons and what goes in 'em and we're with yer," said Curry.

This arrangement was quickly settled on, after which Dick rode back for Felicia and little Abe. When he reached the spot where they had been left, however, he was not a little surprised and alarmed to find they were no longer there. In vain he looked for them. He called their names, but his voice died in the silence of the desolate hollows. There was no answer, and Dick's fears grew apace.

What had become of Felicia and little Abe?

Left to themselves, they fell to talking of the singular things which had happened.

Felicia's horse champed its bit and restlessly stamped the ground.

"That horse acts awful queer," said the boy. "He has got a funny look in his eye, just the same as a horse I once saw that was locoed. You know what that is, don't you?"

Felicia laughed.

"I was born in the West," she said. "Of course I know what it means when an animal is locoed. They have been eating loco weed and it makes them crazy. But I don't think this horse has been doing that."

"Never can tell," said the hunchback.

"Why, it should have shown on him before."

"Not always. Sometimes it breaks out awful unexpected. Look how your horse rolls its eyes. Say, I'm going to——"

Abe did not tell what he was going to do, for, starting his own horse forward, he reached for the bridle of Felicia's animal. To the horse it seemed that the boy's hand was large as a grizzly bear. The animal started back with a snort of alarm, quivering with sudden terror.

"Whoa! whoa!" cried Abe, hastening in his attempt to seize the creature's bit.

These efforts simply served to add to the horse's fear, and suddenly he wheeled and went tearing away, Felicia being unable to check its flight.

Immediately the hunchback pursued, his one thought being to overtake the girl and save her from danger, for he was now confident that something was the matter with the horse.

If the creature was really locoed, Abe knew it might do the most astonishing and crazy things. To a horse thus afflicted a little gully a foot wide sometimes seems a chasm a mile across, or a great ravine, yawning a hundred feet deep and as many in width, sometimes appears no more than a crack in the surface of the earth. Deluded by this distorted view of things, horses and cattle frequently plunge to their death in gorges and ravines, or do other things equally crazy and unaccountable.

Felicia's horse fled madly, as if in fear of a thousand pursuing demons. The girl was a good rider, and she stuck to the animal's back with comparative ease, although unable to check its wild career.

Doing everything in his power to overtake the runaway, the hunchback boy continued the pursuit, regardless of the direction in which it took them. The flying horse turned hither and thither and kept on and on until it was in a lather of perspiration and was almost exhausted to the point of dropping. Mile after mile was left behind them in this manner, Abe finding it barely possible to keep the runaway in sight. At length they came from the hills into a broad plain, and there, in the very midst of the waste, the runaway halted with such suddenness that Felicia barely saved herself from a serious fall. What had caused this sudden stopping of the horse was impossible to imagine, but the beast stood still with its fore feet braced, as if fearing to advance another inch. It quivered in every limb and shook all over.

Felicia heard the clatter of horses' hoofs and turned to see little Abe coming with the greatest haste. The boy cried out to her, and she answered him.

"Oh, Felicia!" he panted, as he came up on his winded horse; "I'm so glad you're safe! Get down, quick—get down! He might run again!"

She slipped from the saddle to the ground, and little Abe also dismounted, but now neither of the horses showed the slightest inclination to run. Both were in such an exhausted condition that they stood with hanging heads, their sides heaving.

"I was afraid you'd be killed, Felicia!" gasped the boy.

Then he saw her suddenly sink to the ground and cover her pale face with her hands. Quickly he knelt beside her, seeking to soothe and reassure her.

"It's all right—it's all right," he said. "Don't you cry, Felicia."

"Where are we, Abe?" she whispered.

"We're right here," was the answer, which seemed the only one he could give.

"Where is Dick?"

"He will come pretty soon. Don't you worry."

"We must find our way back. Can you do that, Abe?"

"Of course I can," he assured stoutly. "Just you trust me."

Then once more he did his best to reassure her, and after a while succeeded in calming her somewhat. To his relief, she did not cry or become hysterical. Over and over the boy assured her that he could find the way back without the least trouble, and after a while he must have convinced her this was true.

"You're so brave, Abe," she half smiled.

"Brave!" he exclaimed. "Me! I reckon you don't know me! Why, I ain't brave at all! I'm just the biggest coward that ever lived."

She shook her head.

"Don't tell me that," she said. "I know better. You're just as brave as you can be."

"Well, I never knowed it before," he said wonderingly. "If I am brave, it is something I never found out about myself. My, but I was scared when I saw that horse run!"

"What will Dick think when he finds us gone?"

"Oh, he will foller us, he will foller us," nodded the boy. "Don't you worry about that. We'll meet him coming."

"But I will never dare mount that horse again."

"Course you won't. You will take my horse. I will ride that critter. Just let him try to run with me!" He said this as if he really fancied he could control the animal in case it attempted to run away with him.

The horses were submissive enough while the hunchback removed and changed their saddles. The animal that had lately seemed crazy and frantic with fear was now calm and docile. Apparently the furious run had worked off the effect of the loco weed.

After a while, Abe did what he could to assist Felicia to mount, and then managed to scramble and pull himself with no small difficulty to the back of the other horse. They turned their animals to retrace the course over which they had come. This, however, was to prove no small task, for the runaway had twisted and turned in a score of different directions during its flight; and, shortly after entering the hills, Abe found himself quite bewildered as to the proper course they should pursue. This fact, however, he tried to conceal from Felicia, knowing it would add to her alarm. So they rode on and on until finally they came to a tiny stream that lay in the little hollows of a broad watercourse. There they found water for themselves and horses.

Now, for the first time, Felicia began to suspect that they were not retracing the course over which they had come.

"I don't remember this place," she said.

"Of course you don't," put in Abe quickly. "It's a wonder you remember anything. By jing! you must 'a' been awful scart when that horse was running so. Course you didn't notice much of anything else."

"But are you sure, Abe—are you sure we're taking the right course?"

"Just you leave it to me," nodded the hunchback.

"But what if we should miss Dick? If we should not find him, what would become of us, Abe? We might starve here, perish from thirst, or be killed by Indians or something."

Abe did his best to laugh reassuringly.

"Don't you go to getting all fussed up that way. We're all right. Let's hurry up now, for it is getting late."

It was getting late. The sun hung low in the west and the afternoon was far spent. In the boy's heart there was a great fear that night would come upon them and find them alone in that wild region. When they sought to push on, the horses barely crept forward, having been badly used up by the mad flight and pursuit.

Lower and lower sank the great golden sun.

"Abe," said Felicia, at last, her face pale and drawn, "we're lost. Don't try to deceive me; I know it."

"Mebbe we are turned round some," he admitted. "But that ain't any reason why you should get frightened. There are lots of mining camps pretty near here. And even if we don't find Dick—which we shall—we will be just sure to find a town."

The girl's chin quivered, and it was with no small difficulty that she kept back her tears. Finally, as the sun dropped behind the western ranges, the horses seemed to give out entirely, refusing to proceed farther.

"No use, Abe!" murmured Felicia. "We may as well give up and stop right here to-night."

"I am just awful sorry," murmured the boy; "but don't you be afraid. I will guard you. I will watch you all night long. There shan't anything touch you, I tell you that."

They were in a long, shallow valley where there was some scanty herbage, and the horses were permitted to find such grazing as they could. The western sky glowed with glorious colors, which gradually faded and passed away, after the bright, silvery stars gleamed forth, and the heat of the day passed before the night was fairly on them.

Felicia lay down in the silence, gazing up at the millions of stars above them. Abe sat near, wondering what he could do to reassure her. At length he thought of his fiddle and pulled it round from his back, where it hung. Lifting the loop of the cord over his head, he held the fiddle to his bosom, softly patting and caressing it. After a time, he found his rosin and applied it to the bow. Then he put the instrument in tune and began to play.

The music was soft, and sweet, and soothing, like the lullaby of a mother over a sleeping child. With this sound throbbing in her ears, Felicia finally slept. When he knew she was fast asleep, the boy slipped off his coat and spread it over her shoulders.

The silence of the night was awesome, and he felt keenly the lonely desolation of their situation. So again he lifted the fiddle to his chin, and again it throbbed with such a soft, sweet melody that even the twinkling stars seemed bending to listen.

CHAPTER XX.

THE FINDING OF THE BABES.

et up yere, pard," said one of the two men who were standing guard over Macklyn Morgan's bivouac. "I sure hears some queer sort of a wild critter a-yowling out yander."

Morgan himself had been eager to push forward through the night toward Merriwell's valley, but the men lately released from the custody of Pete Curry were exhausted by their tramp and refused at nightfall to proceed farther. Therefore, it had been necessary for the party to divide or to stop where they were and make camp. The latter course had been decided upon.

Not feeling positive that Curry and his comrades would not follow them, Morgan had given orders for two of the men to remain constantly on guard through the night. Of course the guard was to be changed at intervals. Now, shortly after nightfall, one of the original two appointed to watch over the camp called his comrade for the purpose of listening to certain strange sounds which came to his ears through the darkness.

They advanced cautiously to the top of a ridge, where they halted and stood listening. The sounds could be faintly heard now and then.

"Whatever does yer make of it, partner?" asked the one who had first heard them.

"Mighty quar sounds for a wild critter to make," declared the other.

"Just what I thought. More like some sort o' music."

"That's it. Dinged if it ain't something like a fiddle!"

"Mebbe we'd better nose out that way and see if we can diskeever what it is."

"We leaves the camp onprotected."

"Only for a short time. There won't anything happen, partner. This yere standing guard is all foolishness, anyhow."

"I reckon you're right."

"Then come on."

Together they advanced in the direction from which the strange sounds seemed to proceed. As they made their way slowly and cautiously into the valley they were able to hear those sounds more and more distinctly, and before long both were satisfied that it was indeed a fiddle.

"Well, wouldn't that chaw yer up!" muttered one. "Whoever does yer reckon is a-playing a fiddle out yere?"

"You have got me."

"Well, we will certain find out. Have your gun ready, pard, in case we runs into a muss."

Pretty soon they saw through the starlight two horses grazing unhobbled and unpicketed.

"Only two," whispered one of the men. "We are as many as they be."

"Whar are they?"

The violin was silent now, and they remained crouching and awaiting until it began again. It led them straight to the spot where little Abe sat playing beside the sleeping girl. So absorbed was he in his music, with his head bowed over the violin, that he failed to observe the approach of the men until they were right beside him and one of them stooped and took him by the shoulder. With a cry of terror, the boy sprang up.

Felicia awoke in great alarm and sat up, staring bewildered at Abe and the two men.

"Oh, ho!" said one of the guards. "What is this we finds? It is a strange bird we diskeevers."

"There's two," said the other. "And, by smoke, t'other one is a gal!"

"Don't you touch her!" shrilly screamed the boy. "Don't you put a hand on her!"

He endeavored to jerk himself from the grip of the man who had seized him, but the strong hand held him fast.

"Whatever is the use to jump around this yere way?" said the man. "We ain't a-hurting you none. Don't git so excited-like. Mebbe it's a right good thing we finds ye yere."

"Who are they, Abe? Who are they?" whispered Felicia.

"I dunno," confessed the boy, filled with regret and despair at his own carelessness in permitting the men to come upon them in such a manner while he was absorbed in his playing. "But they shan't hurt yer. I won't let um."

"Mebbe you tells us what you're doing yere, you two kids," suggested one of the men.

"We're jest lost," said Abe.

"Only that?" laughed the man. "Well, that sure is nothing much. Perhaps if we don't find yer you stays lost. Where did yer get lost from?"

"Oh, I know you won't hurt us!" said Felicia quickly. "Why should you? We can't hurt any one. My horse was frightened and ran away. Abe tried to catch him. That was how we got separated from Dick and the others."

"Dick! Who is this yere Dick?"

Before Abe could check her, Felicia answered.

"Why, Dick Merriwell!"

"Hey?" ejaculated one of the men. "Merriwell! Why, I sure opines that name is a heap familiar. Dick Merriwell! Mebbe you means Frank Merriwell?"

"No! no! I mean Dick Merriwell, his brother."

"His brother?" burst from both of the men.

"Yes," said Felicia.

"Then he has a brother, has he? Well, this is right interesting and no mistake."

"You bet it is!" ejaculated the other. "Where is this yere Dick Merriwell, Hunchy?"

It was the old hateful name which Abe detested, and his soul revolted against it.

"Don't you call me Hunchy!" he shrilly exclaimed. "I won't be called Hunchy!"

In his excitement he actually bristled at the ruffian.

"Ho! ho!" laughed the other man. "What do yer think of that, partner? Why, he is going ter soak me one."

"Ho! ho!" came hoarsely. "That's what he is. Don't let him hit yer hard, for he'll sure fix yer!"

The one who had addressed Abe as "Hunchy" now removed his hat and made a profound bow.

"I begs yer pardon, your royal highness," he said. "If I treads on the tail of yer coat any, I hopes you excuses me. I am not counting to rile you up any, for I reckon you might be a whole lot dangerous."

Abe knew this was said in derision, but he muttered:

"I won't have anybody calling me Hunchy no more. Don't you forget that!"

Felicia was clinging to the cripple now, and he could feel her trembling. He put one of his long arms about her and sought to reassure her by a firm pressure.

"If I hasn't offended your highness," said the man who had asked the question, "perhaps you tells me now where this Dick Merriwell is?"

"Don't tell him, Abe!" whispered the girl. "They are bad men. I'm afraid of them."

"I wist you could tell me," said the boy. "I'd like ter find him myself."

"Then he is somewhere yereabouts?"

"Don't tell!" breathed Felicia again.

"I dunno 'bout that," said Abe. "Mebbe he is two hundred miles away now. I dunno."

"Ef he is so fur, however is it you expects ter find him in a hurry?"

Barely a moment, did the boy hesitate, and then he declared:

"Why, he was a-going through to Californy on the train. We live down on the Rio Verde. Our dad, he's got a cattle ranch down there. Yesterday we started out to go to Flagstaff. They wouldn't let us go alone, so we runned away. We thought mebbe we could find the way there all right, but I guess we can't."

The two men looked at each other in the starlight and shook their heads.

"Sounds fishy," said one, immediately detecting that this statement conflicted with the one made by Felicia.

"A whole lot," agreed the other.

Felicia had gasped when she heard Abe fabricate so glibly. It was a surprise to her, and she was almost sorry she had cautioned him not to tell the facts to those men.

"Well, you certain is off the trail, kids, providing you're bound for Flagstaff. It's right lucky we finds you. We takes you to the camp, and mebbe your dad what you speaks of pays us well if we returns you to him safe and sound. I opines he runs a pretty big ranch."

"You bet," said the boy quickly. "He's got one of the biggest down that way. He has jest heaps of cattle and keeps lots of cowpunchers."

"That being the case," chuckled the man who had grasped the boy's shoulder, "he certain pays liberal when he gits his children back. Now you two come along with us."

He marched them along, one on either side, while his companion set out to catch the grazing horses and bring them.

Felicia slipped from the man's hand and again sought Abe's side, pressing close to him. In his ear she whispered:

"I am afraid we're in awful trouble now, Abe. You remember the bad men we saw in the valley before my horse ran. Perhaps these are two of them."

"Better be ketched by bad men than starve," he returned, with an effort to reassure her. "I have seen heaps of bad men before this, and I am still alive."

One of the horses was easily captured, but, to the surprise of the man, the other one charged viciously at him. When he sought to get at its head, the creature wheeled with a squeal and kicked wildly.

The man swore.

"What ails ye, drat yer?" he growled.

Then he released the docile animal and turned his attention to the other.

To his astonishment, the creature was fierce as a raging lion. It charged on him repeatedly, and he escaped only by the utmost nimbleness. It squealed, and whirled, and kicked in all directions. Apparently it fancied a thousand men were trying to capture it, and its wild gyrations were exceedingly surprising, to say the least.

After a little, the man ran away when he found the opportunity and stood at a distance, with his hands on his hips, watching the cavorting creature.

"The dinged hoss is sure crazy!" he declared. "Why, its a-trying to chew itself up, or kick itself to pieces. Never see but one critter act that way before."

"It's locoed," said Abe to the man with him. Immediately this man called to his companion, saying:

"Let the beast alone. The kid says it's locoed, and ef that's so, I reckon it's no good to anybody."

"Never see no locoed horse feed nateral like this one was," returned the other. "I opines the critter is just ugly, that's all."

But, suddenly uttering snorts and squeals, the horse went dashing off into the distance, as if pursued by some frightful thing. Nor did it stop until it had disappeared far, far away.

CHAPTER XXI.

THE LOTTERY OF DEATH.

Men were lying about on the ground, sleeping where they had dropped. Picketed horses were grazing at a little distance. The most of the men slept heavily, but one or two routed up as the guards brought the boy and girl and the captured horse to the bivouac.

"Whatever has you there?" growlingly asked one of the men who had awakened.

"Some lost children we finds near yere," was the answer.

Macklyn Morgan, wrapped in his blanket, had also awakened. His curiosity was aroused, and he flung off the blanket and got up.

"Children!" he said. "How does it happen that there are children in this wretched region?"

One of the men explained how he had heard the sound of the fiddle, which had led them to the boy and girl. He also repeated Abe's story, adding that it sounded "fishy." The interest of Morgan was redoubled at once. He immediately turned his attention to the hunchback.

"Going to Flagstaff to meet Frank Merriwell's brother, did you say?" he questioned, attempting a kindly manner. "Seems to me that was rather a crazy undertaking, my lad. And what is Frank Merriwell's brother doing in Flagstaff?"

"He jest said he was going there on his way to Californy," declared Abe, trying to stick to his original story and make it seem consistent. "We hope to see him there."

Felicia was silent; but she felt that Abe's yarn was not believed by the men.

"How did you happen to know this Dick Merriwell?" questioned Morgan.

Abe started to reply, but faltered and stammered a little, whereupon Felicia quickly said:

"I am his cousin."

Instantly the man's interest was redoubled.

"His cousin, eh?" he exclaimed. "Now we're getting at it. Curtis, start a fire. I want to look these children over."

While the man thus ordered was complying Morgan continued to question the girl and boy, but now his interest seemed centred in Felicia.

"So you are also the cousin of Frank Merriwell?" he said. "Tell me more about these two Merriwells. I have heard of Frank Merriwell, and I consider him a most excellent young man. I admire him very much."

He endeavored to make his words sound sincere, but little Abe fancied there was a false ring in them.

"You know Dick is Frank's half-brother, sir," said the girl. "He attends school in the East. I was at school in the same place once, but the climate didn't agree with me, and so Frank sent me West for my health."

"Have you seen him lately?"

"Yes, sir."

"When?"

"In Prescott, a few days ago. He was there, but some bad men made a lot of trouble for him and he left."

"This boy is your brother?" asked Morgan, indicating Abe.

"Why, yes, sir!" broke in Abe, quickly, seeing that Felicia would soon be trapped. "I am a sort of brother; an adopted brother, you know."

"Oh, that's it?" said Morgan. "But if you were living on a ranch down on the Rio Verde, how did you happen to be in Prescott when Frank Merriwell was there?"

"Why, we jest went there. Dad he took us there," hastily asserted the hunchback, seeking to maintain the original deception.

"Is that true?" asked Morgan of Felicia.

She was silent.

"Of course it's true!" indignantly exclaimed the boy.

"It seems to me that you are somewhat mixed, my child. Now, I advise you to trust me. It will be the best thing you can do. I advise you to tell me the truth. At this time we're on our way to join Frank Merriwell and help him to defend his new mines. He has many enemies, you know. We might take you directly to him."

"Oh, splendid!" exclaimed the girl, all her suspicions disarmed. "Frank will be so glad! We thought, perhaps, you might be his enemy; that's why we were afraid of you."

Macklyn Morgan forced a laugh, which he tried to make very

pleasant and reassuring.

"You see how wrong you were," he said. "You see now that it's a mistake to try to deceive me. It's best to tell me the truth and nothing else. This story about living on a ranch—how about it?"

"Oh, Abe told you that when he thought you must be Frank's enemy," said Felicia.

"Then it wasn't quite true?"

"No, no."

"And you were not on your way to Flagstaff to meet Dick Merriwell there?"

"No; we left Prescott in company with Dick and some friends, who were on their way to join Frank."

Felicia hastened on and told the entire story.

Abe listened in doubt as to the wisdom of this, shaking his head a little, but remaining silent.

"Now we're getting at the facts," smiled Morgan, as the fire was started and its light fell on his face. "It's much better for us all."

He had assumed a free, benevolent, kindly expression, and to the girl it seemed that he could not be deceiving them. Morgan continued to question her until at length he learned everything he desired.

"Now, my child," he said, "just you rest easy. We will soon join Frank Merriwell, and, of course, this brother of his with his friends will arrive all right in due time."

Morgan then stepped over to where one of the sleeping men lay and aroused him.

"Wake up, Hackett," he said, in a low tone. "Something mighty important has taken place."

He then told the man what had happened, and Hackett listened attentively.

"It seems to me," he said, "that these yere kids are going to be an incumbrance on us."

"That's where you're wrong," asserted Morgan. "With the aid of these children we ought to be able to bring Frank Merriwell to some sort of terms."

"I don't see how, sir."

"Why, it's plain he thinks a lot of this girl. We have her. If that doesn't trouble him some, I am greatly mistaken."

"Mebbe you're right," nodded Hackett. "I reckon I begin to see your little game, Mr. Morgan. Let me look these yere kids over some."

He arose and proceeded to the fire, in company with Morgan, who cautioned him, however, to say little to the boy and girl, fearing Hackett might make some observation that would betray the truth.

"She's some pretty, sir," said Gad, admiring Felicia; "though she's nothing but a kid. I reckon she makes a stunner when she gits older."

"Hush!" said Morgan. "That's nothing to you."

"Oh, I has an eye for female beauty!" grinned Hackett. "It's nateral with me."

Suddenly, to their surprise, without the least warning, a man seemed to rise from the ground a short distance away and walk straight toward the fire. Hackett had his pistol out in a twinkling, but he stood with mouth agape as he saw the newcomer was an old Indian, about whose shoulders a dirty red blanket was draped. It was Felicia, however, who was the most surprised, and a cry left her lips, for she recognized old Joe Crowfoot.

Even as she uttered that cry the eyes of the old redskin shot her a warning look that somehow silenced her. Without giving Hackett as much as a glance, old Joe walked up to the fire, before which he squatted, extending his hands to its warmth.

"Well, dern me, if that don't beat the deck!" growled Hackett. "These yere red wards of the government are a-getting so they makes theirselves to home anywhere. And you never knows when they're around. Now, this yere one he pops right out o' the ground like."

Then he turned savagely on Joe.

"What are you prowling around yere for, you old vagrant?" he demanded threateningly. "Who are you?"

Crowfoot rolled his little beady eyes up at the man.

"Heap flying bird," he answered. "Go through air; go everywhere. Go through ground. White man did him see red snake with horse's head? Injun ride on red snake like the wind."

"What's this jargon?" muttered Morgan.

"Hark!" warned the Indian, lifting a hand. "You hear the flying lizard sing? See that big one up there. See um great green eyes."

Then he stared straight upward, as if beholding something in the air. Involuntarily both men looked upward, but they saw nothing above them save the stars of the sky.

Felicia, who knew old Joe very well, was more than astonished by his singular manner and remarkable words. Her first impulse had been to spring up and greet him joyously, but the look from his black eyes had stopped her. Now, as if she were a total stranger to him, he gave her no attention. Suddenly he thumped himself on the breast with his clinched fist.

"Injun him all iron!" he declared. "Him like pale-face iron horse. When sun he comes up again Injun he go on white man's iron track. He blow smoke and fire and shriek same as iron horse."

"Well, bat me, if the old whelp ain't daffy!" exclaimed Hackett. "He's plumb off his nut, sure as shooting."

"When Injun him lay down to sleep," said Crowfoot, "many stars come and jump like antelope over him. No let him sleep. Him try to scare um away, but star no scare. Bimeby Injun he get sick. He get up and run away. Then star chase um Injun."

"You're right, Hackett," said Morgan, "He's loony, for a fact."

At this point one of the guards came walking up to the fire. The moment his eyes fell on Crowfoot he uttered a shout that instantly aroused every one of the sleeping men.

"By the great horn toads!" he exploded savagely; "that's the old skunk what drugged the whole bunch of us when Pete Curry nabbed us! Whatever is he doing here?"

Without even looking up, Crowfoot began to chant a strange, doleful song in his own language.

"The boys will certain salivate him," asserted the guard, as the men were rising and approaching the fire.

Old Joe apparently heard nothing and saw nothing. That singular chant continued.

"He is dead loony," said Hackett.

"Then mebbe he's been taking some of his own dope," growled the guard. "The boys will knock some o' his looniness out o' him, you bet!"

As the men gathered around, a number of them recognized the aged redskin, and immediately there was a great commotion. Several drew their weapons, and it seemed that Joe would be murdered on the spot. With a scream of terror, Felicia flung herself before the old man, to whom she clung.

"No! no! no!" she cried. "You shall not hurt him!"

In the excitement old Joe whispered in her ear:

"Keep still, Night Eyes. Um bad men no hurt Joe. Him touched by Great Spirit. Nobody hurt um man touched by Great Spirit."

This, then, was the old fellow's scheme. This explained how it happened that he dared venture into the nest of desperadoes. Among the Indians of all tribes a deranged man is regarded with awe as one who has felt the touch of the Great Spirit. No redskin will harm a deranged person, believing the vengeance of the Great Father must fall on whoever does such a thing. Shrewd as he was, Crowfoot had not yet discovered that palefaces did not regard crazed people with such a feeling of awe.

175

"Take the girl away," roared several of the men. "Let us settle with the old Injun."

If Morgan thought of interfering, he was too late, for rude hands seized Felicia and dragged her away, in spite of her struggles. She cried and pleaded, but all her efforts were useless. Crowfoot paid no attention to her, nor did he heed the threatening weapons in the hands of the ruffians. Rising to his feet, he did a solemn dance around the fire, at the same time continuing his doleful chant.

"That yere certain is a death dance for him," muttered Hackett, who realized that the men were aroused to a pitch at which they would insist on wiping the fellow out.

"The black moon him soon come up," said Joe, standing with one hand outstretched as he finished his dance. "Then we see spirits of many dead warriors chase um buffalo over it."

"You will have a chance to take a chase with the rest o' the bunch," snarled one of the men. "Stand back, boys, and watch me cook him."

"Hold on!" cried another, catching the man's wrist. "I opine I am in this yere."

Immediately an argument arose as to which of them should have the satisfaction of killing the Indian who had once fooled them so thoroughly. While this was taking place Joe continued, apparently oblivious of his danger, talking of flying horses and a dozen other impossible creatures. He must have realized that his apparent madness was making no impression on these men, but he seemed determined to play the game through to the finish. At length, he squatted again beside the fire, resuming his doleful chant.

By this time it had been settled that some one of the party should have the privilege of shooting the Indian, for it was agreed that to waste a number of bullets on him was folly. There was some discussion as to the manner of choosing the slayer, but the desperadoes finally decided on drawing lots.

Hackett, who took no part in this demand for the Indian's life, was chosen to prepare the lots, which he did. Then the men eagerly pressed forward to draw. The one who drew the shortest piece was to be the "fortunate" individual. All the while Crowfoot was guarded by men with drawn and ready weapons. Had he made an effort to get away he would have been riddled immediately.

Finally the lots were compared, and a half-blood Mexican, with leathery skin, drooping mustache, deep-furrowed face, and matted black hair, was the one who held the shortest piece. He laughed as he displayed it.

"Stand back!" he cried, flashing a pistol and striding forward to within four paces of the Indian. "I will settle him with one piece of lead."

Then, as this wretch lifted his weapon, old Joe realized at last that his game had failed utterly. There was no escape for him. His long life had led him at last to this, and he believed he stood at the gateway of the happy hunting grounds. Had there been hope of escape he would have made the attempt. Now, as he still crouched by the fire, he drew his red blanket over his head, and from beneath its muffling folds came the sad and doleful chant of the redman's death song.

The executioner stood fair and full in the firelight. He brought his weapon to a level and a shot rang out. It was not he, however, who fired. From somewhere near at hand a report sounded, and the pistol flew from his hand as the bullet tore through his forearm. A yell of pain escaped his lips.

Instantly the ruffians were thrown into the utmost confusion. Feeling that they were about to be attacked, they hastened to get away from the fire, the light of which must betray them to the enemy.

In spite of his age, like a leaping panther, old Joe shot to his feet. With one hand he seized little Abe, whom he snatched clear of the ground. And the next instant the old savage was running for his life. Two or three shots were fired, but in the excitement Crowfoot was untouched.

They were given no further time to turn their attention on him. From out of the shadows came a single horseman, bearing straight down upon them, his weapons flashing. The recklessness of this charge and the astounding suddenness with which it came was too much for the nerves of those men.

Felicia had been released by the man who was holding her as the first shot was fired. This man pulled a weapon and fired once at the shadowy horseman, after which he ran like a frightened antelope, for a screaming bullet had cut his ear. It seemed that the horseman meant to ride Felicia down. In her fear she stood still, as if turned to stone, which was the best thing she could have done.

As he swept past her, the rider swung low to one side in the saddle, and somehow one strong young hand grasped her and snatched her from the ground. She felt herself lifted with such suddenness that her breath seemed snapped away, and then she lay across the horse in front of the rider, who now bent low over her.

Bullets whined, and whistled, and sang about them, but some good fairy must have guarded them, for they were untouched. On they went. The sounds of irregular shooting fell farther and farther behind them.

Felicia had not fainted, although her senses swam and she seemed on the verge of losing consciousness. She could not understand just what had taken place. Suddenly her rescuer began to laugh, and a strange, wild, boyish laugh it was. It thrilled her through and through.

"Dick!" she gasped. "Oh, Dick!"

He straightened up and lifted her, holding her before him with one strong arm.

"Felicia!" he exclaimed, "are you hurt?"

"Oh, Dick! Dick!" she repeated, in wonder. "And is it you?"

"You are not hurt?" he persisted in questioning.

"No, Dick—no."

"Thank goodness!"

"But how was it? My head is swimming; I can't understand. I am dazed."

"Well, I fancy I dazed those fine gentlemen a little," said the boy. "Felicia, I have been searching, searching everywhere for you. We followed your trail as well as we could. When night came we had not found you. I couldn't rest. What fate it was that led me to those ruffians I cannot say, but I believe the hand of Heaven was in it. In their excitement over Crowfoot none of them heard my approach. I was quite near when that brute lifted his weapon to shoot Joe. I didn't want to kill him, and I fired at his arm. It was a lucky shot, for I hit him. He stood between me and the firelight, so that the light fell on the barrel of my pistol. Crowfoot took his cue quickly enough, for I saw him scamper."

"How brave you are! How brave you are!" murmured the girl, in untold admiration. "Oh, Dick, I can't believe it now."

"It was not such a brave thing, after all," he said. "I suppose most people would call it folly. But I had to do it. Why, old Joe saved my life a dozen times when I used to hunt with him years ago. He loved me as a father might love a son. You see it was impossible for me to keep still and see him murdered. I had to do something to save him. He can hide like a gopher on the open plain."

"But Abe, Dick—Abe?"

"I saw Crowfoot snatch him up as he ran. We must leave Abe to old Joe."

"Listen, Dick! Are they pursuing us?"

"We have the start on them, Felicia, and I don't believe they will be able to overtake us if they try it."

Through the night they rode. At the first opportunity Dick turned from his course and doubled in a manner intended to baffle the pursuers.

"It will be a long pull back to Bart and the others, Felicia," he said; "but I think we can make it all right. For all of the time I have spent at school, I have not forgotten the lessons taught me by Crowfoot when I was a mere kid. He taught me to set my course by the stars, the wind, the trees, by a score of things. To-night our guide shall be the stars."

Brad Buckhart was worried and troubled greatly over Dick's long absence, and was on guard where they had camped as night fell. The Texan tramped restlessly up and down, now and then pausing to listen. The others slept. Wiley snored lustily and muttered in his sleep.

"Avast, there!" he mumbled. "Put her to port, you lubber!"

Then, after snoring again in the most peaceful manner, he broke out:

"Right over the corner of the pan, Breck, old boy. Let's see you make a home run off that bender!"

Brad moved still farther away that he might listen without being disturbed by the sailor. Far in the night he seemed to hear a sound. Kneeling, he leaned his ear close to the ground and listened attentively.

"Horseman coming," he decided. "It must be Dick—it must be!"

Finally the hoofbeats of the approaching horse became more and more distinct. Then through the still, clear night came a clear, faint whistle.

"Dick it is!" exclaimed the Texan joyously.

Dick it was, and with him he brought Felicia safely back to them. They did not arouse the others, but she was wrapped in blankets and left to sleep, if possible, through the remainder of the still, cool night. Young Merriwell's story filled the Texan with unbounded astonishment and admiration. He seized Dick's hand and shook it with almost savage delight.

"Talk about a howling terror on ten wheels!" he exclaimed. "Why, you simply beat the universe. You hear me gurgle! Now you just turn in, for I reckon you're a whole lot pegged out."

"Well, sleep won't hurt me if I can corral some of it," acknowledged Dick.

Brad continued to stand guard, thinking that later he would arouse one of the others to take his place. His restlessness and worry had passed somewhat, and after a time he sat down, thinking over the startling things that had happened. It was thus that, exhausted more than he knew, he finally slid to the ground and also slept. The night passed without any of them being disturbed. But in the morning the first man to awaken was Pete Curry, who sat up, rubbing his eyes, and uttered a shout of astonishment. The remaining sleepers awoke and started up.

What they saw astounded them no less than it had Curry, for on the ground near at hand lay little Abe, with Joe Crowfoot's dirty red blanket tucked about him, and within three feet sat the redskin, calmly and serenely smoking his pipe.

Dick flung off his blanket and was on his feet in a twinkling.

"Crowfoot!" he joyously cried, rushing forward with his arms outstretched.

For one who complained of rheumatism and advancing age the redskin rose with remarkable quickness. Usually stolid and indifferent in manner, the look that now came to his wrinkled, leathery face was one of such deep feeling and affection that it astounded every one but himself. The old man clasped Dick in his arms as a father might a long-lost son. To Curry and his companions this was a most singular spectacle. Curry had seized a weapon on discovering Crowfoot. He did not use it when the old fellow remained silent and indifferent after his shout of astonishment and alarm.

That the boy should embrace the Indian in such an affectionate manner seemed almost disgusting to Curry and his assistants, all three of whom held Indians in the utmost contempt. For a moment it seemed that the old man's heart was too full for speech. Finally, with a strange tenderness and depth of feeling in his voice, he said:

"Injun Heart, Great Spirit heap good to old Joe! He let him live to see you some more. What him eyes see make him heart swell with heap big gladness. Soon him go to happy hunting ground; now him go and make um no big kick 'bout it."

"Joe, I have longed to see you again," declared Dick, his voice unsteady and a mist in his eyes. "Sometimes my heart has yearned for the old days with you on the plains and amid the mountains. I have longed to be with you again, hunting the grizzly, or sleeping in the shade by a murmuring brook and beneath whispering trees. Then you taught me the secrets of the wild animals and the birds. I have forgotten them now, Joe. I can no longer call the birds and tiny animals of the forest to me. In that way I am changed, Joe; but my heart remains the same toward you, and ever will."

Now the old redskin held Dick off by both shoulders and surveyed him up and down with those beady eyes, which finally rested on the boy's handsome face with a look of inexpressible admiration.

"Heap fine! Heap fine!" said the old man. "Joe him know it. Joe him sure you make great man. Joe him no live to see you have whiskers on um face, but you sure make great man. Joe him getting heap close to end of trail. Rheumatism crook him and make um swear sometime."

"Don't talk about getting near the end of the trail, Crowfoot," laughed Dick, whose heart was full of delight over this meeting. "You old hypocrite! I saw you last night! I saw you when you took to your heels after I perforated the gentleman who contemplated cutting your thread of life short. Rheumatism! Why, you deceptive old rascal, you ran like a deer! If your rheumatism was very bad, you couldn't take to your heels in that fashion."

Crowfoot actually grinned.

"Injun him have to run," he asserted. "Bullets come fast and thick. If Injun him run slow mebbe he get ketched by bullet."

Little Abe had risen on one elbow, the blanket falling from his shoulders, and watched the meeting between Dick and the old savage. Felicia also was awakened, and now she came hastening forward, her dark eyes aglow and a slight flush in her delicate cheeks.

"Joe! Joe! have you forgotten me?" she asked.

The redskin turned at once and held out his hands to her.

"Night Eyes," he said, with such softness that all save Dick and Felicia were astonished, "little child of silent valley hid in mountains, next to Injun Heart, old Joe him love you most. You good to old Joe. Long time 'go Joe he come to valley hid in mountains and he sit by cabin there. He see you play with Injun Heart. Warm sun shine in valley through long, long day. All Joe do he smoked, and sat, and watched. Bimeby when Night Eyes was very tired she come crawling close up side old Joe and lean her head 'gainst Joe, and sleep shut her eyes. Then old Joe him keep still. When Injun Heart he come near old Joe, him say, 'Sh-h!' He hold up his hand; he say, 'Keep much still.' Then mebbe Night Eyes she sleep and sleep, and sun he go down, and birds they sing last good-night song, and stars shine out, and old Joe him sit still all the time. Oh, he no forget—he no forget!"

Somehow the simple words of the old redskin brought back all the past, which seemed so very, very far away, and tears welled from Felicia's eyes.

"Oh, those were happy days, Joe—happy days!" she murmured. "I fear I shall never be so happy again—never, never!"

"Oh, must be happy!" declared the old fellow. "Dick him make um Night Eyes happy. Him look out for Night Eyes."

"Just the same," she declared, "I would give anything, anything, to be back in that valley now, just as I was long, long ago."

With his head cocked on one side, Cap'n Wiley had been watching the meeting between the Indian and his young friends. Wiley now turned to Buckhart and remarked:

"I am learning extensively in this variegated world. As the years roll on my accumulation of knowledge increases with susceptible rapidity. Up to the present occasion I have been inclined to think that about the only thing a real Injun could be good for was for a target. It seems to my acute perception that in this immediate instance there is at least one exception to the rule. Although yonder copper-hued individual looks somewhat scarred and weather-beaten, I observe that Richard Merriwell hesitates in no degree to embrace him. Who is the old tike, mate?"

"Why, old Joe Crowfoot!" answered Brad. "The only Indian I ever saw of his kind."

Immediately Wiley approached old Joe, walking teeteringly on the balls of his feet, after his own peculiar fashion, made a salute, and exclaimed:

"I salute you, Joseph Crowfoot, Esquire, and may your shadow never grow less. May you take your medicine regularly and live to the ripe round age of one hundred years. Perhaps you don't know me. Perhaps you haven't heard of me. That is your misfortune. I am Cap'n Wiley, a rover of the briny deep and a corking first-class baseball player. Ever play baseball, Joe, old boy? It's a great game. You would enjoy it. In my mind's eye I see you swing the bat like a war club and swat the sphere hard enough to dent it. Or perchance you are attempting to overhaul the base runner, and I see him fleeing wildly before you, as if he fancied you were reaching for his scalp locks."

"Ugh!" grunted old Joe. "No know who um be; but know heap good name for um. Joe he give you name. He call you Wind-in-the-head."

At this the others, with the exception of Wiley himself, laughed outright. The sailor, however, did not seem at all pleased.

"It's plain, Joseph," he observed, "that you have a reckless little habit of getting gay occasionally. Take my advice and check that habit before it leads you up against a colossal calamity."

"Wind-in-the-head he talk heap many big words," said the Indian. "Mebbe sometime he talk big words that choke him."

"That's a choke, Wiley," laughed Dick.

"And that certainly is the worst pun it has ever been my misfortune to hear," half sobbed the sailor. "One more like that would give me heart failure. Did you ever hear of the time I had heart failure in that baseball game with the Cleveland Nationals? Well, mates, it was——"

"We can't stand one of them before breakfast, Wiley," interrupted Dick. "It may prove too much for us. After breakfast we will endeavor to listen while you relate one of your harrowing experiences."

"But this thing is burning in my bosom. I long to disgorge it."

"You have to let it burn, I think. We should be on the move by this time."

Thus Wiley was repressed and prevented from relating one of his marvelous yarns, not a little to his disgust.

CHAPTER XXII.

AN ACT OF TREACHERY.

It was past midday. Guided by Wiley, who seemed to know the way well, the party had pushed on into the mountains and followed a course that led them over ragged slopes and steep declivities.

Finally the sailor paused and turned.

"There, mates," he said, stretching out his hand, "barely half a mile away lies the Enchanted Valley. I have a tickling fancy that we have reached it ahead of that delectable crew we sought to avoid."

Even as he said this, Pete Curry uttered an exclamation and pointed toward the mouth of a ragged ravine or fissure, from which at this moment several horsemen suddenly debouched. They were followed closely by a band of men on foot.

"That's the whole bunch!" exclaimed Curry. "And they're coming as fast as they can chase theirselves. They are heading to cut us off."

"That's right!" burst from Dick. "We've got to make a dash for it. Lead the way, Wiley, and be sure you make no mistake."

A hot dash it was for the fissure that led into the Enchanted Valley. The enemy, yelling like a lot of savages, did their best to cut the party off. Seeing they would fail at this, they opened fire, and a few bullets sang dangerously near the fugitives.

"Oh, bilge-water and brine!" muttered the sailor. "There'll certainly be doings when we attempt to scurry down that crack into the valley! It's going to be a very disagreeable piece of business for us."

Nearer and nearer they came to the fissure for which they were heading. Straight toward the beginning of it they raced, Wiley telling Dick it would be necessary for several of them to halt there and try to stand off the enemy while the rest of the party descended. But as they reached the beginning of the fissure, from behind some bowlders two young men opened fire with repeating rifles on the pursuers. In a moment the hail of bullets sent into the ranks of the enemy threw them into confusion. A horse dropped in its tracks, and another, being wounded, began bucking and kicking. One man was hit in the shoulder.

This unexpected occurrence threw the pursuers into consternation, so that they wheeled immediately and sought to get beyond rifle range.

"Avast there, my hearties!" cried Wiley, as he caught sight of the youths who knelt behind the bowlders. "Permit me to lay alongside and join you in the merry carnage."

"Hello, Wiley!" called Frank, who, aided by Hodge, had checked the ruffians. "It seems that we happened up this way at just about the right time."

"At the precise psychological moment," nodded the marine marvel. "This being just in time is getting habitual with you."

While the enemy was still in confusion Frank and Bart hastened to join the new arrivals and greet them. Of course they were surprised to see Curry and his companions, and the story told by the deputy sheriff, who explained everything in a few words, made clear the cause of his unexpected reappearance at the valley.

"A ministerial-looking gentleman who called himself Felton Cleveland, eh?" said Frank. "He was with the gang that cut loose your prisoners, was he? Well, I am dead sure Felton Cleveland is——"

"Macklyn Morgan!" cried Dick. "I saw him last night. He is the man."

"And Macklyn Morgan is the instigator of this whole business," said Frank. "Wiley, get Abe and Felicia down into the valley without delay. We have got to stand this gang off right here. We can't afford to let them reach this entrance to the valley. We're in for a siege. You will find provisions down there at the cabin. Bring supplies when you return. Abe and Felicia will be safe down there as long as we hold this passage."

"Ay, ay, sir!" said the sailor. "I am yours to command."

Fortunately near the mouth of the fissure there were heaped-up bowlders which seemed to form something of a natural fortress. Behind these rocks the defenders concealed themselves, their horses being taken down into the valley one after another. For a long time the enemy made no offensive move. It seemed to Frank and his friends that the ruffians had been dismayed by their warm reception, and they seemed disagreeing.

"If they will only chew the rag and get into trouble among themselves, it will be greatly to our advantage," said Hodge.

"Let them sail right into us if they are looking for a warm time!" exclaimed Brad Buckhart, who seemed thirsting for more trouble. "I opine we can give them all they want."

Wiley brought a supply of provisions from the valley, and the defenders satiated their hunger while ensconced behind the bowlders.

"This is even better than salt horse," declared Wiley, munching away. "One time when shipwrecked in the South Atlantic, longitude unty-three, latitude oxty-one, I subsisted on raw salt horse for nineteen consecutive days. That was one of the most harrowing experiences of my long and sinuous career."

"Spare us! Spare us!" exclaimed Frank. "We have got to stand off those ruffians, so don't deprive us of our nerve and strength."

"Look here!" exclaimed the sailor, "this thing is getting somewhat monotonous! Whenever I attempt to tell a little nannygoat somebody rises up and yells, 'Stop it!' Pretty soon I will get so I'll have to talk to myself. There was a man I knew once who kept a bowling alley and the doctor told him he mustn't talk; but he kept right on talking. He talked everybody deaf, and dumb, and black, and blue, and stone-blind, so at last there was nobody left for him to talk to but himself. Then he went to talking to himself in his sleep, which disturbed him so that he always woke up and couldn't sleep. The result was that he became so utterly exhausted for the want of rest that it was necessary to take him to the hospital. But even in the hospital they couldn't keep him still until they gagged him. That was the only thing that saved his life. What a sad thing it would be if anything like that should happen to me!"

Late in the afternoon the enemy made a move. Protected by rocks and such cover as they could find, they attempted to close in on the defenders of the valley.

Frank was keenly alert, and he discovered this move almost as soon as it began. Immediately he posted his companions where they could watch, and they agreed on a dead line, across which they would not permit the ruffians to creep without firing on them. As the ruffians drew nearer the cover was less available, and when the dead line was crossed the defenders opened fire on them. Within three minutes several of the enemy had been wounded, and the advance was not only checked, but the ruffians were filled with such dismay that the greater part of them took to their heels and fled. Several of these might have been shot down, but Frank would not permit it.

"I opine that just about gives them all they want for a while," said Brad Buckhart.

It seemed that he was right. The besiegers disappeared amid the rocks, and the afternoon crept on with no further effort in that direction to enter the valley by assault.

Some of the defenders were beginning to wonder if the enemy had not given up when, with the sun hanging low, a man appeared in the distance, waving a white handkerchief, attached like a flag to the end of a stick.

"Whatever's up now?" muttered Pete Curry.

"It is a flag of truce," said Merry.

"Look out, Frank!" exclaimed Bart. "It may be a trick."

Merry rose and stood on a mound of bowlders, drawing out his own handkerchief and waved it in return.

"What are you going to do?" asked Hodge.

"I am going to find out what they are up to," was the answer.

"I tell you it may be a trick."

"We will see."

The man in the distance with the flag of truce immediately advanced alone. Barely had he walked out into full view when Merry said:

"It is Macklyn Morgan, or my eyes are no good!"

"Old Joe he fix um," said the aged Indian, carefully thrusting his rifle over the rocks and preparing to take aim.

"Stop him!" exclaimed Merry. "Don't let him fire on a man with a white flag!"

The old savage seemed greatly surprised and disappointed when he was prevented from shooting.

"When um Morgan man he is killed that stop all trouble," said Joe. "Good chance to do it."

"Watch him close, Dick," directed Frank. "I am going out there to meet Morgan."

"Let me go with you."

"No; he's alone. I will go alone. He is taking his chances. If anything happens to me, if one of those ruffians should fire on me, Morgan knows my friends here will shoot him down. Still, there may be some trick about it, and I want every one of you to watch close and be on the alert."

"Depend on us, Frank," said Dick. "Only I'm sorry you won't let me go with you."

A few moments later Merriwell strode out boldly from the rocks, with the white handkerchief still fluttering in his hand, advancing to meet Morgan, who was slowly coming forward.

They met in the centre of the open space near the little heap of bowlders. In grim silence, regarding his enemy with accusing eyes, Merry waited for Morgan to open the conversation.

"This is a very unfortunate affair, young man," said the hypocritical money king. "I am sorry it has happened."

"Are you?" asked Frank derisively.

"I am, I am," nodded Morgan. "It's very bad—very bad."

"If you feel so bad about it, sir, it's the easiest thing in the world for you to bring it to an end."

"But you are the one to terminate it, young man."

"How do you make that out?"

"You know how you can settle this affair without delay. You heard my proposition in Prescott."

"I believe I did. It was very interesting as the proposition of a thoroughly unscrupulous man."

"Don't get insulting, Mr. Merriwell. I am doing my duty. Milton Sukes was my partner. Do you think I can conscientiously ignore the fact that he was murdered?"

"I fail to understand what that has to do with me."

"You know I have proofs," said Morgan sternly. "You know they will convict you."

"I know nothing of the sort. You have no proofs that are worth being called that."

"Everything points accusingly and decisively at you. You were Mr. Sukes' bitter enemy. It was to your advantage that he should be put out of the way. He annoyed you. He gave you great trouble."

"And I fancy, Macklyn Morgan, that I annoyed him a little. But why do you pretend that it is on his account you are carrying out this lawless piece of business? You know its nature. You know in your heart that you are a hypocrite. You have even offered, if I turn over my property to you here, to make no proceeding against me. Is that the way you obtain justice for your dead partner? Is that the sort of justice you are looking for, Morgan? Don't talk to me of justice! I know the sort of man you are! I know you from the ground up!"

"Be careful! Be careful! You are making a mistake, young man. Mr. Sukes annoyed you and harassed you because he believed you held property that he should possess—property that rightfully belonged to him. He obtained no satisfaction from you. If I am willing to settle with you by securing possession of this undeveloped mine here, which I now offer to do, you ought to think yourself getting off easy. It is not often that I enter into an affair of this sort. It is not often that I take hold of it personally. I allow my agents to carry such things through under my directions. In this case, however, I have considered it best to see the matter to an end myself. I confess that it seemed probable that you might be too slick for my agents."

"No thanks whatever for the compliment. Have you anything new to propose, Mr. Morgan?"

"My proposition is this: that you and your companions retire at once from this vicinity, and if you do I give you my word that you will not be molested. It is an easy and simple way to settle this whole affair. If you comply, we will let the Sukes matter drop where it is. You will escape prosecution for murder. Think well of it—think well. It is the best thing you can do. You are trapped now. You are penned in here and you can't get out. If we see fit, we can lay siege to this place and keep you here until we starve you out. In the end you will be compelled to surrender. In the end you will lose everything. If you force me to such a course, not only will I obtain possession of this undeveloped mine, but I tell you now that I shall do my best to see you hanged for the murder of Milton Sukes."

Frank laughed in the man's face.

"It's plain," he said, "that even now, Macklyn Morgan, you don't understand me. It's plain that you still fancy it possible to frighten me. You are wasting your time, sir. Go ahead with your siege and see what comes of it."

This seemed to enrage Morgan, for suddenly he violently shook the flag at Frank and cried:

"Then take the result of your obstinacy!"

Instantly there were several puffs of white smoke from beyond the distant rocks and Frank pitched forward upon his face.

At the same moment Macklyn Morgan made a spring and dropped behind a little pile of bowlders, where he was fully protected from the defenders of the valley.

Apparently Frank had been treacherously shot down in cold blood while under the flag of truce.

The watchers of the defense were horrified as they saw Frank fall. Dick uttered a savage cry and would have rushed out from behind the rocks had he not been seized by Brad Buckhart.

"Steady, pard—steady!" warned the Texan, finding it difficult to detain young Merriwell.

"Let go!" panted Dick. "Don't you see! My brother! The dastardly wretches have shot him!"

"And do you propose to prance out there and let them shoot

189

you up, too? Do you propose to let these measly galoots wipe out the Merriwell family in a bunch? Cool down, pard, and have some sense."

Bart Hodge had been no less excited than Dick, and nothing could have prevented him from rushing forth to Frank had he not suddenly made a discovery as he sprang up. His eyes were on his chum of school and college days, and he saw Frank quickly roll over and over until he lay close against a bowlder, where he would be protected in case the enemy fired again. Then, as he lay thus, Merry lifted the hand that still clutched the white handkerchief and waved it in a signal to his friends.

Hodge was shaking in every limb.

"He is not killed!" he exclaimed.

"Heap keep still," came from old Joe. "No shot at all. Him all right. Him see gun flash, him drop quick, bullets go over um. Him fool bad palefaces a heap."

"What's that?" fluttered Dick. "Do you mean that he wasn't hurt, Joe?"

"No hurt him much," asserted the old savage, "Strong Heart he have keen eye. He watch all the time. He see gun flash. He see smoke. He drop quick."

It was not easy to make Dick believe his brother had not been hurt, but Frank managed to convey to them by signals that he was all right. Their relief was unbounded. Indeed, Dick's eyes filled with a mist of joy, although his anxiety was intense, for he feared that his brother might still be in a position where the enemy could get further shots at him. Frank, however, hugged the rocks closely, and there was no more shooting.

On the other side of the bowlders lay Macklyn Morgan, his evil heart filled with triumph, for he believed Merriwell had been slain. His astonishment was unbounded when he heard Frank's voice calling his name.

"Morgan," called Merry, "can you hear me?"

"Yes, I hear you," answered the astounded villain. "So they didn't kill you outright, did they?"

"Hardly that," returned Merry. "They didn't even touch me."

"What did you say?" burst from Morgan. "Why, those men were the best shots in our party! They were carefully chosen for this piece of business."

"A fine piece of business, Macklyn Morgan!" contemptuously retorted Merry. "And you planned it, I presume! You are a smooth-faced, hypocritical man of wealth, known far and wide and greatly respected because of your riches. Yet you have descended to a piece of business like this! Sukes was bad enough, Morgan; but you're a hundred times worse. You have failed in your most dastardly plot, just as you will fail in everything. Lie still, Macklyn Morgan. Keep close to those rocks where you are, for if you show yourself you will be riddled by my watching friends. From this time on your life will not be worth a pinch of snuff if they get a chance at you."

So the two men, the fearless youth and the treacherous money king, lay each sheltered by the bowlders while the sun sank in the west and day slipped softly into night. When the shadows had deepened sufficiently, Frank crept away on his stomach toward the valley, taking the utmost pains not to expose himself, and, through his skill in this, returned at last in safety to his friends, who welcomed him joyously.

"Heap well done!" grunted old Joe. "But now Strong Heart him know more than to trust um bad men. No do it some more."

Dick was able to repress his emotion, although Frank read in the few words his brother said the intense anxiety he had felt.

"What will be their next move?" exclaimed Hodge.

"They will attempt to overpower us by some sudden move to-night," said Frank. "We must remain on the alert every moment."

The stars came out bright and clear, as they always do in that Southwestern land, and, if possible, their light seemed more brilliant than usual. The night advanced, and still the enemy before them remained silent. It was Curry who discovered something down in the valley that attracted his attention and interested him. He called the attention of Frank, who saw down there a light waving to and fro and then in circles.

"Whatever does yer make of that, pard Merriwell?" asked Curry.

"It's a signal," said Frank—"a signal from Abe and Felicia. They are seeking to attract our attention. I must go down there at once."

"There's trouble of some sort down there, Frank," said Dick, who had reached his brother's side. "Let's go quickly."

Merry found Bart and directed him to take charge of the defense at that point and be constantly on the alert. With Dick close behind him, he hastened down the fissure leading into the valley. In the narrow place through which they descended the starlight was dim and uncertain, yet they hastened with reckless speed. Reaching the valley, they made straight for the cabin, where the signal light was still waving. As they drew near, they saw the grotesque figure of little Abe swinging a lighted torch over his head and then waving it round and round. The flaring torch revealed

Felicia, who stood near.

"What's the matter, Abe?" demanded Frank, as he dashed up.

"I am glad you saw it! I am glad you came!" said the boy. "Frank, those men are trying to get into the valley another way."

"Where? How?"

"Felicia saw them first. Some of them are on the other side."

"But there is no entrance save the one we are defending."

"They are planning to get in by descending the face of the precipice. We saw them creep down over the rocks, three or four of them, and it took them a long time. They have reached a precipice that is perpendicular."

"That should stop them."

"I watched them through your field glasses, which I found in the cabin. They were letting themselves down with the aid of ropes."

"Ropes?" exclaimed Dick.

"A new game," said Frank.

"Can they descend that way?" questioned the boy.

"It's possible," admitted Frank. "Show us where they are, Abe. Drop that torch and lose not a moment."

The hunchback led the way, running on before them, and they followed him closely. As they came at length to the vicinity of the precipice, they saw through the pale starlight that Abe had spoken truly, for already long lariats had been spliced together, and, by the aid of these, which now dangled from the top of the precipice to the bottom, one of the men had already begun to descend. They saw the shadowy figure of his companions waiting above, and it seemed that the men did not dare trust themselves more than one at a time upon the spliced rope.

"We've got to stop that, Frank!" panted Dick.

"We will stop it," said Merry. "Don't attract attention. Let's get nearer."

They stole forward still nearer, watching the man as he came down slowly and carefully. This man had descended almost half the distance when a sudden rifle shot broke the stillness of the valley. Immediately, with a cry, the dark form of a man dropped like a stone.

Frank and his companions had been startled by the shot, but Merry instantly recognized the peculiar spang of the rifle.

"Old Joe!" whispered Merry.

As they stood there a silent figure came slipping toward them, and the old Indian stopped close at hand.

"Bad men no come down that way," he said quietly. "Joe him shoot pretty good—pretty good. Joe him think mebbe he shoot four, five, six times, he might cut rope. Joe him shoot once, him cut rope. Joe him got rheumatism. Him pretty old, but him shoot pretty good."

"Was that what you fired at?" asked Merry, in astonishment. "You didn't shoot at the man on the rope?"

"Plenty time to shoot man when Joe him find out he no cut rope," was the retort. "When rope him cut one man he come down pretty fast. Him strike, bump! Mebbe it jar him some."

"The fall must have killed him instantly," said Frank. "If you cut that rope, Joe, you have spoiled their attack on this side of the valley. Stay here. Watch sharp, and make sure they don't resume the attempt. If they do, Abe can signal again."

"All right," said Crowfoot. "Me watch."

With this assurance, Frank felt safe to return again to the defenders above, and Dick returned with him. When he told what had taken place in the valley Cap'n Wiley observed:

"I had it in for Joseph Crowfoot, Esquire, for calling me Wind-in-the-head; but I will overlook the insult. Evidently the old boy is a whole army in himself."

As they lay waiting for the attack they fully expected must take place, there came to their ears from the direction in which the enemy was supposed to be the sounds of shots, followed immediately by hoarse yelling and more shooting.

"Well, what do you make of that, Merry?" cried Hodge. "There seems to be a ruction of some sort going on over there."

Frank listened a few moments. The sound of the shooting receded, and the yelling seemed dying out in the distance.

"It may be a trick," he said; "but I am in hopes those ruffians have quarreled among themselves. If it is a trick, we will keep still and wait. Time will tell what has happened."

Time did tell, but all through the rest of the night they waited in vain for the attack. When morning finally dawned the mountains lay silent in the flood of light which poured from the rising sun. Nowhere was the enemy to be discovered.

Old Joe came up to them from the valley and declared that the men on the other side had been driven away. The fate of their comrade seemed to dishearten them, and they had crept back like snails over the rocks and vanished during the night.

It was the old Indian who set out to find what had happened among the besiegers led by Morgan. He slipped away among the rocks and brush and vanished like a phantom. He was gone an hour or more when he suddenly reappeared and beckoned to them.

"Come see," he invited.

They knew it was safe to follow him, and they did so. Where the enemy had been ensconced they found one man, sorely wounded and in a critical condition. That was all. The others, to the last rascal of them, had vanished.

"Where have they gone, Joe?" exclaimed Frank.

"Ask him," directed the Indian, motioning toward the wounded man. "Mebbe he tell."

This man was questioned, and the story he told surprised and satisfied the defenders beyond measure. Disgusted over their failure to get into the valley, the ruffians had plotted among themselves. A number of them had devised a plan which to them seemed likely to be profitable. Knowing Macklyn Morgan was a very rich man, they had schemed to take him personally, carry him off, and hold him in captivity until he should pay them handsomely for his freedom. Not all the ruffians had been taken into this plot, and when the schemers started to carry Morgan off there was an outbreak and some shooting, but they got away successfully.

With Morgan and the leading spirits of the affair gone, the others quickly decided to give up the assault on the valley, and that was why they had departed in the night, leaving the wounded man behind to such mercy as Merriwell and his friends might show.

"Well, what do you think of that?" exclaimed Dick.

"Think?" said Frank, with a laugh. "Why, I think Macklyn Morgan has been caught in his own trap. Now let him get out of it!"

CHAPTER XXIII.

NEW RICHES PROMISED.

hen a week had passed Frank and his friends began to feel that all their troubles were over, for the time being, at least. Old Joe Crowfoot, who had been scouting in the vicinity, reported that he found no signs of probable marauders and himself settled down contentedly to smoke and loaf in the warm sunshine of the valley. With Dick and Felicia near, where he could watch them occasionally or hear their voices, the peaceful happiness of the old fellow seemed complete.

Cap'n Wiley likewise loafed to his heart's content And if ever a person could make a whole-souled and hearty success of loafing it was the cap'n. He became so friendly with Crowfoot that old Joe even permitted him sometimes to smoke his pipe.

One beautiful morning the entire party was gathered in front of Merriwell's cabin talking things over.

"There seems nothing now, Frank, to prevent us from securing miners and opening up this new claim," said Hodge. "Macklyn Morgan seems to have disappeared off the face of the earth."

"Perhaps he has learned that it is dangerous for a man like him to attempt dealing with the ruffians of this part of the country," put in Dick. "It seems certain now that he was actually carried into captivity by the very gang he employed to seize these mines."

"But he will get free all right," declared Frank. "He will turn up again sometime."

"If they don't kill him any," said Buckhart.

"They won't do that," asserted Merriwell. "They can make nothing out of him in that fashion; but they might make a good thing by forcing him to pay a large sum for his liberty."

"Well, now that everything seems all right here, Frank," said Dick, "I suppose Brad and I will have to light out for the East and old Fardale."

"Waugh! That certain is right!" exclaimed the Texan. "We must be on hand, pard, when Fardale gets into gear for baseball this spring."

"Baseball!" cried Wiley, giving a great start. "Why, that word thrills my palpitating bosom. Baseball! Why, I will be in great shape for the game this season! My arm is like iron. Never had such a fine arm on me before. Speed! Why, I will put 'um over the plate like peas! Curves! Why, my curves will paralyze 'um this year!"

"Ugh!" grunted old Joe. "Wind-in-the-head blow a heap. Him talk a lot with him jaw. Mebbe him jaw git tired sometime."

"Look here, Joseph," expostulated Wiley, "I don't like sarcasm. If I didn't love you as a brother, I might resent it."

"Great horn spoon!" cried Buckhart, scratching vigorously. "These fleas are the biggest and worst I ever saw. You hear me murmur!"

"What, these?" squealed Wiley, in derision. "Why, these little creatures are nothing at all—nothing at all. They just tickle a fellow up a bit. Fleas! Say, mates, you should have seen the fleas I have beheld in my tempestuous career. You should have seen the fleas I met up with in the heart of darkest Africa. Those were the real thing. Don't 'spose I ever told you about those fleas?"

And he told them a long and wonderful story about African fleas.

"Ugh!" grunted the old Indian, when Wiley had finished. "Wind-in-the-head biggest blame liar old Joe ebber see."Some days later, with the exception of Hodge and Crowfoot, Frank and the rest of his party arrived in Prescott. Hodge and the aged redskin were left, together with one of Pete Curry's men, to guard the valley after a fashion. Besides going to Prescott for the purpose of seeing his brother and Buckhart off, Frank had several other objects in view. With him he brought considerable ore, taken from the quartz vein they had located in the valley, and also a small leather pouch that was nearly filled with dull yellow grains and particles washed from the placer mine. With these specimens Frank proceeded direct to an assayer, who was instructed to make an assay and give a report.

Following this, Frank set about picking up some genuine miners who knew their business and who could be relied on. It was his purpose to keep a few men at work on the claims while he completed the plans talked over by himself and Hodge and arrange for the transportation to the valley of such machinery as they needed to work the mines. As far as the placer was concerned, this was not such a difficult problem. With the quartz mine, however, it was quite a serious matter, as the valley was far from any railroad and extremely difficult of access.

Frank knew very well that it would cost a big sum of money to begin practical operations on the quartz claim, and already, for a young man of his years, he had his hands pretty full. Hodge, however, had been enthusiastic, and Merry felt that Bart would, with the greatest readiness and satisfaction, remain where he could oversee everything and carry all plans out successfully.

Merry felt that he was greatly indebted to Wiley, and he saw that the sailor had one of the best rooms in the best hotel of Prescott and was provided with every comfort the house could afford. This was not the only way in which Frank intended to reward the captain.Wiley himself was somewhat "sore" because he had declined to accompany Frank and Bart at the time they had returned to the valley and successfully located Benson Clark's lost mines.

"'Tis ever thus," he sighed wearily, when the matter was spoken of. "I will bet eleventeen thousand dollars that I have lost more than a barrel of good opportunities to become rotten with wealth during my sinuous career. Not that I haven't felt the salubrious touch of real money to an extensive extent, for sometimes I have been so loaded down with it that it rattled out of my clothes every step I took. When I sauntered carelessly along the street in days past I have shed doubloons, and picaroons, and silver shekels at every step, and I have often been followed by a tumultuous throng, who fought among themselves over the coin that rained from my radiant person. Still to-day here I am broke, busted, while the world jogs on just the same, and nobody seems to care a ripityrap. Excuse these few lamentations and wails of woe. By and by I will take a little medicine for my nerves and feel a great deal better."

"Don't worry over it, Wiley," said Frank, laughing. "It will all come out in the wash. I don't think you will die in the poorhouse."

"Not on your tintype!" cried the sailor. "I propose to shuffle off this mortal coil in a palace."

"Wiley," cried Frank, "I believe you would joke in the face of old Death himself!"

"Why not? I regard life as a joke, and I don't propose to show the white feather when my time comes. I will have no mourning at my funeral. I propose to have my funeral the gayest one on record. Everybody shall dress in their best, and the band shall play quicksteps and ragtime on the way to the silent tomb. And then I shall warn them in advance to be careful, if they want to finish the job, not to pass a baseball ground where a game is going on, for just as sure as such a thing happened I'll kick off the lid, rise up, and prance out onto the diamond and git into the game."

"Don't you worry about what will become of you, cap'n," advised Merry. "For all that you failed to stick by us in relocating those claims, I fancy we shall be able to make some provisions for you."

"That's charity!" shouted Wiley. "I will have none of it! I want you to understand that little Walter is well able to hustle for himself and reap his daily bread. Not even my best friend can make me a pauper by giving me alms."

"Oh, all right, my obstinate young tar," smiled Merry. "Have your own way. Go your own course."

"Of course, of course," nodded Wiley. "I always have, and I always will. Now leave me to my brooding thoughts, and I will evolve some sort of a scheme to make a few million dollars before sundown."

Wiley's schemes, however, did not seem to pan out, although his brain was full of them, and he had a new one every day, and sometimes a new one every hour of the day. Knowing they were soon to be separated again, Dick and Felicia spent much of their time together. It was Merriwell's plan, of which he had spoken, to take Felicia to Denver and find her a home there where she could attend school.

The assay of the quartz Merry had brought to Prescott showed that the mine was marvelously rich. Beyond question it would prove a good thing, for all of the great expense that must be entailed in working it. On the day following the report of the assayer, Merry was writing letters in the little room of the hotel provided for such use when a man entered, approached him, and addressed him.

"Excuse me," said this man, who was middle-aged and looked like a business man from the ground up. "I suppose you are Mr. Frank Merriwell?" "That's my name."

"Well, my name is Kensington—Thomas Kensington. Perhaps you have not heard of me?"

"On the contrary, I have heard of you, Mr. Kensington. I believe you have a mine in this vicinity?"

"Yes, and another in Colorado. I hear that you have lately located a promising quartz claim. I understand that the assay indicates it is a valuable find."

"Perhaps that's right," admitted Merry; "but I am at a loss just how you acquired the information."

"My eyes and ears are open for such things. I am in Prescott to have a little assaying done myself, and I happened, by the merest chance, to hear Mr. Given, the assayist, speaking with an assistant about the result of his investigation of your specimens. You understand that it was barely a chance."

"I presume so," said Merry. "I don't suppose that Given would talk of such matters publicly."

"And he did not, sir—he did not. I assure you of that. I have also learned, Mr. Merriwell, that you have other mines?"

"Yes, sir."

"And this new claim of yours is inconveniently located at a distance from any railway town?"

"That is correct."

"Now, I am a man of business, Mr. Merriwell, and if you care to have me do so, I would like to investigate your property with the possibility of purchasing this new mine of yours."

Frank was somewhat surprised.

"I am not at all certain, Mr. Kensington, that I wish to sell. Besides that, I have a partner who would have to be consulted in the matter."

"But we might talk it over, sir—we might talk it over. Are you willing to do so?"

"I have no objections to that."

Kensington then drew up a chair and sat down close by the desk at which Merry had been writing.

"If I were to make you an offer for your property, on being satisfied with it as something I want," he said, "would you consider it?"

"It's not impossible. But you must remember that my partner is to be consulted in the matter."

"Of course, of course."

"He might not care to sell. In that case I can do nothing."

"You might use your influence."

Frank shook his head.

"I wouldn't think of that, sir. I would leave the question entirely to Hodge, and he could do as he pleased."

"Do you fancy that there is a possibility that he might be induced to sell in case the offer seemed an advantageous one?"

"Yes, I think it possible."

"Good!" nodded Kensington. "That being the case, we can discuss the matter further. Do you mind showing me the report of the assayer?"

"Not at all. Here it is."

Merry took the paper from his pocket and handed it to Kensington, who glanced over the figures and statements, lifted his eyebrows slightly, puckered his lips, and whistled softly.

"Do you mean to tell me, Mr. Merriwell, that this assay was made from an average lot of quartz from your mine, or was it from specially chosen specimens?"

"Mr. Kensington, I had this assay made for myself, and not for the public. I had it made in order that I might find out just how valuable the mine is. That being the case, you can understand that I would not be foolish enough to pick what appeared to be the richest ore. On the contrary, sir, I took it as it came."

Again Kensington whistled softly, his eyes once more surveying the figures.

"How far is this mine from the nearest railroad point?"

"Just about one hundred miles."

"And in a difficult country as to access?"

"Decidedly so," was Merry's frank answer.

"It will cost a huge sum to open this mine and operate it."

"There is no question on that point."

"Still, this report shows it will be worth it, if the vein pans out to be one-half as promising as this assay of your specimens."

Merry laughed.

"Mr. Kensington," he said, "it is my belief that we have not fully uncovered the vein. It is my conviction that it will prove twice as valuable as it now seems when we get into it in earnest."

For some moments Kensington continued to whistle softly to himself. It seemed to be a habit of his when thinking.

"Are your other mines valuable, Mr. Merriwell?"

"Yes, sir."

"As valuable as this one?"

"I believe they are."

"And you have them in operation?"

"I have one of them in operation."

"That is the Queen Mystery, I believe?"

"Then you have heard of it, sir?"

"There is not much going on in mining matters in Arizona that I have not heard of. It's my business to keep posted. You have never thought of selling the Queen Mystery?"

"Mr. Kensington, the Mystery is opened and is in operation. I have not contemplated selling it, and I do not think I shall do so. If you wish to talk of this new mine, all right. I can listen. Nothing whatever may come of it, but I see no harm in hearing whatever you have to say."

"Now we're getting at an understanding, Mr. Merriwell. Of course, I wouldn't think of making you any sort of an offer for your mine unless thoroughly satisfied as to its value. I should insist on having it inspected by men of my own choice, who are experts. Their report I can rely on, and from that I would figure."

"That would be business-like," Merry nodded.

"And you would have no objections to that, of course?"

"Certainly not, sir. Still, you must not forget that I have a partner who might object. It will be necessary to consult him before anything of the sort is done."

"All right, all right. Where is he?"

"He is at the mine."

Kensington seemed somewhat disappointed.

"I was in hopes he might be in Prescott."

"He is not."

"Another point, Mr. Merriwell. Are you certain your title to this property is clear?"

"Absolutely certain, sir."

"I am glad to hear that. Of course, I should look into that matter likewise. Unless the title was clear, I wouldn't care to become involved."

"In that case," said a voice behind them, which caused them both to start slightly, "I advise you, Mr. Kensington, to let that property alone."

Merriwell turned quickly and found himself face to face with Macklyn Morgan!

"Morgan!" exclaimed Frank.

To the ministerial face of the money king there came a smile of grim satisfaction, for he knew he had startled Frank.

"Yes, Mr. Kensington," he said, "you had better be careful about this piece of business. There are some doubts as to the validity of this young man's claim to that mine."

Kensington did not seem pleased, and immediately he demanded:

"How do you happen to know so much about it, sir?"

"Because I am interested. My name is Macklyn Morgan. It is barely possible you have heard of me?"

"Macklyn Morgan!" exclaimed Thomas Kensington. "Why, not—why, not——"

"Exactly," nodded Morgan. "I belong to the Consolidated Mining Association of America. You may know something of that association; it's quite probable that you do."

"I should say so!" exclaimed Kensington, rather warmly. "I

know that it's a trust and that it has been gobbling up some of the best mines in the country."

"Very well. You know, then, that the C. M. A. of A. makes few mistakes. As a member of that association I warn you now that you may involve yourself in difficulty if you negotiate with this young man for this mine which he claims."

Frank rose to his feet, his eyes flashing with indignation.

"That will about do for you, Morgan!" he exclaimed. "I think I have stood about as much from you as I am in the mood to stand. Mr. Kensington, this man does belong to the Consolidated Mining Association. That association attempted to get possession of my Queen Mystery and San Pablo mines. I fought the whole bunch of them to a standstill and made them back water. They have given up the fight. But after they did so this Mr. Morgan, in conjunction with another one of the trust, did his level best to wring the Queen Mystery from me.

"The matter was finally settled right here in the courts. They were beaten. It was shown that their claims to my property were not worth a pinch of snuff. Since then Sukes, this man's partner, met his just deserts, being shot by one of his tools, a half-crazed fellow whom he led into an infamous piece of business. This Morgan is persistent and vengeful. He has trumped up some silly charge against me and tried to frighten me into giving up to him my Queen Mystery or my new mine. It is a pure case of bluff on his part, and it has no further effect on me than to annoy me."

Both Kensington and Morgan had listened while Frank was speaking, the latter with a hard smile on his face.

"You can judge, Mr. Kensington," said Morgan, "whether a man of my reputation would be the sort to take part in anything of that kind. When it comes to bluff, this young fellow here is the limit. I tell you once more that you will make a serious mistake if you have any dealings with him. Any day he is likely to be arrested on the charge of murder, for there is evidence that he conspired in the assassination of my partner. It even seems possible that he fired the fatal shot. That's the kind of a chap he is."

"Mr. Kensington," said Frank, with grim calmness, "this man, Morgan, has done his level best in trying to blackmail me out of one of my mines. This murder charge he talks about he has trumped up in hopes to frighten me; but I fancy he has found by this time that I am not so easily frightened. I can prove that he employed ruffians to jump my claim—to seize these new mines. We were forced to defend it with firearms. Morgan himself tried to have me treacherously shot, but he was not the kind of a man to deal with the ruffians he had employed, and he fell into a trap, from which he has now somehow escaped. He was captured and carried off by those same ruffians of his, whose object it was to hold him until he should pay a handsome sum for his liberty. Either he has managed to escape or he has paid the money demanded by those rascals."

Morgan laughed.

"It is not possible, Mr. Kensington, that you will believe such a ridiculous story. I give you my word—the word of a gentleman and a man of business and honor—that the whole thing is a fabrication."

"Morgan," said Frank, "I propose to make this statement public just as you have heard it from my lips. If it is not true, you can have me arrested immediately for criminal libel. I dare you to have me arrested! If you do, I shall prove every word of what I have just said and show you up as the black-hearted rascal you really are. Instead of having me arrested, it is more than likely that you will employ some ruffian to shoot at my back. I'll guarantee you will never try it yourself. If I were to step out here now and make a similar charge against Mr. Kensington, what would be the result?"

"By thunder!" burst from Kensington, "I'd shoot you on sight!"

"Exactly," nodded Frank. "And so would Macklyn Morgan if the statement were false and if he dared."

Morgan snapped his fingers.

"I consider you of too little consequence to resort to any such method. I am not a man who shoots; I'm a man who crushes. Frank Merriwell, you may fancy you have the best of me, but I tell you now that I will crush you like an eggshell."

As he said this his usually mild and benevolent face was transformed until it took on a fierce and vengeful look, which fully betrayed his true character. Quickly lifting his hand, Merry pointed an accusing finger straight at Morgan's face.

"Look at him, Mr. Kensington!" he directed. "Now you see him as he is beneath the surface. This is the real Macklyn Morgan. Ordinarily he is a wolf in sheep's clothing, and it is only the clothing he reveals to those with whom he has dealings."

Instantly the look vanished from Morgan's face, and in its place there returned the mild, hypocritical smile he sometimes wore.

"I acknowledge that my indignation was aroused," he said. "And I know it was foolish of me. I have said all I care to. I think Mr. Kensington will have a care about making any negotiations with you, Merriwell. Good day, Mr. Kensington."

Bowing to Frank's companion, Morgan coolly walked away and left the room.

CHAPTER XXIV.

WHAT HAPPENED TO DICK.

ust at dusk a horse came galloping madly up toward the front of the hotel, bearing on its back an excited, frightened, pale-faced girl. It was Felicia. Brad Buckhart happened to be leaving the hotel as the girl pulled up her sweaty horse.

"Oh, Brad!" she cried, and her voice was filled with the greatest agitation and distress.

The Texan made a bound down the steps.

"What is it, Felicia?" he asked. "Whatever is the matter? My pard—he went out to ride with you! Where is he now?"

"Oh, where is he? Oh, where is he?" cried Felicia.

"You don't know? Is that what you mean? Oh, say, Felicia, don't tell me anything has happened to my pard!"

"Brad! Brad!" she gasped, swaying in her saddle, "a strange thing has happened. I can't account for it."

In a moment he lifted her down in his strong arms and supported her, as he tumultuously poured questions upon her.

"What's this strange thing, Felicia? What has happened? Where is Dick? Tell me, quick!"

"Oh, I wish you could tell me!" she retorted.

"He went out with you?"

"Yes, yes!"

The Texan made an effort to cool down.

"Look here, Felicia," he said. "We're both so excited we don't hit any sort of a trail and stick to it for shucks. If anything whatever has happened to my pard, I want to know it right quick. Keep cool and tell me all about it. What was it that happened?"

"But I tell you I don't know—I don't know," came faintly from the girl. "We rode some miles to the south. It was splendid. We laughed, and chatted, and had such a fine time. Then, when we turned to come back, I challenged Dick to a race. My horse was just eager to let himself out, and we raced. I had the lead, but my horse was so hard-bitted that I couldn't look back. Two or three times I called to Dick, and he answered. I heard his horse right behind me, and felt sure he was near. Once I thought he was trying to pass me, and I let my horse out more.

"I don't know how far I went that way, but it was a long, long distance. After a while his horse seemed letting up. He didn't push him so hard. Then I pulled up some and called back to him again, but he didn't answer. I had to fight my horse, for he had the bit in his teeth and was obstinate. After a while I managed to turn, and then I saw something that gave me an awful jump. Dick's horse was a long distance away, and was going at a trot, but Dick was not in the saddle. The saddle was empty, and Dick was nowhere to be seen."

"Great tarantulas! Great horned toads! Great Panhandle!" exploded Buckhart. "You don't mean to tell me that my pard let any onery horse dump him out of the saddle? Say, I won't believe it! Say, I can't believe it! Why, he can ride like a circus performer! He is a regular centaur, if I ever saw one! Whatever is this joke you're putting up on me, Felicia?"

"No joke, no joke!" she hastily asserted. "It's the truth, Brad—the terrible truth! Dick was not on the horse. I don't know what happened to him, but he wasn't there. As soon as I could I rode back to find him. I rode and rode, looking for him everywhere. I thought something must have happened to him that caused him to fall from the saddle. I wondered that I had heard no cry from him—no sound."

"And you didn't find him?"

She shook her head.

"I found nothing of him anywhere. I rode until I was where we started to race. After that I had called to him, and he had answered me more than once. I know that, at first, he was close behind me."

"Jumping jingoes!" spluttered Brad. "This beats anything up to date! You hear me warble! You must have missed him, somehow."

"It is not possible, Brad. I stuck to the road and followed it all the way through the chaparral, beyond which we had started to race this way."

"Then you raced through a piece of woods, did you?"

"Yes, yes."

"Do you remember of hearing him answer any to your calls after you had passed through those woods?"

"I don't remember."

"Oh, Brad, what if he was thrown from his horse and some wild animal dragged him into the chaparral after he fell senseless on the road! You must find him! Where is Frank? Tell Frank at once!"

"That's good sense," declared the Texan. "But wherever is Dick's horse?"

"I don't know where the animal is now. I paid no further attention to it after I found Dick was missing."

By this time the Texan had heard enough, and, lifting Felicia clear off her feet, he strode into the hotel with her, as if carrying a feather. Just inside the door he nearly collided with Cap'n Wiley.

"Port your helm!" exclaimed the sailor. "Don't run me down, even if you are overloaded with the finest cargo I ever clapped my eyes on."

"Hold on, Wiley!" commanded Brad. "Just you drop anchor where you are. I want you."

"Ay, ay, sir!" retorted the marine. "I will lay to instantly. Ever hear the little story about the captain who ran out of provisions and, getting hard up, decided to have eggs for breakfast and made his ship lay two?"

"Cut your chestnuts out, now!" growled the Texan. "Where is Frank?"

"I last saw his royal nibs in close communion with a gentleman who is literally rotten with money."

"Not Macklyn Morgan?"

"Well, hardly. He is not chumming with old Mack to any salubrious degree. It was Thomas Kensington."

"Do you know where Frank is now? If you do, find him instantly and tell him something has happened to Dick."

"Ay! ay!" again cried Wiley. "Just you bear off and on right where you are, and I will sight him directly and bring him round on this course."

The sailor hurried away, leaving Brad to question Felicia still further about the road they had taken outside of Prescott.

Fortunately Frank was easily found, and Wiley came hurrying back with him.

"What is it, Brad?" asked Merry, controlling his nerves and betraying little alarm, for all that he saw by the appearance of Felicia that some serious thing had occurred.

"Oh, Frank—Dick!" she panted. "You must find him—you must!"

The Texan quickly told Merry what had happened as related by Felicia.

Frank's face grew grim and paled a little—a very little. His jaw hardened, and his eyes took on a strange gleam

"I opine I know just the road they took," said Buckhart. "She has told me all about it. I am dead certain I can go straight back over that trail."

"Wiley," said Merry, still with that grim command of himself, "get a move on and have some horses saddled and made ready."

"Leave it to me," cried the sailor, immediately taking to his heels and dusting away.

By this time others in the hotel knew what had happened, and a number of people had gathered around. Unmindful of them, Frank took Felicia on his knee as he sat on a chair and questioned her.

"Oh, Frank!" she suddenly sobbed, clasping him about the neck. "You will find Dick, won't you?"

"As sure as I am living, Felicia," he asserted, with that same confident calmness. "Don't you doubt it for a moment, dear. Rest easy about that."

"You don't think some wild animal has got him?"

"I hardly fancy anything of that sort has happened to my brother."

Merry called for the housekeeper, who soon came and he turned Felicia over to her, saying:

"Look out for her, Mrs. Jones. Take care of her and don't let her worry more than can be helped."

"Lord love her sweet soul!" exclaimed the housekeeper, as she received the agitated girl from Frank and patted and petted her. "I will look after her, Mr. Merriwell. Don't you be afraid of that. There, there, dear," she said, softly stroking Felicia's cheek. "Don't you take on so. Why, they will find your cousin all right."

"You bet your boots!" muttered Brad Buckhart, who was examining a long-barreled revolver as he spoke. "We will hit the trail and find him in less than two shakes of a steer's hoof."

Wiley now came panting back into the room, struck an attitude, and made a salute.

"Our land-going craft are at the pier outside."

Frank paused only to kiss Felicia and whisper a last word in her ear. As he turned to leave the room, he came face to face with Macklyn Morgan near the door.

Morgan looked at him in a singular manner and smiled.

"Excuse me, sir. You seem to be in a great hurry about something."

Merry stopped short and stood looking straight into the eyes of his enemy.

"What is your next low trick, Morgan?" he said. "Let me tell you here and now, and don't forget it for an instant, if ever any harm comes to me or mine through you, you'll rue it to the last moment of your miserable life."

With which he strode on out of the hotel.

Away out of Prescott they clattered, and away into the gathering darkness of a soft spring night. The cool breeze rushed past their ears and fanned their hot cheeks. Frank was in the lead, for Wiley had taken pains to see that Merriwell's own fine horse was made ready for him.

"Is this the road, Buckhart?" the young mine owner called back. "This is the one Felicia told us to take, isn't it?"

"Sure as shooting!" answered the Texan.

"We don't want to make any mistake in our course," put in the sailor. "That would be fatal to the aspirations of our agitated anatomy. At the same time we want to keep our optical vision clear for breakers ahead. We may be due to strike troubled waters before long."

"That's what we're looking for!" growled Buckhart, who seemed hot for trouble of some sort.

Onward they rode along the brown trail. Beneath them the ground seemed speeding backward. The lights of the town twinkled far behind them. Frank's keen eyes detected something that caused him to drop rein and swerve from the road. At a short distance from the trail a horse was grazing. This animal shied somewhat and moved away as Merry approached, but Frank's skill enabled him, after a little, to capture the creature, which proved to be saddled and bridled.

"Dick's horse," he said. "Hold him, Buckhart. I want to make an examination."

Brad took the creature by the head, and a moment later Frank struck a match, which he protected in the hollow of his hand until it was in full blaze. He then examined the saddle and the creature's back. Several matches were used for this purpose, while both Buckhart and Wiley waited anxiously for the result.

"What behold you, mate?" inquired the sailor.

"Nothing," answered Frank. And it seemed there was relief in his voice.

"Whatever did you expect to find?" questioned the Texan.

"I hoped to find nothing, just as I have," was the answer. "Still, I thought it possible there might be blood stains on the horse. It is not likely there would be hostile savages in this vicinity. Indeed, such a thing is almost improbable; yet it was my fancy that Dick might have been silently shot from his saddle."

"How silently?" asked Brad. "Shooting is pretty certain to be heard, I opine."

"Not if done with an arrow."

"But the Injun of this day and generation is generally provided with a different weapon."

"That's true; but still some of them use the bow and arrow even to-day."

"I don't reckon a whole lot on anything of that sort happening to my pard," asserted the Texan.

"Nor I," admitted Frank. "But I thought it best to investigate." The horse was again set at liberty. They had no time to bother with it then. Once more they found the trail and rode on.

Before them loomed the dark chaparral, into which wound the road they followed. On either hand the tangled thicket was dark and grim.

"A right nasty place for a hold-up!" muttered Buckhart, whose hand was on his pistol.

"If any one tries that little trick," observed Cap'n Wiley, "it's my sagacious opinion that they are due to receive a surprise that will disturb their mental condition and throw their quivering nerves into the utmost agitation. I am ready to keep the air full of bullets, for in that way something will surely be hit. Reminds me of the time when I went gunning with Johnny Johnson. We came to a promising strip of forest, and he took one side and I took the other. Pretty soon I heard him banging away, and he kept shooting and shooting until I grew black in the face with envy. I reckoned he was bagging all the game in that preserve. In my seething imagination I saw him with partridges, and woodcock, and other things piled up around him knee-deep.

"For just about an hour he kept on shooting regular every few seconds. At last I came to him, for I didn't find a single measly thing to pop at. Imagine my astonishment when I found him idly reclining in a comfortable position on the ground and firing at intervals into the air. 'John, old man,' says I, 'what are you doing?' 'Wiley,' he answered, 'I am out for game. I haven't been able to find any, but I know where there is some in this vicinity. I arrived at the specific conclusion that if I could keep the air full of shot I'd hit something after a while, and so I am carrying my wise plan into execution.' Oh, I tell you, John was a great hunter—a great hunter!"

"Better cut that out," said Frank. "This is a first-class time for you to give your wagging jaw a rest, cap'n."

"Thanks, mate; your suggestion will be appropriated unto me."

Through the chaparral they went, their eyes searching the trail and noting every dark spot on the ground. At length they came to the farther border of the thicket, but without making any discovery.

"Here's where Felicia said the race began," said Brad. "We haven't found a thing, Frank—not a thing."

Still Merry led them on a little farther before halting and turning about.

"What's to be done now?" anxiously inquired the Texan.

"We will follow the trail back through the chaparral," said Frank. "We will call to Dick. That's the only thing it seems possible for us to do."

Having decided on this, they rode slowly back; calling at intervals to the missing lad. The thick chaparral rang with their voices, but through it came no answer. The cold stars watched them in silence. By the time they had again debouched from the chaparral Brad was in such a state of mind that reason seemed to have deserted him. He actually proposed plunging into the thicket and attempting to search through it.

"You couldn't make your way through that tangle in broad daylight," declared Merry. "Don't lose your head, Buckhart."

"But, Frank—my pard, we must find him!"

"We will do everything we can. We may not find him to-night. But I will find him in time."

"What has become of him?" groaned the Texan.

"It's my belief," said Merry, "that he is in the hands of my enemies. This is a new blow at me. I saw something of it in the eyes of Macklyn Morgan when I faced him in the hotel just before we started. There was a look of triumph on his face."

"Whoop!" shouted Brad. "Then he's the galoot we want to git at! It's up to us to light on him all spraddled out and squeeze the truth out of him in a hurry. Just let me get at him!"

"And you would simply make the matter worse than it is. You must leave this thing to me, Buckhart. You must hold yourself in check unless you want to injure Dick. I will deal with Macklyn Morgan."

"You," said Wiley. "I fancy you have hit on the outrageous and egregious truth. I don't know just what egregious means, but it sounds well there. Morgan has scooped Richard and proposes to hold him hard and fast until he can bring you to terms."

"I think very likely such is his plot," nodded Merry.

"He ought to be shot!" exploded Brad. "It was a whole lot unfortunate that the ruffians who carried him off did not keep him."

"How do you think the trick was done?" questioned Wiley.

"I haven't decided yet," admitted Frank. "But I feel sure my brother is nowhere in this vicinity now. It's my object to see Morgan again without delay."

With this object in view Merriwell lost no further time in riding straight toward Prescott. When the town was reached he set out immediately to find Morgan, having first told Brad to see Felicia and do his best to soothe her fears.

Felicia was waiting. She started up as the Texan tapped on her door.

"There, there, child!" exclaimed Mrs. Jones, who was still with her. "Sit down and keep quiet. I will see who it is."

When the door was opened and Buckhart entered, Felicia cried out to him:

"Dick—you have found him?"

"Well, not exactly that," said the Texan; "but I opine Frank will find him pretty quick now."

The girl was greatly disappointed.

"Then you know what has become of him?" she asked.

"I opine we do," nodded Buckhart.

"He is safe?"

"You bet he is. He is all right, Felicia. We know well enough that he isn't hurt a bit."

She seized his hands.

"Tell me," she pleaded, "tell me all about it."

Brad was placed in an awkward position, and he felt that it was necessary to draw on his imagination.

"Why, there is not a great deal to tell," he said. "I reckon Dick's horse must have stumbled and thrown him. It stunned him some, of course. Then there were some gents what happened along and picked him up, and that's about all."

She looked at him in doubt and bewilderment.

"But I didn't see any one. Why didn't I see them?"

Buckhart coughed behind his hand to get a little time for thought.

"Why, these yere gents I speak of," he said, "were afraid to be seen, for they have been up to some doings that were not just exactly on the level. That being the case, they took him up all quietlike and stepped into the chaparral with him, and doctored him, and fixed him O. K. Of course, they will want to be paid for that little job, and that's why they are keeping him. You leave everything to Frank. He will settle with them and bring Dick back as sound as a nut. You hear me chirp?"

Having made this statement, the Texan felt greatly relieved. He had managed to get through it some way, although it was a hard strain on him. Still, Felicia was not entirely satisfied, and her fears were not fully allayed.

"If these men are bad men," she said, "won't they harm Dick some way?"

"Ho! ho! ho!" laughed Brad. "What a foolish notion to get into your head, Felicia. Whatever good would it do them to harm him? What could they make out of that? It's up to them to take the best care of him, so Frank will feel like coughing up liberal when he settles. You can see that easy enough. So don't worry over it any more."

"No, don't worry over it any more, child," put in Mrs. Jones. "Just go to bed. The strain on you has been severe, and you must rest."

"Oh, I'm afraid I can't rest until I see Dick! Don't you think I may see him soon? Don't you think Frank will bring him here right away?"

"Oh, mebbe not," said Brad. "It may take some time, for Frank thought likely Dick had been carried to Goodwin, or Bigbug, or some place. You see, we didn't find out just where they had taken him. All we found out was that he had been taken somewhere and was all right. You let Mrs. Jones tuck you in your little bed, and you just close your peepers and get to the sleeps. That's the best thing for you to do."

Fearing she might suspect that he had not stuck by the truth if she questioned him further, Brad now made the excuse that he had to hurry away, and quickly left the room. In the meantime Frank had been searching for Morgan. He fully expected to find Morgan without trouble, and in this he was not disappointed. The money king was talking with Thomas Kensington in the hotel bar.

"I beg your pardon, Mr. Kensington," said Merry. "If I'm not interrupting an important matter, I'd like a word or two with this man."

Morgan lifted a hand.

"You will have to excuse me, sir," he said. "I am quite busy now."

"On the other hand," said Kensington, "we have finished our business. Mr. Morgan followed me here and wished to talk of mining matters. I am in no mood to discuss such matters tonight."

He bowed to Frank and turned away.

Morgan gave Merriwell a defiant look.

"I cannot waste my time on you, young man," he said. "It's altogether too valuable."

"You have wasted considerable time on me in the past, and I have been compelled to waste some on you. This night has brought matters to a climax. I know your game; but it will fail, just as every trick you have tried has failed. I have a few words to say to you. My brother is missing."

"What's that to me? I care nothing about your brother."

"Yet you attempted not so very long ago to hold him as a hostage. It was your scheme to force me into dealing with you by holding my brother a prisoner in the hands of your ruffians."

"Be careful, young man! Don't accuse me of anything like that! If you do, I'll——"

"You'll what?" demanded Merry, grim as flint and cold as ice. "Now, what will you do, Macklyn Morgan?"

"I'll make you smart for it!"

"It's about time you learned, sir, that your threats have no effect on me whatever. As I have said, my brother is missing. If he is not in Prescott to-morrow morning, it will be the worse for you. Do you know how I dealt with Milton Sukes? Do you know that I investigated his business methods and found out about his crooked dealings, so that when I was ready to expose him he was driven desperate? Macklyn Morgan, are you immaculate? Do you mean to tell me that your career as a maker of millions has been unspotted? Do you mean to tell me that you never have been concerned in any crooked schemes? I know better, Morgan. I know how a man like you makes his money. As I dealt with Sukes, so I will deal with you! I will investigate. I will learn the truth, and then I will expose you. To-day you may be concerned in several questionable projects. If those schemes are rotten, the world shall know it. I shall take hold of this thing in earnest, and I'll do for you what I did for Sukes."

"That's a threat on my life!" cried Morgan, turning to the others who were near. "Gentlemen, I call on you to bear witness that this man has threatened my life."

"You know better, sir, I have threatened nothing but your crooked business. Your life is safe as far as I am concerned. But you will see that my brother is in Prescott to-morrow, or I'll hold you up for the inspection of the whole country and show people what a thoroughbred scoundrel you are! That's all I have to say to you, sir. Good night."

Frank turned his back on Morgan and walked out of the room.

CHAPTER XXV.

HOW WAS IT DONE?

hat had happened to Dick? Intentionally he had permitted Felicia to keep the lead in the race through the chaparral. It is possible he might have overtaken her had he tried. He had no thought of danger, and he was wholly unprepared when out from the shadows of the chaparral shot a twisting, writhing coil, the loop of which fell over his shoulders and jerked him like a flash from the saddle. The shock, as he struck the ground, drove the breath from his body and partly stunned him. Before he could recover he was pounced upon by two men, who quickly dragged him into the edge of the thicket, where a third man—a half-blood Mexican—was coiling the lariat with which the boy had been snatched from the horse's back.

These men threatened Dick with drawn weapons.

"Make a sound or a cry, kid," growled one of them, "and we sure cuts you up!"

The boy's dark eyes looked fearlessly at them, and he coolly inquired:

"What's your game? I have not enough money on me to pay you for your trouble."

"Ho, ho!" laughed one of the trio. "We gits our pay, all right, younker. Don't worry about that. Tie his elbows close behind him, Mat. Mebbe we best gags him some."

"No, none of that," declared the one called Mat. "If he utters a cheep, I'll stick him sure."

But the other insisted that Dick should be gagged, and this they finally and quickly did. With his arms bound behind him and a gag between his teeth, he was lifted to his feet and forced into the depth of the thicket. The Mexican, who was called Tony, seemed to know a path through the chaparral, although it was dim and indistinct, and this they followed.

Thus it happened that when Felicia missed Dick and turned back she found no trace of him. On through the thick chaparral they threaded their way, now and then crouching low to push through thorny branches, their progress necessarily being slow. For a long time they tramped on, coming finally to an opening.

Several horses were grazing there. No time was lost in placing the captive boy on the back of a horse and fastening his feet together beneath the animal's belly. Already it was growing dusky, but those men knew the course they would pursue. The Mexican and Mat mounted one animal and followed Dick, while the biggest man of the party, who had once been addressed as Dillon, now took the lead.

Starry night came as they still pushed on, but they had left the chaparral behind and were on the trackless plain. Finally it was decided that the captive should be blindfolded. By this time his jaws were aching, and he was greatly relieved when the gag was removed. They seemed to think there was little danger of his cries being heard should he venture to shout for help. Dick did not shout; he felt the folly of it.

Long hours they rode, and the bandage over the boy's eyes prevented him from telling what course they followed. At last they halted. The cords about his ankles were released, and he was unceremoniously dragged from the saddle to the ground. Following this, he was marched into some sort of a building. There at last the bandage was removed from his eyes, and even his arms were set free. Dillon and Mat were with him. The Mexican had been left to care for the horses.

"Now, kid," said the big man, "you makes yourself comfortable as you can. Don't worry none whatever; you're all safe here. Nothing troubles you, and we looks out for you. Oh, yes, we looks out for you."

"Why have you brought me here?" asked Dick.

"We lets you guess at that a while. It amuses you perhaps, and passes away the time."

"If my brother finds out who did this——"

"Now, don't talk that way!" cried Mat. "We don't bother with your brother any. We does our business with other parties."

"So that's it—that's it!" exclaimed Dick, "My brother's enemies have paid you for this piece of work."

"That's one of the little things you has to guess about," hoarsely chuckled Dillon. "Thar's a bunk in the corner. I sure opines this place is stout enough to hold you, and all the while Mat or I sits in the next room. If we hears you kick up restless-like, we comes to soothe you. We're great at soothing—eh, Mat?"

"Great!" agreed Mat.

"If you has a good appetite," continued Dillon, "in the morning we gives you a square feed. Oh, we treats you fine, kid—we treats you fine. We has orders to be ca'm and gentle with you. We're jest as gentle as two playful kittens—eh, Mat?"

"Jest so," agreed Mat.

"Of course, you being young, it disturbs you some to be introduced to us so sudden-like. Still, you seems to have a lot of nerve. You don't git trembly any, and you looks a heap courageous with them fine black eyes of yours. By smoke! I almost believes you has it in yer ter tackle us both, kid; but you'd better not—you'd better not. It does no good, and it ruffles our feelings, although we is so ca'm and gentle. When our feelings is ruffled we are a heap bad—eh, Mat?"

"Sure," agreed Mat.

"That's about all," said Dillon. "Now we bids you a pleasant good night, and we hopes you sleeps sweet and dreams agreeable dreams—eh, Mat?" "We does," nodded Mat.

Then they backed out through the door behind them, which led into the front room of the building, leaving Dick in darkness, as the door was closed and barred.

Dick knew there was very little chance for him to escape unaided from the clutches of those ruffians. Still, he was not the sort of a boy to give up, and he resolved to keep his ears and eyes open for any opportunity that might present itself. Left without a light, there was no hope of making a satisfactory examination of his prison room until the coming of another day.

He flung himself down on the couch and meditated. But for the fact that he was in fine physical condition, his fall when jerked from the saddle might have injured him seriously. As it was, he had simply been somewhat shaken up. He felt a slight soreness, but regarded it as of no consequence. Of course, he understood the game the ruffians were playing. Beyond question he was to be held as a hostage in order that Frank's enemies might force Merry into some sort of a deal concerning the mines.

His one satisfaction lay in the belief that Felicia had escaped. As he lay there on the bunk, he could hear the mumbling voices of his captors in the next room. After a time his curiosity was aroused, and he felt a desire to hear what they were saying.

Silently he arose and stole over to the partition between the rooms. This partition was strangely thick and heavy for a building in that part of the country. Seemingly it had been constructed for the purpose of safely imprisoning any one who should be thrust into that room. Although he pressed his ear close to the partition, he was unable for some time to understand anything the men were saying. He moved softly about, seeking a place where he might hear better, and finally found it in a crack beneath the massive door, through which shone a dim light.

Lying flat on his back, with his ear near this crack, the boy listened. To his satisfaction, he was now able to hear much of the talk that passed between the men. Plainly but two of them, Mat and Dillon, were in the outer room.

"This piece of work certain pays us a good thing, Mat," said Dillon. "The gent what has it done is rotten with coin, and we makes him plank down a heap liberal."

"What does yer know about him, pard?" inquired Mat. "Whoever is he, anyhow?"

"Why, sure, I hears his name is Morgan, though I deals with him direct none at all myself."

"Well, partner, this is better and some easier than the railroad job."

"All the same, Dan gets a heap sore when he finds we has quit t'other job. And, as for this being less dangerous, I am none certain of that."

"Why not?"

"Well, this yere Frank Merriwell they say is a holy terror. Dan hisself has had some dealings with him, you know. He knocks the packing out of Dan down at Prescott not so long ago."

"Down at Prescott," thought the listening boy; "down at Prescott. Why, I supposed it was up at Prescott. If it's down, Prescott must be to the south. In that case these fellows doubled and turned north after scooping me in."

This was interesting to him, for one thing he desired to know very much was just where he had been taken. As he was meditating on this, Dick missed some of the talk between the men, for in order to understand what they were saying it was necessary for him to listen with the utmost intentness.

"Do you allow, Dillon," he finally heard Mat say, "that Dan will stick to his little plan to hold up that train?"

"I opine not. He won't be after trying it all by his lonesome. One man who holds up a train and goes through it has a heap big job on his hands."

"So that's the kind of a railroad job they were talking about!" thought Dick. "They surely are a tough lot."

"Mebbe he comes searching for us," suggested Dillon.

"Mebbe so. Ef he does, we has to deceive him."

"He gits a whole lot hot, I judge."

"You bet he does. And when he is hot we wants to keep our eyes peeled for a ruction."

"That's whatever."

Although Dick listened a long time after this, the conversation of the ruffians seemed of no particular importance. Finally they ceased talking, and evidently one of them at least prepared to sleep. Dick arose and returned to the bunk, where he lay trying to devise some possible method of escape. Scores of wild plans flittered through his brain, but he realized that none of them were practical.

"If I could get word to Frank," he thought. "But how can it be done—how can it be done?"

Such a thing seemed impossible. At last he became drowsy and realized that he was sinking off to sleep, in spite of his unpleasant position. He was fully awakened at last by sudden sounds in the outer room. There came a heavy hammering at the door, followed by the voice of one of Dick's captors demanding to know who was there. Dick sat upright on the bunk, his nerves tingling as he thought of the possibility that the ruffians had been followed by a party of rescuers, who were now at hand.

The one who was knocking seemed to satisfy the men within, for Dick knew the door was flung open. He swiftly crossed the floor and lay again with his ear near the crack beneath the door.

"Well, you two are a fine bunch!" declared a hoarse voice that seemed full of anger. "You keeps your dates a heap well, don't yer! Oh, yes, yer two nice birds, you are!"

This was the voice of the newcomer.

"Howdy, Dan?" said Mat. "We thinks mebbe yer comes around this yere way."

"Oh, yer does, does yer?" snarled the one called Dan. "Why does yer think that so brightlike? Why does yer reckon that when you agrees ter meet me at Win'mill Station I comes here to find you five miles away? That's what I'd like to know."

"Windmill Station," Dick said to himself. "Five miles from Windmill Station, and Windmill Station is some twelve or fifteen miles north of Prescott."

"You seems excited, Dan," said Mat, in what was intended to be a soothing manner. "Mebbe we has reasons why we didn't meet you any."

"Reasons! If you has, spit 'em out."

"Yes, we has reasons," quickly put in Dillon. "Dan, we finds we